Beautiful Chaos

ALEX TULLY

Niki —
Enjoy!
Alex Tully

One hundred octillion =

100,000,000,000,000,000,000,000,000,000

(or a one with twenty-nine zeros after it)

CHAPTER 1

He had probably done it a hundred times, but it never got any easier. As soon as Brady O'Connell pulled open the back door to McGuire's Pub, the all-too-familiar smells hit him in the face: corned beef soaking in sauerkraut, sweat-stained flannel on top of smoke-filled denim, beer breath laced with whiskey, and always a hint of Old Spice thrown in for good measure.

The bar was packed and loud, as it was every Thursday at six. Jimmy Rainey, a short, stocky guy with a crazy-long beard, spotted him first. Just like the illuminated McGuire's sign hanging in the window, Jimmy was a permanent fixture there. Waving his can of Budweiser in the air, he called out, "Brady! Look, everybody, Brady's here!"

Brady gave Jimmy his customary wave and quickly moved on to Pete, an old Irishman with thinning red hair and a thick accent. "Brady!" He lifted his mug in salute, the dark amber liquid sloshing over the sides. "How are ya, my boy?"

"Good." Brady nodded. "Good to see you, Pete."

He moved like a politician through the crowd. "Hey, Joe," a nod, "Liam," a nod. Like a lot of the regulars at McGuire's, they both worked at Union Steel, one of the area's biggest employers. The rank odor of molten steel lingered around them, a nasty byproduct of their jobs.

Next, he got a quiet "Hey, kid" from 'Eagle Ears' Bob. Although Bob didn't say much, he still seemed to know everything about everybody, thus earning himself the nickname. Brady had asked him once, just for fun, why they called him Eagle Ears.

Bob shook his head. "You know what, kid? I have told these idiots a million times that an eagle's hearing is no better than any other damn bird's." He pointed to the corner of his right eye. "It's the eagle's eyes that are special." Then he put his hand on Brady's shoulder, his expression dead serious. "I told them they should be calling me 'Pigeon Ears' because pigeons have an exceptional sense of hearing. Did you know that?"

Brady had to hold back a laugh. "No, I didn't know that."

He gave Bob a nod and continued down the bar. "Quinn," a nod, "Mike," a fist-bump—he was one of the few guys under the age of thirty.

He finally came to the end, to the seat at the front of the bar—the seat reserved for him. Before he even had a chance to sit down, Maggie scurried over to him, moving quicker than most sixty-year-olds, her crazy orange hair bouncing behind her.

"How's my favorite customer?!" she squawked.

His shoulders tensed. "Hey, Maggie." He gave her his nicest smile, even though his insides were cringing. Brady had been making these weekly visits to McGuire's for over a year and he still hadn't gotten used to the attention. It was always embarrassing.

She wiped her hands on her apron and leaned over the counter. "Come here, you!" She wrapped her skinny arms around him, squeezing hard, and he patted her on the back awkwardly in return.

A chorus of "oohs" and "aahs" reverberated throughout the bar.

"Oh, don't you pay attention to them." She waved a hand dismissively. "What can I get for you, honey? You want a sandwich, or maybe some soup? Navy bean today— Eddy makes the best ever."

"No, thanks, Maggie, I'll just have a pop."

"Just a pop, always a pop," she mumbled as she made her way to the cooler.

Brady sat up a little straighter in his stool and folded his hands in front of him, trying to act as casual as possible, when a voice boomed from clear across the bar. "Hey,

Brady!" Jimmy shouted. "How old are you now? Sixteen? Seventeen?"

Here it comes. Brady smiled and played along. "Seventeen!" he yelled back.

Jimmy was the stereotypical loudmouth, all bark and no bite. He was the guy everybody rolled their eyes at, but secretly missed if he wasn't around. He just provided too much entertainment.

"Hey! You find yourself a nice little lassie yet?" Jimmy howled in self-amusement, like he had said something everyone hadn't heard a hundred times before.

Brady usually let Jimmy have his fun. Showing respect for the guys at McGuire's was the smart thing to do, the only thing to do. But for some reason, that particular time, he decided to yell back, "Not yet, Jimmy, but what about you?!"

Apparently the guys thought that was hilarious, because a thunderous roar of laughter followed. Brady knew Jimmy was around fifty years old and had never been married. No shocker there.

"I told you, Brady, trouble, them girls," he said, his deep voice dangerously close to a slur. "They be nothing but trouble."

Maggie was back with a can of Coke. "Now don't you let them boys get to you." She poured some Coke into a glass with ice, and then said over her shoulder, loud enough for everyone to hear, "They just all wish they were young and handsome like you."

Oh God, there was no end to it. His body automatically sank lower into his chair, and he felt the heat in his cheeks burn into a full-on flush.

Quinn raised his bottle of beer. "To Brady!" he proclaimed. "You know we love ya, kid!"

The rest of the guys followed, raising their bottles, cans and glasses in unison. "Hear, hear! To Brady!"

Then Quinn added, "And if you ever do find a little lady, I got one piece of advice for you—don't ever bring her in here!"

Laughter erupted once again as the guys nodded to each other in agreement.

Brady managed a tight smile and reciprocated the gesture, holding his glass of Coke in the air. "Thanks, guys! Especially for all of the great advice!"

These weekly visits were tortuous, but it was all just part of the job. Business was business. At six o'clock on Thursdays, at McGuire's Pub on Bridge Street, Brady O'Connell was the most important person in the world— the big cheese, the top dog, the king shit.

He sipped his pop, reached into his pocket, and reminded himself that it would all be over soon.

CHAPTER 2

Busting through the back door, Brady stepped over the huge pile of dirty clothes in the laundry room. "Dad! I'm back!" He made his way into the kitchen and went straight for the bag of Lay's on the counter.

"Hey! Don't be eating my stuff! Take your own!" *Shit.* It was like his dad was telepathic.

"Okay...fine." He grabbed a bag of Doritos instead and headed to his bedroom.

While getting a big slap on the back from one of the guys at McGuire's, he had also gotten a big dousing of Miller Lite. He scanned the floor for a shirt and found a crumpled-up flannel in the clean pile. He had never gotten used to the idea of folding his own clothes, let alone putting them away in drawers. Pointless. The 'clean pile-dirty pile' system worked just fine for him.

Besides, Dad didn't really care what his room looked like, as long as he kept his door shut. Other than fighting over snacks, which had resulted in the 'my snack-your snack' system, they made good roommates.

Mom and Dad had gotten divorced when Brady was thirteen. One day at the dinner table, his mom had just broken the news, as casually as if she was talking about the weather. "Jennifer, Brady," she'd said calmly. "Your father and I love you very much, and this decision is extremely hard for us. But we have decided to get a divorce."

Boom. Ka-pow.

Brady's jaw dropped, mid-chew, kernels of corn falling from his bottom lip. *What? What did she just say?*

He immediately looked over at his dad, head down, shoveling another spoonful of mashed potatoes into his mouth.

Jen spoke first. "What do you mean? Why?" The shock in her voice made Brady's heart sink further. His sixteen-year-old sister was obviously as clueless as he was.

It didn't make sense. Mom and Dad seriously didn't argue about anything. Everything seemed fine. Everything *was* fine.

Mom sighed. "It's complicated, and I don't expect you to fully understand it, but people change and feelings change. It's just not easy to explain...it's complicated."

"So, that's it?" Brady could feel a swell of anger rising up inside of him—toward his mom. He glared at her with all the intensity he could muster. "That's all you have to say?" He saw the surprise in her eyes, but he didn't care. "So let me get this straight. Dad almost, like, *dies...*" His voice cracked and he took a deep breath. "And he's..." He couldn't get the words out. "And now you're just going to leave him?!"

Dad slammed his fist on the table, his good fist. "Brady! Watch it!" He pointed his fork in warning. "You don't talk to your mother that way."

Brady raised his hands in the air. "I'm sorry, but I just don't get it!" He waited for some kind of explanation, but his parents just exchanged glances.

He couldn't believe his dad wanted this—it wasn't possible. "So, Dad, you're okay with this?"

His dad sighed heavily. "Brady, it's what we both feel is best."

Oh my God, the clichés just keep on coming. He looked over at Jen, who seemed resigned to the bullshit announcement. Her eyes were on her plate, but he could see a single tear dripping down her cheek.

"Best!? For who?" he shouted. And he pushed himself away from the table and ran for the stairs.

When Brady looked back on that time, it was a pretty typical scenario: parents tell kid they're getting a divorce, kid freaks out, then kid mopes around for weeks giving parents the silent treatment.

Maybe if his parents had fought, or even raised their voices once in a while, he wouldn't have been so shocked. But there had been no screaming or yelling, no mean glares or tense silence.

In fact, things had seemed much better since the accident. Dad didn't have to work the long hours at the steel plant anymore, and they all got to spend more time together. Shit, they even did family game night. Everything had seemed fine, and that was why the big reveal felt like such a brutal punch in the gut.

Brady quickly learned an undeniable truth: parents can be masters of façade. Kids have no clue what's actually going on between good ol' Mom and Dad. If he learned anything from the divorce, he learned that.

Dad moved into a little bungalow on the other side of Fulton. Brady and Jen would visit him every Wednesday and Saturday. Dad would order a pizza and they all would sit around and Netflix binge. Jen would clean Dad's bathroom and he would give her twenty bucks. She was definitely getting ripped off.

This went on for a few weeks and things seemed okay, but every time Brady had to leave his dad, he got a sick feeling in his stomach. His dad always put on a happy face and acted like he was fine, but Brady knew he was miserable. Who wouldn't be? His wife had divorced him— yes, Brady would bet his Xbox it was all Mom's decision. He hobbled around with a limp and had enough prescription bottles in his bathroom to fill a pharmacy. He couldn't work anymore, and he was too proud to go out and see any of his old work buddies. He was alone— completely and totally alone.

Brady had made up his mind. He would move in with Dad—it was the perfect arrangement for both of them. He could help Dad out and keep him company, and Brady would have more freedom without Mom always in his face.

At first, both Mom and Dad had resisted the idea.

Dad said, "Brady, you don't need to worry about me. I'm fine. You should stay with your mother."

Mom asked, "Brady, who will do your laundry? Remind you about homework?"

Not very strong arguments. For one, he was an A/B student, and two, doing laundry didn't seem exactly mind-bending. He knew his mom was sad about it, but she still had Jen at home. And she also had Tony, her new boyfriend, who she had tried very unsuccessfully to keep under the radar.

It wasn't long before Brady was packing up his things and moving in with Dad. Four years later, it was still working out great.

Brady went into his dad's office and found him in the usual spot. He was sitting at his desk with his back to the door, staring out the dirty bay window. His shoulders slumped to the left, his right hand twiddling a pen between his fingers. He always appeared deep in thought. "Everybody show?"

"Yep." Sometimes there was a no-show at McGuire's, but it was rare.

A small tuft of Dad's silver hair stuck out over the high-back chair. He had been gray as long as Brady could remember, and he wasn't that old—forty-nine. A few years ago, Brady had casually asked at what age he had started looking like Colonel Sanders. That was a big mistake.

"Well, when you're thirty, and all of your friends are going bald, you will be going gray, but you will still have your hair. See?" He stuck his hand in his thick, bushy hair and messed it up.

"And guess what else, smart-ass? You can put stuff in your hair and make it any color you want—black, blond, hell, you can make it goddamn purple, but at least you'll have your hair! You'll be thanking me!"

Brady was sorry he had asked.

Collapsing into the La-Z-Boy, he put his feet up. "What you looking at?"

"You know, that jackass is out there every day," Dad muttered. "Honest to God."

Brady looked out across the street and saw Mr. Davis kneeling down in his front lawn. He was tending to his pride and joy—his grass. The summer had been brutal, and while most sane people had surrendered their straw-like grass to the perpetual falling of leaves and acorns, Mr. Davis had not. His lawn was as green as the neon sign hanging outside McGuire's bar.

Dad sighed. "Anyway, no problems, then?" Back to business.

"No problems. Everyone says hi." Brady grabbed the remote and started flipping through channels. "That Sutton guy, he's interesting."

All of the regulars at McGuire's fit into a pretty standard mold: blue-collar guys going to the local watering hole after a hard day's work. But Sutton was different; he was always dressed in a suit, drank imported beer, and drove a Lexus.

15

Dad turned in his swivel chair, his left leg dragging slightly behind his right. "Yeah, he's got money—some hotshot lawyer."

"Where'd he come from?"

"Remember Lonnie?"

"Yeah, he hasn't been at McGuire's in forever."

"That's because he got one DUI too many. Sutton was his lawyer. Must've heard about me through him." Dad added, "But Sutton's a good customer. One of those guys who thinks he's smarter than the rest of us. Wish I had more like him."

Brady reached into the inside pocket of his jacket and pulled out a stack of white envelopes. "Well, he didn't stay long. He's always in and out." He fingered through the envelopes. "I don't think McGuire's is his kind of establishment."

Dad laughed. "Well, he better get used to places like that. The way he's going, he won't be hanging out at those fancy country clubs much longer. Let me see his envelope."

Brady handed him the envelope with 'Sutton' written in red ink across the front. "No indeed." Dad pulled out the small stack of crisp green bills and fanned them out in his hand. "Not when you're dishing out a grand a week."

Then he smiled and began counting out the hundred-dollar bills. "Pretty soon McGuire's Pub is going to start looking like a goddamn five-star restaurant."

CHAPTER 3

Brady sat on his bed tearing through his calculus homework when his phone started buzzing. He reached over to see a familiar face light up the screen—his best friend Jay. Eyes bulging, and flaming-red cheeks puffed out like he had eaten a couple of softballs—it was priceless. Jay had repeatedly tried to delete the image, but Brady kept copies, of course.

Jay was the kid in school who would try anything. Brady dared him to do ridiculous things and he never refused. And even more impressive, Jay didn't demand anything in return. He just did it for the hell of it. So one day, after doing some online research, Brady had brought a little something extra in with his school lunch: a Carolina

Reaper, one of the hottest peppers on the planet. All of their friends sat around the table in the cafeteria when Brady offered his best friend the curious-looking novelty and dared him to take a bite.

"YOLO," Jay said, popping it in his mouth. What happened next wasn't pretty. Jay had lost his taste buds for weeks and insisted the inside of his mouth was permanently scarred.

Jay had retaliated by finding a fifth-grade picture of Brady after he had just gotten braces. The braces protruded so much, Brady couldn't even close his mouth completely. Jay used that pic as a screen saver and liked to flash it around as much as possible.

"What's up, Jay?"

"Brady, you are never going to believe this!" His voice was frantic. "I scored tickets to New Dogma at the Q next week!"—a quick breath—"And not only that—get this—I got backstage passes to see the band before the show!"

"What? Seriously—how?"

"My dad got them from some guy at work." Jay's dad was the purchasing manager for a plastics company, and that job came with a big perk—kiss-ass sales people trying to get on his good side with free tickets to sporting events and concerts.

"I thought your mom wouldn't let you go to concerts." Although Jay was seventeen, his mom was ridiculously overprotective and treated him like a five-year-old.

"Dude, my dad gave me the tickets and already said I could go. She isn't going to say shit."

Brady did love New Dogma, and the show had been sold out for months. "What night?"

Jay hesitated. "That's the thing, it's Thursday."

Brady began running his hands through his hair in frustration. "You know that's McGuire night."

"I know, I know, but this is backstage, dude! Maybe your dad can change the day just this once?"

Jay knew all about the business. He had even accompanied Brady to McGuire's a couple of times, loving the idea of being able to sit in a bar like he was legal. And even though Jay acted like a complete clown most of the time, he was extremely loyal and knew when to keep his mouth shut.

Brady quickly went through a rundown of options in his head, but nothing seemed feasible. "Jay, you don't get it. It's always Thursday at six—no exceptions. These guys have very set routines and they do not deviate. I can't just change the time!"

Jay's voice turned into a high-pitched squeal. "Asshole, we are going to meet the band! Do you not get that?"

"Yes, I get that, Jay."

"Bro, this is serious. What about the bar lady with the crazy hair?"

It took Brady a second. "Maggie? No, she told me a long time ago she didn't want to get involved. Like a 'no see, no tell' policy. She looks the other way because we bring her a lot of customers, but I could never ask her."

Think of something, Brady. "What time do we have to be backstage—like exactly when?"

"Hold on, let me grab the passes." Suddenly the latest New Dogma single came blaring through the other end. "For your listening enjoyment," Jay said. Brady could hear things being thrown around.

"Okay. It says to be at stage entrance B at seven forty-five p.m. for security check before meet-and-greet. No admittance after eight o'clock."

The Q Arena was in downtown Cleveland and a thirty-minute drive with no traffic. With heavy traffic, it could take an hour, plus parking. But he tried to sound optimistic. "I think we'd be okay if we left by seven."

"What?! Dude, we'll never make it. Six thirty at the latest."

"Jay, you don't understand. I don't meet those guys until six. Most of them show on time, but some come in a little later. Seven is the best I can do. I'm always done by seven."

Jay let out an exaggerated sigh. Brady knew he was pissed, but he also knew Jay wasn't going to ask anyone else to go.

"Okay, but as soon as you're done with business, we need to go. We need to haul ass out of there, no effing around."

"I promise you," Brady assured him. "I promise you we will get to the concert on time."

***

"You promised, asshole."

They sat inside McGuire's, watching the red illuminated numbers change on the digital clock over the bar. The seven turned into an eight—6:58.

"Just chill out, okay?" But Brady was worried. He took another sip of his Coke and looked over at the entrance for the hundredth time, hoping to God he would walk in.

Sutton, the rich asshole, the lawyer guy with the fancy suits. He was the person Brady was waiting for. And it was unusual. Sutton always walked in at 6:15, like clockwork. He ordered his bottle of Heineken and drank it fast. Then they exchanged envelopes, short and sweet, and then he left. In and out—no pats on the back, no "Brady boy!" no socializing like the other guys.

"Dude, we have to go—like now! Can't you just tell your dad Sutton was a no-show?"

Brady sighed. "I'm sorry, Jay. My dad said I had to deliver them all. He doesn't give a shit about the meet-and-greet. He said I should be happy he's letting me go to the concert at all."

"I can't believe this, Brady. This is a once-in-a-lifetime opportunity and you're going to blow it."

Just then Maggie came over. "You boys sure you don't want a sandwich or something?"

Brady attempted a smile. "No, thanks, Maggie. We're good."

As she walked away, Jay began mumbling under his breath. "Good, Maggie...we're just effing awesome, Maggie...things couldn't be better, Maggie."

Brady ignored the tantrum and put his head in his hands. He closed his eyes. *Think, Brady.*

An idea immediately came to him; but it was a risky one. "Hey, Maggie, do you by any chance know where Sutton lives?"

She turned around, her wrinkled face scrunched into a frown. "Sutton?"

"Yeah, the rich lawyer guy. He's always wearing a suit?"

Her eyes lit up in recognition. "Oh! The Heineken guy!" She put her finger to her lips. "You know what? He doesn't really say too much when he comes in. Sorry."

"Hey, Brady," a familiar voice piped in from a couple of barstools down. It was Eagle Ears Bob. "The last time the suit was here, I heard him telling Quinn he lived over in Richmond."

Richmond was an upscale suburb, only fifteen minutes away from Fulton. And, it was on the way to downtown, with the highway passing right through it. Maybe they could just stop on the way, drop off the envelope, and his dad would never even know…

"Thanks, Bob." Brady didn't think about it any further. "C'mon, let's go."

Jay was on his phone googling Sutton before they even reached the car. "Okay, there's an attorney named Sutton living in Richmond. Jeff Sutton—here's a pic." Jay held up the phone. "Is this the guy?"

Sutton's face filled the screen, a huge cheesy smile plastered across it. "Yep, that's him."

"Okay, just a few more seconds to get the home address." Jay could find anything on the internet—

anything. It was kind of scary, actually. "Okay, got it. Not too far off the highway either, only like five minutes out of our way."

But the first thing they had to do was stop at home and drop off the envelopes with his dad. Keeping all that cash in the car was not an option, especially downtown. Luckily, McGuire's was only a block from his house.

Brady crept in through the back door, hoping his dad had dozed off. He carefully set the envelopes on the kitchen table and turned to leave. Just when he was about to make his exit, he heard Dad yell from the office, "Hey! Everybody show?"

Brady's shoulders tightened. He had never lied to his dad—ever. He'd just never had a reason to. He hesitated and then yelled back, "Uh, yeah!"

"Good! Go have fun, and don't do anything stupid!"

"Okay, Dad!" Brady felt a pang of guilt in his chest. "I'll see you later!"

And he was out the door.

CHAPTER 4

They drove to Richmond as fast as they could without risking a ticket. The pink sky had already faded to a dusky gray. The days were getting shorter, and in a couple of weeks the clocks would be turned back, making the night come even earlier.

They got off the highway and took a couple of turns, ending at a newer housing development. At the entrance, an illuminated brick pillar read Brittania Estates.

"Wow, fancy," said Jay.

"Yep." It was exactly the kind of neighborhood Brady had thought a lawyer would live in. Nothing but winding concrete streets and perfect treeless lawns. And mega-giant houses, of course.

Jay drove slowly along the glow of the streetlamps while Brady looked for Sutton's address. When he found it, they parked on the curb across the street.

Luckily, the car they were driving fit right into the neighborhood. Jay's mom had insisted they take her new Volvo, one of her conditions of letting Jay go to the concert. Which wasn't a bad deal when the only other option was Brady's old Focus.

Brady looked across the street and surveyed the house. It looked just like all the others—an obnoxiously big rectangle of red brick. He noticed a couple of cars in the driveway, and the porch light was on.

In the hurried decision to just 'drop off' the envelope, he hadn't exactly thought through how he would do it. "Now what? Should I just go knock on the door?" he asked Jay.

"You're kidding, right? How can you be so smart and so stupid at the same time?" Jay shook his head. "Not a good idea, genius. Try explaining to Mrs. Sutton who you are."

"I'm regretting this decision already." Brady's eyes found the mailbox at the end of the driveway, sitting on a square pedestal made of matching brick. "I guess maybe I could put it in the mailbox."

"Yes." Jay slowed his words, as if talking to a two-year-old. "Go over and put it in the mailbox. That's the black shiny thing sitting on top of the little chimney-looking thing."

Brady had a sudden urge to punch Jay. "I'm aware of that."

But he was also overwhelmed with a feeling that he was about to do something incredibly stupid. "It's a lot of cash. Maybe we should just nix this idea. I don't know if I'm comfortable just leaving it there."

"Jesus Brady! The clock is ticking! No one in this neighborhood is going to be out robbing mailboxes tonight!"

Brady's stomach was in knots. "But what if someone else opens it?" A very real possibility.

"Here." Jay reached over and grabbed a pen out of the console. "Write on the envelope—'Attorney Jeff Sutton, legal documents enclosed,' like all professional. Whoever gets it will think it's just work shit."

"What if we have the wrong address?" A less likely possibility, but still a possibility.

"Look!" Jay was pointing at the black mailbox. Brady could barely make it out in the dark, but it was there— *Sutton* written in fancy gold letters across the side.

Brady felt paralyzed. "I just have a bad feeling."

In one quick motion, Jay reached over and tried to grab the envelope out of his hands. "Give it to me, you pussy!"

"No! I'll do it!" Without thinking about it any longer, Brady took the pen and printed as neatly as he could on the front of the envelope:

Jeff Sutton, Attorney-at-Law
Legal documents enclosed

He made sure it was tightly sealed, got out of the car, and quickly carried it over to the mailbox. He was just about to open the little hatch when he heard a door slam.

It was the front door of the Suttons' house. Someone was walking down the front lawn, and they were moving fast.

Shit! Brady's mind raced as he stuffed the envelope back into his jacket.

"Hey! Excuse me? Can I help you?" It was a girl.

A really pretty girl, with long, dark red hair and pale skin. She was wearing jeans and a blue sweatshirt with the words "Richmond High" across the front. Brady got a weird nervous feeling in the pit of his stomach.

She cracked a smile. "Can I help you?" she repeated.

Shit, shit, shit. Think, Brady.

"Uh, yeah, hi. Mr. Sutton lives here, right?" He was practically stuttering for Christ's sake. "Your dad is Jeff Sutton? He's a lawyer, right?"

She folded her arms in front of her, still smiling. "Right…"

He pulled the envelope out of his jacket. "Well, see, I promised my dad I would get these papers to Mr. Sutton—your dad—and I forgot to mail them. And my dad will kill me if—well, I was just going to leave them in the mailbox."

She took a step toward him. "Oh, well, he's not home right now, but I can take them for him." She held out her hand in front of her. "I'll make sure he gets them as soon as he gets back."

Brady hesitated for only a second when the car horn blasted behind him. "C'mon, Brady! Let's go!" Jay yelled.

"Just a minute!" he yelled back.

"It's okay, Brady." She was still holding her hand out. "I'll give it to him, I promise."

Hearing her say his name did something to him, and he suddenly lost all rational thought. It was like his brain had suffered a malfunction. He handed over the envelope and then stood there frozen. She wasn't moving either, like she expected him to say something.

Another blast of the horn.

Brady gave her a short wave. "Okay, well, thanks," he said, and turned on his heel. As he walked back to the car, he had the overwhelming urge to turn around and ask her name, but he just kept walking.

Jay was hanging out the driver's-side window, and even in the dark, Brady could see the whites of his teeth—his big mouth smiling in amusement. "Awww, Brady! I think you like her!"

Brady gave him the finger and got in the car. "Don't say a word, asshole."

CHAPTER 5

As soon as Vivienne got back in the house, she shoved the envelope into her jeans pocket. Excessive curiosity had always been her biggest weakness, and that Brady boy's story was curious indeed.

"Hey, Vivs!" Chad emerged from the kitchen. "Where the hell were you?"

He stood with a big plastic bowl in his hands, his face already suspicious. "I got the popcorn. Are we going to watch this movie or what?" The bowl was gigantic, but next to Chad's body it seemed oddly normal-sized.

"Sorry, I thought I heard Oscar outside." She gave him her most sincere smile. Not a complete lie. She had heard something; it just wasn't the cat. "Go ahead and start the movie. I'll be there in a minute. I just gotta use the bathroom."

"Well, hurry it up." Chad didn't like to wait.

She whipped open the bathroom door and locked it behind her. Sitting on the toilet, she stared at the crumpled white envelope and squeezed it between her hands. God, she wanted to know what was inside—maybe she would just take a peek. She carefully began peeling back the seal on the envelope. A wad of green bills came into view. *Holy crap.*

She began counting the fifty-dollar bills. "One, two, three…" All the way to eighteen. Nine hundred dollars! *Legal documents, my ass.*

"Vivs!" Chad shouted. "What the hell are you doing in there?"

"Coming!" She quickly folded the envelope and stuck it back into her pocket. "Just one sec!" She checked herself out in the mirror and nervously smoothed down her hair. She took a deep breath. "You can do this, Vivienne." She had already made up her mind that it was now or never. Tonight was the night; she couldn't put it off any longer.

Chad sat in the great room on the enormous leather sectional. He was definitely pretty to look at. One of the most popular guys at school, he fit all the stereotypes. He was tall and good-looking, he drove a nice car, he was the star quarterback of the football team—okay, not exactly, but he was the star wide receiver. And he was nice. Everyone liked him. Students liked him, even teachers liked him—that kind of nice.

Too bad it was all a charade.

She forced a smile. "Sorry, it must have been the burritos they served at lunch. Went right through me. Not pretty."

His face fell. "Oh my God, Vivs, that's disgusting! I didn't need to know that."

"What's disgusting? Poop?" She grabbed a handful of popcorn and sat on the edge of the couch. "Guess what, Chad? Everybody poops. Every single person on the planet. Even the"—she tried to think of what would set him off the most—"those Victoria's Secret models. Yeah, they have to sit on the toilet and poop just like everybody else!"

He stared at her like she had three heads. "What is wrong with you?"

"Nothing." She sat down, making sure to leave a generous space between them. She needed to stay focused. Getting him angry wouldn't help anything.

They had only been dating two months. Vivienne was surprised when he'd asked her out, but not because she didn't deem herself worthy—although she was sure that's what other people were thinking. She just didn't really get it. He was a senior and they didn't exactly hang out in the same circles.

Chad was sort of an enigma. He had been dating Kristen Lane for almost two years and then she'd moved to Phoenix. Over the summer, he had become the new fascination of every girl at school. And because he wasn't a player who went through girls like underwear, it made him all the more attractive.

So on that hot afternoon in late August, while hanging out at the lake, she was seriously shocked when Chad stopped next to her group of friends and said, "Hey, Vivienne, would it be okay if I called you sometime?"

The simultaneous gasping of girls around her was embarrassing, and she could literally feel the anticipation hanging heavy in the air. She'd smiled and said as nonchalantly as possible, "Sure."

Only thirty seconds into their first date, Vivienne knew it was a mistake. He came to pick her up and when she answered the door, he looked her up and down and frowned. He frickin' frowned!

"Is there something wrong?" she blurted out, the big red flag waving over his head.

"Oh no!" He seemed to catch himself. "I just thought you might get chilly in that skirt."

Really? On a first date, he was analyzing her clothing choices. Was he really concerned about her catching a chill, or was he worried that she showed too much skin? She quickly realized it was the latter.

She tried to give him the benefit of the doubt and overlooked a lot of the obvious signs of a possessive boyfriend. He critiqued her clothes, asked who she was texting, and put her friends down in subtle ways. He acted arrogant and entitled, and had zero sense of humor. After only a couple of weeks, she had known she had to break it off, but it was easier said than done.

Kendra, her best friend and biggest confidante, said it would be social suicide. The hate talk would be harsh. "Can you believe Vivienne did that? Who does she think she is?

She's not even in the same league..." would be the general consensus.

But they didn't know Chad—the *real* Chad. They only knew the image that he had expertly created, the image he put on display for everyone to see.

And when Vivienne had finally thought she had enough courage to do it—to break it off for good—homecoming came. Chad was on the homecoming court, and of course he asked her to go, and of course she said yes. She knew it was weak, but she had always wanted to go, and it wasn't like anyone else was going to ask her at that point.

Kendra, her best friend, had a brilliant idea. She said Vivienne should use homecoming as an opportunity. They had been looking at the whole situation completely wrong. Maybe it was time to use reverse psychology; maybe she should try to get Chad to break up with *her*.

He had already been pushy in the sex department, and he would probably expect something that night. So when they sat in the limo after the dance and he began kissing her, she let things get a little heated. Then she pulled away, took his hand in hers, and said, with all the sincerity she could muster, "Chad, I want you to know that I believe sex is a holy union between man and woman and only after the sacrament of marriage can that sacred union take place."

She tried not to crack a smile when his face contorted with confusion and he asked, "What does that mean?"

"Chad," she said in a somber tone, "that means I won't have sex with you." And then she paused. "At least not until after we're married."

Vivienne and Kendra figured most guys would go running for the hills after that revelation. Or at least the mention of marriage would surely be enough to get him out of the picture for good.

They were wrong.

To her immense disappointment, Chad called her the next day, acting like nothing had happened. Acting like he hadn't given her the silent treatment the whole way home, like he hadn't looked at her with anger and disgust, like he hadn't almost slammed her leg in the door as she got out of the limo because he couldn't get rid of her fast enough.

No, he acted as if everything was just fine. But it wasn't fine, it was worse. He had an edge to him, a newly acquired look in his eyes that actually scared her.

It had been five days since homecoming—and there they were. She had no choice. Whether it was social suicide or not, she had to break up with him right there, right then.

"Vivs! Hello?"

Another thing she didn't like about him, he insisted on calling her Vivs. When she told him she didn't like it, he said 'Vivienne' took too much effort and went right back to it.

"Are you going to sit way over there?" He smiled and patted the empty spot on the couch next to him.

Vivienne looked at the space between them but didn't move. Her eyes wandered to the big screen, where a prison brawl was unfolding. A man in an orange jumpsuit was beating a guard over the head with a pipe, blood shooting into the air like a fountain.

"Chad..." Her heart began racing, and the nervous tingle stirring in the pit of her stomach turned into an all-out frenzy. *Just do it.*

She stood up and took a deep breath. "I want to say something."

CHAPTER 6

It all started a couple of years ago. They were having their Saturday breakfast—bacon and eggs—a once-a-week ritual.

"Brady, I want to show you something." Dad seemed excited, which was unusual. He limped into his bedroom and came back with a black three-ring binder. He pulled out a sheet of paper and put it on the table between their empty plates.

There were rows and rows of numbers written in Dad's scrawl, some in black ink and some in red.

Brady was immediately intrigued. "What's this?" His brain was drawn to numbers like a moth to light.

"I'm going to show you." Dad was smiling. No—he was beaming. Brady had seriously never seen him like that before. "Okay, forget this for a minute." He flipped the paper over. "Boy genius, see if you can figure this out."

Brady was no genius. The truth was, his freakish ability to analyze numbers was offset by a disability in regards to anything subjective. So while he had always gotten straight A's in math, he was terrible in things like English and art. Ask him to proof the Pythagorean Theorem, no problem. Ask him to draw a picture of a flower, big problem.

"If I bet a hundred dollars on the Browns and they win the game, what do I get?"

"The shock of a lifetime?"

"Ha-ha. Just play along, smart-ass."

Brady shrugged his shoulders. "A hundred dollars?"

Dad nodded. "Right, and if I lose?"

"Uh—you lose a hundred dollars?"

"No!" Dad picked up the paper and waved it in Brady's face. "Not necessarily. If I made a bet with Jimmy down at the steel plant, yes. But if I made the bet with a bookie, I'd have to pay him a hundred and ten."

"Like a fee."

"Exactly! See, if I really wanted to win a hundred dollars with a bookie, I'd have to front a hundred and ten. So the ten bucks is the juice—if the bookie wins a bunch and loses a bunch, he still comes out ahead because of the juice."

Brady thought he knew where Dad was going next. "Don't people just bet online now?"

"Of course they do." Dad smiled. "But you see, Brady, a lot of my buddies from the plant, especially the old-timers, don't trust computers. Hell, some of them don't even know how to turn one on."

He played dumb. "So why are you telling me all this?"

Dad sighed. "I'm going to start calling you boy idiot instead of boy genius."

Brady was silent for fear of further ridicule.

"You can have good days and bad days, but over time, I've made some real cash."

He felt a twinge in his chest. "Wait—so you're a bookie, like, now?" How had he not noticed?

"Well, yeah, I've only been doing it for a couple of months, and I only have a few guys. But I'd like to take on more."

Brady wasn't sure what to say, but he knew one thing. He had never seen his dad as happy and excited as this. "Well, isn't it…like, illegal?"

Dad laughed. "Trust me, Brady, no one is going to care about little old Sean O'Connell taking a few bets from some work buddies. And personally I don't think there is a damn thing wrong with it."

His dad leaned back in his chair. "Like you said, everyone bets online now. And think about the casinos popping up all over. Those are the real crooks. Feeding on people who are spending their entire paychecks—giving them false hopes."

Brady's curiosity was piqued. "So is it hard to keep track of all the bets and stuff? Lots of numbers, huh?"

Dad raised his hands up in the air. "I am so glad you asked that!"

And so Dad gave Brady the ins and outs of betting. He taught him about spreads and straights, favorites and dogs, points and parlays, limits and layoffs. Brady's brain was in overdrive mode and he loved it.

And that was how he became Dad's business partner and "numbers guy." He even created a computer program sophisticated enough to do the calculations automatically. Each week Brady entered in the numbers and printed off sheets full of mistake-free wagers. Dad took the calls and brought in new customers. Business grew and the money grew.

But exchanging money at the house wasn't practical anymore, which presented a new problem. Since the accident, Dad had pretty much become a hermit. Whether he was physically able to or not, Dad hardly ever left the house. And it was obvious he didn't want to.

But Brady thought of the perfect solution. "I can pay out and collect at McGuire's," he volunteered. McGuire's was just down the block, and all the guys from the steel plant went there almost every day. Problem solved.

And everything had worked perfectly—until Sutton.

***

As soon as Brady walked in the door from school, he knew something was wrong. Before he could even set his backpack down, Dad was calling him. "Hey, Brady! Come here, would ya?" His voice sounded uneasy.

Brady walked tentatively to the office and found his dad in his usual spot, folded hands on his desk, staring out the window. "Hey, I got a call from Sutton this afternoon."

Brady's heart sank and he suddenly felt light-headed. He sat down in the La-Z-Boy.

Dad slowly turned to face him. "He said he went to McGuire's, but you weren't there. The other guys told him you had already left." Dad's face looked concerned, but not angry—yet.

"Okay, Dad, see"—his voice faltered—"we did leave McGuire's a little early."

Dad closed his eyes and slumped down further into his chair.

"But, Dad…" His mouth was so dry, he could barely get the words out. "I found out where Sutton lived and I went to his house—"

"Stop!" Dad held up his hands in front of him. "Brady, stop right there. Did you just say you went to his house?!" he asked incredulously.

"I know, but—"

"No! Don't say another word." Dad stood up. "Please tell me this is what happened next. Please tell me you realized Sutton wasn't home, you kept the money, and now that nine hundred dollars is in your room, tucked away safe and sound. Please tell me that, Brady." He paused. "Because Sutton told me he never got the money."

"What?!" The word came out in a raspy shriek. "No, that's impossible. I…I," he stuttered, trying to make sense of it. "Wait, are you sure?"

Wrong choice of words. Dad gave him a look of such...*contempt* was the only word that came to mind, that Brady actually felt scared. He had never been afraid of his dad before, but at that moment he was.

Brady's head was spinning. "I gave it to his daughter. She promised she would give it to him. She—"

"You what!?" His dad's face turned purple.

"She must've just forgotten!" *Of course, she just forgot!* "Just call Sutton back and tell him his daughter has it— yeah, I'm sure she just forgot to give it to him!"

But Dad lowered his head and collapsed back into his chair. "Christ, Brady, I thought you were smarter than this."

The feelings that had been simmering inside of Brady since the night before—the guilt over lying to his dad, and the fear that his dad would find out—had been realized. He swallowed hard. "Dad, I'm really sorry, but she said she would give it to him. I know she has it."

His dad was hunched over in his chair, his elbows resting on his knees. "Well, we've got a real big problem."

Brady was afraid to say anything more. His chest was so constricted with worry, it was getting hard to breathe.

"You'd be surprised at how well I get to know my customers, Brady. Some of them like to talk, especially that asshole Sutton. He might not say much at McGuire's, but he sure as shit does on the phone."

Dad sighed and looked up at Brady. "And one thing I know for certain—Sutton doesn't have a daughter."

CHAPTER 7

"I want to say something."

Chad stopped shoveling the popcorn into his mouth and looked at her. *Now or never, Vivienne.* She tried hard to keep her eyes on his. He needed to know she meant it. "Chad, I don't think we should go out anymore."

For a few seconds he didn't say anything, his face remaining blank. But then a look came over him, one she'd never seen before. It was amusement, but in a mocking way. "You're serious?"

To anyone on the outside, it did seem ridiculous. How could Vivienne not-even-in-the-same-league Burke be breaking up with perfect Chad Sutton? It just didn't make sense.

Chad slowly got up from the couch and walked toward her, and Vivienne promptly stepped backwards. "C'mon, Vivs, what's bothering you? I'm sure we can work it out." He towered over her, his white smile as ominous as it was perfect.

"It's just...Chad, I don't think it will work. I think maybe we're not such a great fit for each other."

"Why is that?"

She wasn't prepared for the question. "I don't know, really, it's just—"

Suddenly his hands were on her arms, his fingers pressing in hard. "A great fit?" His left cheek was pulsating. "Really, Vivs, you couldn't come up with something better than that?"

Before she knew what was happening, his grip tightened even more and she was being pulled toward the front door. "Let go, Chad!" she yelled as pain radiated through her arm. "You're hurting me, asshole!"

Chad whipped open the door and pushed her through it. Pushed her. She stumbled onto the brick walkway and caught herself right before she did a face-plant. She turned to see him standing in the doorway, his face empty— emotionless.

She wanted to scream at him, but she was so shocked at what he had done, she was speechless.

"Be careful, Vivs," he said, his voice completely flat. "Don't want to hurt yourself."

Her feet began back-pedaling beneath her, and she turned to her car in a full-on sprint. Before she could get the door open, she heard him yell behind her, "Be safe, Vivs!"

She got in, hit the lock button, and fumbled to get her key in the ignition. Then she peeled out of the driveway, not daring to look back.

She didn't even get to the end of the street before the tears came. And they came hard. She realized then that 'possessive boyfriend Chad' was more like 'certified psycho Chad.' Something was seriously wrong with him.

It wasn't until she was halfway home that she remembered she had an envelope full of cash in her pocket—cash that belonged to Mr. Sutton. *Crap!*

Vivienne couldn't turn back, though. She was shaking so hard that all she could think about was getting home. And when she got there, she ran straight up to her room and shut the door. She flopped down on the bed and stared up at the ceiling. She couldn't believe Chad had just done that! She closed her eyes and tried to calm herself but the image of him and his threatening smile immediately popped into her head.

She sat up and took a deep breath, reminding herself that the hard part was over. Chad obviously got the message. The next order of business was hiding the envelope.

Vivienne was the first to admit she was a slob. And her room was a treasure trove of girl's essentials, scattered around ripe for the picking. Morgan, her fourteen-year-old sister, was a serious mooch. Maybe Vivienne was being a little hypocritical, considering she had just taken an envelope full of cash that didn't belong to her—but her sister took everything. Nothing was off-limits. And when her Raspberry Essie nail polish disappeared, she was horrified to learn that Morgan wasn't even the culprit. It was actually her nine-year-old sister Tess, who seemed to be following in Morgan's footsteps. That's when Vivienne knew things had gotten serious.

She had begged for a lock on her door, but the Burke household had an "open-door" policy—no secrets in their house. Maybe if Morgan and Tess started raiding Mom's room, she would change the policy, but Mom lived in L.L. Bean and didn't wear makeup, so she really didn't have anything to worry about.

Vivienne realized she would have to get creative with her hiding spots. Forget about underwear drawers, jewelry boxes, or beneath the mattress—definitely the first places little thieves would look.

No, she decided the best way to hide something valuable was to disguise it with the junk, and so far, it had worked beautifully. She had a pile of old purses and backpacks that had accumulated over the years, filling the space in the bottom of her closet. One of the backpacks, a pink vinyl monstrosity with a big sequin V on front, had been her favorite when she was like eight. And she knew her sisters would never go near it.

Inside, a convenient zipper pocket made the perfect hiding spot for her most cherished possessions. Lots of items had occupied the space, from the gold earrings she got on her sixteenth birthday to her MAC lipstick.

But for the last seven months, she'd kept only one thing there—the thing that was more important to her than any of that other stuff. And now it would have a neighbor—well, more like a visitor—the envelope. She slipped it into the pocket and zipped it up.

Last order of business: call Kendra. Vivienne really didn't want to relive the whole breakup with Chad, but she knew she couldn't keep it bottled up any longer. Kendra would make her feel better; she always did.

She answered on the first ring. "What happened? Did you do it?"

Vivienne sighed. "It was bad, Kendra—really bad."

"Oh my God, did he cry?!" she shrieked.

"No. He didn't cry." She could visualize Kendra's disappointed face. Vivienne began chewing her nails. "He pushed me out his front door." She even surprised herself at how calmly it came out.

"What?!" Another shriek. "Are you okay?"

"Yes, but he was crazy, Kendra. I was actually scared."

"Okay, hold on. Back up. Start from the beginning."

And so Vivienne told Kendra the whole story from start to finish—almost. She didn't know exactly what to say about the envelope full of cash that she…had she stolen it? She hadn't meant to take it…she had forgotten about it…and then she'd been scared…and then she'd panicked…

The realization hit her. She had stolen nine hundred dollars! There was no point in sugar-coating it. "There's something else I need to tell you about."

"What is it?" asked Kendra.

Vivienne was mentally exhausted, and so she told Kendra she would give her every little detail later, but she only had enough energy for the abbreviated version.

Kendra: Okay...so where did you get it?

Vivienne: From a boy named Brady.

Kendra: Who the hell is Brady?

Vivienne: I'm not sure, but he was cute.

Kendra: Like how cute?

Vivienne: Really cute.

Kendra: Uh-oh.

Vivienne: Just let me finish the story.

Kendra: Okay, sorry.

Vivienne: So I was on my way to the bathroom and I saw him outside putting something in Chad's mailbox, so I went out there.

Kendra: And he just gave it to you?

Vivienne: Well, he thought I was Mr. Sutton's daughter.

Kendra: Did you tell him that?

Vivienne: No, he said, 'Your dad is Mr. Sutton? He's a lawyer, right?' and I said 'right,' so technically I didn't really lie.

Kendra: Semantics, Vivienne. Okay, so then what?

Vivienne: I went in the bathroom and opened it.

Kendra: Can I ask why you opened it?

Vivienne: I was curious.

Kendra: Of course you were. Okay, so why didn't you give it to Chad then?

Vivienne: Okay, because when I came inside, he asked me what I was doing, and I lied and said I was looking for Oscar.

Kendra: Who's Oscar?

Vivienne: Chad's cat. I'm gonna miss him.

Kendra: Okay…

Vivienne: So, I was so nervous about breaking up with him, I just wanted to get that over with, and then I was going to put the money in the mailbox when I left.

Kendra: And then Chad scared the crap out of you.

Vivienne: Exactly. I freaked out and took off. I didn't even remember about the envelope until I was almost home.

Kendra: So are you going to take it back?

Vivienne: Of course. But it's getting late and I'm really tired. First thing in the morning.

Kendra: Well, at least it's finally over with Chad.

Vivienne: Yeah. (Pause) Kendra?

Kendra: Yeah?

Vivienne: Do you think what I did was stealing?

Kendra: No…maybe unintentional stealing.

Vivienne: Unintentional stealing. Great.

Kendra: Get some rest, Vivienne. No worries.

Vivienne: Okay.

Pulling her blanket up, she rolled over onto her side and let her head sink into the pillow. She was still holding the phone when she fell asleep.

CHAPTER 8

The day did not go how she had planned.

Vivienne woke up to Morgan whipping her door open and screaming, "Vivienne! You're gonna be laa-ate!"

She hadn't moved all night. She was in exactly the same position she had fallen asleep in. She jumped out of bed and got ready in record time, squeezing an hour-long routine into twenty minutes. Thank God for dry shampoo.

After arriving at school ten minutes late, she spent most of the day avoiding Chad. At lunch, she glanced at him once. He was sitting at a table with all the other football players, but unlike his obnoxious cohorts, he wasn't laughing and shouting through mouthfuls of pizza. He was looking at her. And smiling. Not a nice smile—a crazy smile.

Before she even left school, she got a text from her mom saying there was a crisis at work and Vivienne would have to pick up Tess from Richmond Elementary. Because of that delay, which consisted of waiting in a line of minivans like twenty miles long, she was late to her job at Shady Oaks and thus felt a little guilty about leaving there exactly at the end of her shift.

So she got home later than she was supposed to, and found herself rushing once again. Kendra would be there in half an hour to pick her up for the football game. She threw off her musty work clothes and jumped in the shower. She blow-dried her hair and then changed into her customary jeans and sweater.

Her phone beeped with a text from Kendra: *I'll be there in 5.*

Crap! She quickly checked her makeup, the little that she wore, adding a little mineral powder over the smattering of freckles across her nose and cheeks. They had been cute when she was ten; now she would do anything to get rid of them. Mom said they gave her character—code word for ugly. She'd also told Vivienne that the freckles would fade in her twenties, like somehow that was comforting.

"They're very unique," she'd say. "I learned to like mine, and I even missed them when they were gone. You will too."

Sorry, Mom. No chance in hell.

Vivienne got another text from Kendra: *Beth is coming.*

Noooo! What was she thinking?! Vivienne called her immediately.

"Hey," she answered, Ellie Goulding playing in the background.

"Did you pick up Beth yet?"

"Well, I'm sitting in her driveway waiting for her. Why?"

"Kendra!" she yelled. "We were supposed to go to Chad's and drop off the envelope!"

"Oh yeah." A pause. "We can still do that, Beth won't care."

"No, you're right, Beth won't care. In fact, she would love it. You know she has the biggest mouth in the whole school. And she's obviously in love with Chad. I don't want her to know anything about it—even remotely."

Bottom line, Vivienne didn't trust Beth. There had just been too many instances of things said in confidence suddenly circulating throughout school and social media. Vivienne had learned real quick to keep her mouth shut, especially when Beth pried for info about Chad. She always gave her generic answers like, "it's good," "he's good," "we're good," when she really wanted to say, "it's bad," "he's bad," "we're bad," and most of all, "you can have him."

Vivienne's head began throbbing. "Kendra, why'd you even invite her?"

"I'm sorry, okay? She just came right out and asked me, and what was I supposed to say, no?"

Vivienne took a deep breath. "I'm sorry. I'm just so stressed out right now."

"It's okay, I wasn't thinking. Do you want to drop it off yourself and then meet us at the game later?"

"My mom took the car to run errands." As soon as Vivienne had walked in the door, her mom was walking out. "She'll probably be gone for a while."

"Hmmm..." Kendra was thinking. "How about we drop it off after the game? I'll just take Beth home first."

"Okay, right after the game though."

"Oh crap. Beth's coming. I'll see you in a bit."

Vivienne took the envelope out of her jeans pocket and put it back into the zipper pocket of the backpack. She ran down the stairs and into the kitchen to grab a bottle of water. Every cabinet door was open, and pots and pans were stacked in piles all over the floor. Morgan was sitting at the kitchen table behind a tower of boxes and garbage bags.

"What's this?" Vivienne asked.

Morgan shrugged. "She's on one of her cleaning kicks. This one seems pretty intense."

"Well, I'm heading out."

"Did you clean your room?" Morgan asked. She loved asking questions she already knew the answers to.

"Tell Mom I will tomorrow. I promise."

"She's gonna be pissed," Morgan said in her 'you'll be sorry' voice.

"Whatever." Vivienne heard tires screech out front and a car horn beep. "I've got to go."

She grabbed her jacket and walked outside into the cool autumn air. The sun had just set below the horizon and a breeze rustled through the trees sending leaves tumbling across the lawn. The faint sound of a marching band could be heard playing in the distance. A picture-perfect Friday night.

That was until she saw Beth, hanging out the passenger-side window, all smiles. Kendra must've told her about the breakup with Chad.

"Hey, Vivienne!" she called out.

"Hey, Beth."

She jumped into the backseat and Kendra turned the stereo up. As they drove off, Vivienne decided she was going to forget about Chad, and the envelope, and just try to have a good time. The three of them sang out loudly to the music, so preoccupied with their own amusement that none of them noticed the car following closely behind.

CHAPTER 9

"Holy shit, that chick's a terrible driver," Jay laughed.

Brady watched as the white SUV pulled out of the driveway. "Yeah, just make sure you don't lose them."

As soon as Brady was finished apologizing profusely to his dad and promising him repeatedly that he would get the money back, he called Jay over for an immediate brainstorming session.

Even without a name, it was easy to find her. Brady's dad had two valuable pieces of information: one, although Sutton didn't have a daughter, he did have a son; and two, his son was a star football player. Of course he was.

A quick Google search for *Richmond Ohio football Sutton* brought up the Facebook page of one Chad Sutton. He looked like Brady had thought he would, the typical all-American pretty boy. In a relationship with Vivienne Burke. There was a picture of the two of them dressed up, probably homecoming. A pretty redhead with an innocent smile. Nobody would ever figure her for a thief.

Then Jay did some quick hacking, looking up Burkes in Richmond, and within minutes they had her home address. At first, Brady had just wanted to go to her house and confront her face-to-face. But Jay had advised wisely that doing it on her home turf wasn't a good idea. She could just deny it, or tell her parents, or God knows what else. And what was he supposed to say? "I'll call the police"? Not an option.

"What if she gave the envelope to Chad, and he pocketed it?" Jay asked.

Brady had already considered that. "It's a possibility. But I have to start with her."

They decided the element of surprise was key—Brady needed to catch her off-balance, and what better way than in front of a bunch of people? The football game was the perfect opportunity. He figured the odds were pretty good that she would be there to watch Mr. All-American, but just to be sure, they would stake out her house, watch, and wait.

First, around 7:05 p.m., they saw Vivienne pull into the driveway in a minivan and run into the house. A few minutes later, Mrs. Burke (he would assume) ran out of the house and jumped into the minivan. Then, twenty minutes after that, at approximately 7:30 p.m., the white SUV came barreling down the street and screeched to a halt in

Vivienne's driveway. He wondered how many times that girl had flunked her driving test.

"You want a drink, O'Connell?" Andrew asked, reaching back and handing him the plastic Sprite bottle. "Seven and Seven, or I guess I should say, Seven and Sprite."

Brady grabbed the green bottle and took a huge swig. The drink tasted more like Seagram's Seven with a dash of Sprite, and he almost spit it out. "Jesus, that's strong!" The liquid burned as it went down his throat.

Andrew was Jay's older brother, a senior at Fulton High, and their secret weapon. They figured Vivienne might try to play dumb and walk away, and the last thing they wanted to do was cause a scene. But what if they had something that would make it impossible for Vivienne's friends to walk away?

That was where Andrew came in. No girl had ever turned away from Andrew—ever. He looked like he should live in Hollywood, not in the burbs of Cleveland. He was a walking cliché—tall, dark and handsome to the extreme. Women gawked at him; old ladies smiled at him approvingly. When he entered a room, the girls came running. Brady had witnessed it, and the term 'they threw themselves at his feet' would not be an exaggeration.

Which just made it all the funnier that Andrew was gay.

"Where'd you get that?" Jay asked.

Andrew smiled. "Where do you think? The liquor cabinet."

"When are you going to tell me where the key is, asshole?"

"Yeah, right, Jay—all I need is you two dipshits cleaning out the liquor cabinet and giving mom a coronary. I'll get the blame—I always do." He took another drink. "I have one more year in this hellhole, and I'm not letting anything screw that up."

Andrew had been accepted at NYU to study architecture and had already secured a part-time modeling contract. He was counting the days until graduation.

Then he added, "I'll tell you where the key is as soon as my plane lands in New York. Fair enough, little brother?"

"Whatever."

Brady and Jay knew upfront Andrew wasn't going to participate in their plan without bribery. So they promised him fifty dollars, as soon as Brady got the envelope back. After they gave Andrew all of the details of the plan, he changed his mind and said he wanted a hundred. They settled on seventy-five.

"So remind me exactly what you want me to do?" Andrew asked.

"Bro, all you have to do is flirt with the girls a little— you know—don't be gay," Jay said. "Go back into the closet for a couple of hours."

Andrew took another drink. "Shit, I can't believe I'm following a bunch of chicks in a car."

"I really can't thank you enough for doing this, man," Brady said quickly. Andrew was critical to the plan.

"Just so long as I get my seventy-five bucks." He shook his head.

"You will."

"So how pissed was your dad, O'Connell?"

"How pissed?" Brady thought about the look on his dad's face. He would never forget it, and never wanted to see it again. His dad had told Sutton there was a mix-up, apologized, and gave him his envelope full of money. A nine-hundred-dollar loss. "No. I wish he would've been pissed. He just looked—disappointed."

Andrew finished off the last of the liquid at the bottom of the green bottle. "Oh, man, do I know *that* look."

As they came to a stop, Brady looked out the window and saw Richmond High Stadium, home of the Rockets, aglow with lights. The white SUV was parked a couple of rows ahead and there were three girls walking away from it.

Jay put the car in park. "Well, boys, we're he-re!"

"Jesus," Andrew mumbled. "I better get that money, O'Connell."

"You will, you will, trust me. I am not going home tonight without that envelope. I don't care what I have to do."

The three of them waited inside the car for a couple of minutes and then got out and made their way toward the entrance. Brady believed what he said. He was going to get the money back, no matter what.

And the first thing to do—find Vivienne Burke.

CHAPTER 10

"Touchdown Rockets!" the announcer's voice boomed from the loudspeakers. All of the Richmond High fans jumped to their feet, cheering in unison. "A forty-three-yard touchdown pass from Bell to Sutton gives your Richmond Rockets a fourteen-to-seven lead at halftime!"

"I'm freezing," said Kendra. "Do you guys want to get some hot chocolate?"

Vivienne and Beth both nodded. It must've dropped ten degrees since they got to the game. They made their way down the bleachers with the rest of the crowd. Walking to the concession stand, Beth asked, "So, Vivienne, what happened with you and Chad? You broke it off?"

Vivienne was actually impressed. Beth had made it through a whole first half without asking her about the breakup. She thought about him smiling at her in the cafeteria and a chill went down her spine.

Beth went on, "I mean, he is so hot, and looks so good in that uniform. And he seems really sweet."

Vivienne's frustration was at a breaking point. People had no clue what the real Chad Sutton was like. Why shouldn't she just tell the truth about him? Why shouldn't she just tell Beth that he was a narcissistic, overbearing, psychotic, control freak? And he wasn't even a good kisser!

"Look, Beth, the uniform part is definitely true, but in regards to the rest, let's just say things aren't always as they seem."

Not good enough for Beth. "What do you mean? What happened?"

"Let me ask you something," Vivienne retorted. "You don't wear a lot of makeup, right?"

"What?" Beth looked taken aback. She didn't need it; she was one of those lucky people with flawless skin, not a freckle in sight.

"Makeup—you don't wear a lot of makeup."

"Uh…yeah. I mean, no, I don't. My skin is really sensitive and so I try—"

Vivienne cut her off. "Well, that would be unacceptable to Chad."

She saw the hurt on Beth's face, but she didn't stop. It was like all of the anxiety from the last few weeks had culminated into a giant stress ball and she needed to get it out with every word, every breath, or she would explode.

"He would tell you that you're beautiful, but you could look even more beautiful with some make-up, maybe some brighter color on your lips," Vivienne rambled. "And then, after you spent all day at Macy's roaming around the cosmetic counters looking for that perfect shade of brilliant red, he would take one look at you and say, 'It looks great, I was just hoping you would've picked something a little more pink.'"

Beth and Kendra were staring at her.

"*That* is Chad."

Kendra made her 'whoa' face. "Okay, then, Vivienne."

"I definitely get it," Beth snapped.

Vivienne caught her breath and put her hands on top of her head. She sounded like a raving bitch. "Crap, I'm sorry. I'm sorry, Beth. It's just frustrating because everyone thinks Chad's like this god, and he's not."

Kendra quickly tried to smooth things over. "Hey, did you guys see Madison White with Connor Phillips?"

No one answered. They stood in awkward silence at the end of the concessions line—a line that had already started wrapping around to the back of the small brick building. Halftime would be over before they ever got served, but Vivienne could care less about the game. All she cared about was the hot chocolate, and getting warm. Hopefully she could convince Beth and Kendra to leave early.

"Hey, Vivienne!" a guy's voice shouted behind her, a voice she didn't recognize.

She turned around and saw some guys moving through the crowd, toward her. She squinted as they got closer, trying to make out their faces. And then her stomach dropped.

She recognized the one in the middle. It was Brady, the boy from last night, the boy she took—stole—the money from. *Crap, crap, crap!*

She felt a sharp pain in her side as Beth jabbed her with an elbow. "OMG, Vivienne! You know these guys!?"

Her mind was blank. *Oh God. Think, Vivienne. Think!*

"Holy crap! That guy is so hot," Kendra said excitedly.

They were getting closer.

"Shhh! Calm down!" Vivienne urged under her breath. "Just chill out, okay?"

The three boys were suddenly standing in front of the three girls: on the left side, a shorter guy with spikey blond hair, wearing a plaid flannel down to his knees; on the right side, a tall, dark-haired, ridiculously gorgeous guy who sported a dark wool coat.

And, appropriately, in the middle stood Brady, average height, brownish-blondish hair, in a blue hoodie and jeans. He had his hands in his pockets, and he was smiling. He didn't look anything like the shy, uncertain Brady she'd met the night before. He looked confident and determined and, well, he looked hot.

Her stomach did a flip-flop. "Hey." It was all she could manage to get out.

"Wow, what are the chances?!" Brady's voice was loud and orchestrated. "I thought that was you! How are you, Vivienne?"

She tried to steady her voice. "Good…uh, I'm good."

"Oh, hey, I'm so rude." He smiled at her friends. "I'm Brady, and these are my friends, Jay and Andrew."

Both of the guys nodded. "Hey."

Immediately Beth and Kendra were on flirt-alert, all smiles. "Hey, I'm Beth."

Then Kendra waved. "Kendra." She nudged Vivienne.

"Oh yeah, sorry." Vivienne couldn't think; her brain was muddled. "Beth and Kendra."

Andrew smiled. "Good to meet you ladies."

With those simple words, Vivienne could feel the air being sucked in around her as her friends gasped in delight.

"So, Vivienne…" Beth was bubbling with enthusiasm. "How do you guys know each other?"

"Um…" *Oh crap.* There was nothing there. Her mind was completely, utterly, one hundred percent blank. She wanted to run. She looked over toward the bathrooms. She could say she was sick, she could—

Brady piped in suddenly, "Oh, well, it was a brief meeting, really. See, I had left my dad's debit card in the ATM like an idiot." He watched her closely as he spoke. "Anyone behind me could have gone in there and taken out a lot of cash, but luckily Vivienne was nice enough to tell me about it."

Vivienne wanted to fall into a hole.

Then he added, "She saved me from a possible shit-kicking by my dad."

At that, Vivienne looked to Kendra for help, and in return she got a look that said, *I guess we don't have to worry about going to the mailbox anymore.*

Beth was too awestruck by the Greek god named Andrew standing in front of her to even have a clue about what was really going on. "Do you guys go to Garfield?" she asked. Home of the Bulldogs—the opposing team.

"Yep, Garfield," said Jay. "We're from Garfield."

Vivienne knew that was probably a lie. Brady had found out who she was and had come there to confront her. She wanted to kick herself for being so stupid! If only she'd had the guts to turn around last night and put the frickin' envelope in the frickin' mailbox, none of this would've happened.

Beth was going to make the most of their 'chance' meeting with the boys. "Hey, do you guys want to go to a party? There's supposed to be a keg."

Jay didn't hesitate. "Absolutely."

"You know what?" Kendra tried to do damage control. "I'm not sure if I'm feeling up to it."

Beth instantly swung her head in Kendra's direction. "What do you mean? You just told me you wanted to go. It's freezing out here."

Brady's eyes were still on Vivienne, a smug look on his face. "Well, we love a good party but…" He shrugged.

She needed to get him alone and explain herself. "No, you know what, Kendra? Let's go. It'll be fun."

"Awesome!" Beth quickly pulled out her phone and took a step closer to Andrew. "It's at my cousin Kirby's house and it's kind of out in the boonies. I'll give you the address." She read it off quickly and then added, "And maybe you should give me your number—you know, just in case."

While Vivienne was consumed with shame, Beth obviously had none.

Brady's gaze was still focused on her. "We'll follow you. You know, just in case."

Vivienne turned away and the six of them began making their way toward the exit. Kendra was quickly at her side. "It's all good," she said quietly. "You were right. Brady's hot, but more importantly, he seems really nice."

"Would you keep it down?" Vivienne urged under her breath, her heart racing, palms sweating. She felt like she was going on trial, or being led to a public flogging. Okay, maybe that was a little extreme, but the point was, she didn't know what Brady was planning. Would he make a big scene at the party? Did he want to exact revenge and humiliate her in front of everyone?

"Look," Kendra went on, "you have nothing to worry about. I am a hundred percent sure Brady will understand."

"I'll understand what?" Brady asked, now on the other side of Vivienne, walking with her in stride, so closely that his arm brushed up against hers.

"Oh, hey, Brady," Kendra quickly said. "What part of Garfield did you guys say you're from?"

Brady smiled. "I think you already know we're not from Garfield." He picked up his step and joined Andrew and Jay, where Beth walked between them babbling like an idiot.

Vivienne looked at Kendra, and her best friend gave her a tight-lipped smile. "Okay, I'm ninety-nine percent sure he'll understand."

CHAPTER 11

Kendra pulled the car alongside the dark, wooded road. Kirby lived in the least desirable part of Richmond, right next to the highway, with the closest neighbor over half a mile away. It was isolated, but not quiet. The non-stop whirring of cars and trucks on I-90 filled the air, which made it the perfect place for a party.

They got out and stood in front of the old dilapidated house, lit up from the inside and thumping with some kind of rap music.

"Not many cars yet. We're early," said Vivienne nervously.

"Yeah, but as soon as the football game's over it will be insane," Beth said proudly.

Kirby's parties were the place to go, but really they were the *only* place to go. No one in high school could get away with parties like his. Kirby was twenty-one and went to the local community college. His mom, Beth's aunt, was divorced and tended bar at a nightclub downtown. She didn't come home much on the weekends.

Vivienne looked down the road and could see Brady and company walking toward them.

"Should we wait for them?" Kendra asked.

"Uh, yeah...we did invite them," Beth answered as if it was the dumbest question in the world.

All three guys walked up with smiles on their faces. Vivienne could only imagine what they'd talked about on the way over. Maybe something like, "Wow, so that's the little thief that took your dad's money! How embarrassed must she be?"

She couldn't look any of them in the eye.

"After you ladies." Andrew waved his arm toward the front door. Beth and Kendra looked at each other and giggled. Giggled! *Unbelievable.*

When they walked into the house, Vivienne immediately smelled the pot. Kirby was sitting on the couch with a couple of his cronies, passing around a giant purple bong. Great, now they could all go home smelling like weed.

Kirby got up, his long curly hair tucked behind a knitted beanie. "Oh, hey! My favorite cousin!" He hugged Beth and then turned back to the guys on the couch. "Hey! Put that shit away, we have guests."

"It's okay." Beth laughed.

"So is the game over already?" he asked, the stupid grin never leaving his face.

"No, but it was kind of lame," she said. "Sorry we're so early. I hope it's okay."

"Of course! Always happy to see my little cuz!" he laughed, teetering on his heels. Obviously he'd been smoking for a while.

"Oh." Beth loved taking center stage. "And these are my friends, Andrew, Jay and Brady."

Vivienne cringed and glanced at Kendra who was rolling her eyes behind Beth's back.

"Cool. Well, make yourselves comfortable, there's a keg in the kitchen."

"Thanks, man," Jay said first, and Brady and Andrew followed with guy nods.

"No problemo!"

They made their way through the small hallway and into the kitchen. A group of girls from Richmond High sat around a table talking and laughing. They were seniors, and Vivienne only knew one of them by name—Delaney—but as soon as they saw Andrew, and probably Brady too, their eyes lit up. "Hey, girls!" said Delaney in her friendliest voice. Vivienne would bet her iPhone that she had no clue what any of their names were.

"Hey!" chirped Beth. This time though, Beth didn't want to offer any introductions.

They all crowded around the keg without a word, much to Delaney's disappointment. Andrew took up bartending duty, filling their red plastic cups with cheap beer. Brady was standing so close behind Vivienne she could feel his breath on the back of her ear, giving her goosebumps.

She didn't know what made her do it, but it was as if she couldn't help herself—she casually turned around, and as nonchalantly as possible, glanced up at him. That was a mistake. His eyes were fixed on her and he grinned, or maybe smirked.

She whipped her head back around, her cheeks burning. All she could think of in that moment was, *He has the cutest dimple in his chin…oh my God, get a grip Vivienne!*

"Hey! Earth to Vivienne," Beth said. "Give Andrew your cup!"

"Oh, sorry." She reached over, handed her cup to Andrew and tried to pay attention to what Beth was saying, "So, yeah, we're cousins, but we're really like brother and sister." *Oh no, please no more Kirby talk.*

"Oh, and Kirby always has a killer Halloween party. You guys should definitely come to that."

"For you." A red cup suddenly appeared in front of her. Brady was holding it.

"Thanks," she said without looking at him and took a gulp. She hated the taste of beer, but at that moment she had an overwhelming urge to drink. He was standing right next to her and she had to say something—she needed to finally end the tension. "Brady, I want to—"

"Hey, guys!" Before she could finish, Kendra was yelling from the back door. "Come check this out!"

Brady turned and walked away like everyone else, leaving her standing there. "Explain," she finished, to herself. He wasn't going to make it easy on her, was he?

She made her way out back and took in a breath of cold, weed-free air. It had turned into a crisp and cloudless night and the first thing she noticed was the bonfire. But all of the lawn chairs scattered around it were empty.

"Vivienne, over here!" she heard Kendra call out.

Toward the back of the yard, everybody was sitting at a couple of small picnic tables in the grass. Kendra was lying on the seat of one of the tables, looking up. "Come see, Vivienne! It's amazing!"

Vivienne took another gulp of her beer. With the glow of the fire behind her, it got darker as she walked, and she took careful steps through the bumpy grass. All she needed was to fall and humiliate herself even further.

Beth and Andrew sat opposite Kendra at one table, Jay was sitting in a reclining lawn chair, and Brady sat at the other table by himself. Of course he did. If she didn't sit there, it would be way more awkward than it already was.

Vivienne took a seat across from him and avoided his eyes by immediately looking up at the sky. "Wow!" It just slipped out. She couldn't remember a time when she had ever seen so many stars. For a few seconds she actually forgot about where she was, lost in the beauty of it.

"Hey, Rain Man!" Jay yelled, breaking her dreamlike trance. "Why don't you give us all an astronomy lesson?"

Beth almost spit out her beer. "What did you call him?"

Jay laughed. "Rain Man. You know, like the movie."

Beth shook her head no. She was leaning so far into Andrew, she was practically sitting in his lap.

Vivienne had seen the movie, but there was no way she was participating in that conversation. She looked at Brady, who was staring down at his cup of beer.

"Well, Google it," Jay said. "Brady's a savant."

Kendra sat up. "What does that mean exactly?"

Andrew piped in, "It means he's brain-damaged. Tell 'em, O'Connell."

Brady's wouldn't look up. "Stop it, assholes."

But Jay had no intention of stopping. "No, seriously, check this out. Brady, what's thirty-seven thousand, nine hundred and eighty-two, times four hundred fifty-six?"

"Stop." He glared at Jay, "seriously."

Vivienne watched Brady's face. When she was curious about something, she couldn't let it go, which sometimes got her into trouble, present situation included. And she was definitely curious about the boy sitting in front of her. "Do you know the answer?"

He looked up at her and said without skipping a beat, "Seventeen million, three hundred nineteen thousand, seven hundred and ninety-two."

"No way!" Beth shrieked. She had already typed it into her calculator app. "He's right!" She held it up for everyone to see.

Kendra practically jumped up from her table and slid into the seat next to Brady. "Wow. That's pretty impressive. Have you always been able to do that?"

Vivienne quickly put down her beer and got up from the table. "Hey, Brady, can I talk to you for a minute?"

He smiled, a smile she still couldn't read. "Sure."

As she began walking toward the house, she could feel him following on her heels. The stupid charade had gone on long enough. Everyone probably knew the truth, and nobody really seemed to care. While she was freaking out and worrying about what would happen next, everyone else was just having a good time on a Friday night.

She walked to the side of the house, where she wouldn't have to shout over the blaring music. When she stopped and turned, he was right there. Close—really close. She took a step back.

Brady crossed his arms in front of him, leaned one shoulder against the house and waited. He wasn't smiling anymore; he obviously wanted answers.

It was impossible to look him in the eye. "Okay, first off, I'm really sorry." She could hear a tremble in her own voice and hated it. "I have the envelope. It's a long story, but I was going to put it in the mailbox tonight. I swear."

She managed a quick glance at his face which remained expressionless. "Anyway, I'm not a bad person. I would never just—take money like that. Honestly, I was going to put it in Chad's—."

"Your boyfriend," Brady interrupted.

"My ex-boyfriend," she corrected. "See, we got in this fight and I—"

"Look," he cut her off again, "do you have the money or not?"

"Not right now, of course. It's at my house. It's safe, trust me."

He shook his head. "Trust you? Really?"

"Okay, bad choice of words, but I'm telling the truth. My friends and I can just go to my house and pick it up."

"Whatever." He sighed, but seemed satisfied. "But we'll be following right behind you again."

Before he walked away, she needed to ask him something that had been bothering her. "Why didn't you just say something at the game? I mean, why come to the party and everything?"

"I don't know." He shrugged. "We never pass up a good party."

And then she saw it—a glimpse of the shy Brady from the night before, his eyes a little softer, his voice a little more forgiving. "And it was kind of fun to watch you squirm."

And flip-flop went her stomach.

CHAPTER 12

Vivienne told her friends, who were now sitting around the warm campfire, that she wanted to leave. "Hey, guys, I'm not feeling great."

Beth immediately got up and led Vivienne away from the fire. "We'll be right back." She dug her fingers into Vivienne's arm so viciously, she knew she'd have bruises in the morning. "Vivienne, we can't leave now. I am begging you! Can we please hang with them a little longer?"

"I'm sorry, but I feel like crap," she said, not a complete lie.

Beth wasn't giving up. She turned and yelled over to the fire, "Kendra, couldn't she just take your car? I'm sure Jay could give us a ride, he's a DD. You wouldn't mind giving us a ride home later, would you Jay?"

Oh my God. Absolutely zero shame.

"Uh, yeah, I could do that." He looked at Brady and shrugged. "Sure."

But there was a big problem with that idea. Vivienne needed to get the money to Brady somehow. "I don't know if I feel good enough to drive by myself, though."

As soon as she said it, Brady was at her side. "I can take you. I only had a few sips of my beer."

"Perfect." Beth skipped back to the fire and pulled her lawn chair closer to Andrew's. Kendra came over, reached into her coat pocket and pulled out her keys. "Here." She looked at Vivienne and winked. "Hope you feel better."

"Thanks."

Brady was already two steps ahead of her, walking toward Kendra's car. Vivienne suddenly contemplated what she was doing. For some reason, even though she barely knew him, she completely trusted Brady. But she also realized that was stupid. Most psychos came off as perfectly nice people. Any girl with half a brain in her head, and she'd like to think she had more than just a half, would take some precautions.

When they got to the car, she threw him the keys and opened the rear door.

"What are you doing?" he asked.

"Sitting in the backseat."

He stared at her. "Why?"

"Oh, and I always carry pepper spray with me, just so you know." She jumped into the backseat and shut the door.

He stood outside the car for a couple seconds before he opened the door and got into the driver's seat. "Unbelievable," he said under his breath.

"I'm sorry, but think about this: what if you had a daughter? What would you want her to do? That's what my mom asked me once, and she makes a really good point."

Brady shook his head. "I'm not sure how to even begin to respond to that." He turned around and looked at her. "But I can assure you, the last thing on my mind is trying to make a move on you. I just want my money back. And once I get that, you will never see me again."

"Fine." But she felt a pang of disappointment. She wasn't sure why, but she did.

He started the car. "Where to, ma'am?"

"Ha-ha."

The ride to her house was only ten minutes, but it already felt like forever. Brady had driving to preoccupy him; she used her phone. She texted Kendra.

Vivienne: *Sitting in backseat. Awkward. He called me ma'am.*

Kendra: *LOL* ☺ *Beth all over Andrew. I don't think he's feelin' it.*

Vivienne: *What a shocker. Text me later.*

Kendra: *Bye!*

Vivienne couldn't stand the silence. She could only imagine what Brady thought of her. She had to say something. "So, Brady, how did you know I had the money? I mean, I could've given it to Chad and he could've taken it."

"True, I didn't know. But I had to start with you. And when I got to the game and saw the look on your face...well, it was pretty funny, actually."

Vivienne could feel her cheeks getting hot. "I was scared, okay? And embarrassed."

For some inexplicable reason, she wanted him to understand. She didn't want him to think she was some horrible person. "Can I please explain to you what happened?"

"Fine," he sighed. "Explain it to me, *please*."

She ignored his sarcasm. "Okay, well, last night I decided I was going to break up with Chad—and that's a whole other story. I should've given him the envelope right away, but I kind of lied and told him I was outside looking for Oscar—that's his cat. I just didn't want any distractions, so I decided I would break up with him first, and then put the envelope in the mailbox on my way out."

"But..." Brady prompted.

"But when I told him I wanted to break up, he completely flipped out and threw me out of his house. Literally, he grabbed me by the arm and pushed me out the front door!" She took a one-second breather. "And then I was so freaked out, I mean, he had this completely psycho smile on his face, and I just—"

"Okay, okay, I get it." Brady's voice was quiet, and strangely comforting. "You don't need to explain anymore. Really." He shook his head. "God, what an asshole."

"Yeah, a real big asshole."

She could see Brady smile at that.

Just then they arrived at 28513 Sycamore, home sweet home. Should she invite him in? It would be the polite thing to do. "Do you want to come in?" she asked.

"Uh, no. I'm good here."

"Right." She gave him a weak smile.

She ran up to the house, and as soon as she entered the front door she could hear girls laughing in the family room. She peeked in to find Tess was having a sleepover—again. Vivienne went straight up the steps to her room and whipped open the door.

What the hell?

She must be in the wrong room. The bed was made, the floor was clean—everything looked spotless. Her eyes immediately went to the closet floor, where shoes and shoeboxes were stacked in neat little rows. Above them, newly installed hooks held purses and bags and...

Where was it? She began ripping off the purses and bags one by one. She pushed aside the hangers full of clothes, then got on her knees and began pushing through boxes. She looked under the bed, in the dresser drawers, in the closet again.

It was gone.

She ran down the stairs so fast she fell on her ass halfway down. "Tess!" She was screaming. "Tess!"

She went into the family room, where she found a circle of nine-year-olds lying on the floor in their sleeping bags. They were watching *Pitch Perfect.*

"Tess! Did you borrow my backpack? The pink one with the big V on it?!"

They all stared at her, wide-eyed. One girl pulled a pillow up in front of her face.

"You know, the old one—it was in my closet!" Vivienne searched the room as she asked.

"What's your problem, Vivienne?" Tess yelled back. "We're trying to watch a movie here. I didn't touch your stupid backpack!"

That sent the girls into a giggling frenzy. She took a deep breath. "Where's Morgan?"

"I don't know."

"Where's Mom?"

"I don't know, Vivienne! I don't keep tabs on everybody!" Tess rolled her eyes and there was more laughter. Vivienne wanted to smack her.

She walked away and frantically called her mom. She answered on the third ring. "Hey, honey."

"Mom! What did you do with the stuff in my room?"

"Vivienne slow down. I can barely understand you."

She exhaled loudly and cleared her throat, which felt like it was closing up on her. "Mom, when you cleaned out my room, I had this pink backpack in my closet, it had a big silver V on it. What did you do with it?"

"Oh, I'm sorry, hon. I took a few things I didn't think you used anymore. You had so much clutter in that room, Vivienne, and I've been telling you for weeks to clean it up."

She suddenly felt like she couldn't breathe. "Where is the backpack?! The pink one?"

"What do you want with that old thing, anyway? You haven't used it since the third grade."

"Mom, can you just tell me what you did with it?"

"Well, I'm sorry, hon, but I dropped it off a couple of hours ago with all of the other stuff."

*No, no, no...*Vivienne closed her eyes. "Where, Mom?"

"At Goodwill, of course."

CHAPTER 13

As soon as Vivienne left the car, Brady felt his whole body relax. He reached into his pocket and pulled out a fresh piece of peppermint gum. He wiped his sweaty hands on the front of his jeans and took a deep breath.

He thought he had done a pretty good job of playing it cool most of the night, but inside he was a ball of nerves. Vivienne put him on edge, and he wasn't sure why. He had always been very comfortable in his own skin, never really caring what other people thought of him. But he did care what Vivienne thought. And that was new, unfamiliar to him.

After a few minutes, the gum began to lose its flavor, and he started to lose his patience. What the hell could she be doing in there? He waited another five minutes and then got out of the car.

He knocked on the front door and a little girl answered—maybe ten if he had to guess—a miniature

Vivienne. An entourage of girls in pajamas and ponytails appeared behind her.

"Can I help you?" asked mini-Vivienne. The girls couldn't contain themselves and erupted into laughter.

He felt like a jackass. "Uh, I'm looking for Vivienne?"

"Oh, well, come on in." She opened the door further. "Vivienne! You have a visitor!" she screamed in an earsplitting voice.

Brady stepped inside and all of the girls scampered away in hysterics.

Vivienne appeared at the top of the stairs, and the second he saw her he knew something was wrong—she was white, not just pale, but sickly white.

As she walked down the stairs, she held on to the rail like she needed to steady herself. "Can we talk outside for a minute?" she asked. Her hands were empty. Where was the envelope?

A bad feeling crept into his stomach as he walked outside.

She immediately started rambling. "Brady before you say anything, please just hear me out… I don't have the money right this minute, but I know where it is and—."

"What!?" he erupted. "You're not serious, are you?" But he knew she was.

She held her hands up. "I know where it is. It's at the Goodwill in Fulton."

WTF? He stared at her in disbelief. "The Goodwill store? How in the hell did it end up at Goodwill?"

"I hid the envelope inside this old backpack I had." She went into pace mode, back and forth, back and forth. "And my mom is a complete neat freak, like crazy about it, and she cleaned out my closet, and took it to Goodwill."

"Wait!" A dull pain began spreading over his eyes, muddling his thoughts. "Let me get this straight. That all happened tonight? While you were at the game?" Was she for real, or was she just screwing with him?

Vivienne looked like she was going to cry. "Yes. Sometimes my mom goes on these Goodwill runs and she just scours the house for junk, and tonight she went into my room and the backpack was really old and—"

"Just stop!" he yelled. He ran his fingers through his hair and looked up at the sky. "This can't be happening."

"Brady, I'm so sorry."

"You're sorry?" He bit his lip before he really went off on her. "What does the backpack look like?"

"It's bright pink, like plastic, and has this big silver V on it."

He turned and walked away—to where, he didn't have a clue. But he had to get away from her.

"Wait! Brady, wait!" She started following him. "They open at nine tomorrow, so I just have to—"

"You?" He whipped around and looked at her pale, pleading face. He had no sympathy. "No, Vivienne, *you* don't have to do anything." And then he added, "I think I can take it from here."

"Brady, I feel so bad about this. I am really sorry."

He turned his back on her again and started down the sidewalk. He couldn't listen to it anymore. She was sorry? What if somebody had already bought the backpack? What if the money was gone for good?

His dad—after the initial shock had worn off—had been surprisingly cool about the whole thing. He had told Brady to just let it go, learn a lesson from it, and move on.

But then his dad started blaming himself. "I never should have gotten you involved in the first place," he said. And then, the thing that Brady dreaded most. "Maybe I need to rethink the whole damn business."

Well, there was no way Brady would let that happen. He knew how much the business meant to his dad and he needed to prove he could handle it. He owed his dad that much.

As soon as Brady began texting Jay, a car came cruising down the street, honking its horn—Jay's Volvo. It pulled up alongside him. "Everything square?" Jay was driving with Andrew in the passenger seat; Vivienne's two friends were in back.

Brady walked over to the car and opened the back door. "Get out." He sounded like an asshole, but he didn't care.

"Wow, you don't have to be rude about it." The first girl got out and the really annoying one was still saying her goodbyes to Andrew. "So, talk to you soon? You can text me anytime."

Andrew nodded. "Sure thing."

"Jesus Christ," Brady mumbled, and then he stopped before getting into the car. "Hey, one more thing!" he called over to the girls.

They turned around, waiting eagerly. "I just thought you guys should know"—he paused for effect—"Andrew's gay."

The look on their faces was almost enough to make him smile—almost. Brady slammed the car door and they took off down the street.

CHAPTER 14

Vivienne arrived at the Fulton Goodwill at 8:30 a.m. just in case they would let her in early. She stood by the entrance doors and waited until 8:45 a.m. when the first employee showed up. An older woman, a little on the plump side with a bouffant of white hair, greeted her. "Good morning." She smiled. "Is there something I can help you with?"

Vivienne noticed the name tag on her blue vest. "Yes—Bonnie, uh, do you think there is any way I could go in a little early? My mom dropped off something of mine by mistake and I really need to find it as soon as possible."

Bonnie frowned. "You know what, honey, I've got a few things I have to do inside first, and then I'll come and get ya, okay?"

Vivienne knew Brady would be there soon and she was dreading having to face him again. She had worried about it all night. But she needed to find that backpack as much as he did. Not only was there the envelope inside, but more important to her was the thing tucked right alongside it.

At 8:55 a.m., Bonnie still hadn't let her in, and a small black car pulled into the mostly empty parking lot. It was Brady. As he got out and walked toward her, she felt her heartbeat pick up speed, the flutter in her chest fluttered faster, the flip-flop in her belly flopped harder. She couldn't control it—it just happened.

There was just something about him, the way he carried himself, the way he talked, the way he smiled, the way he looked at her—even when he was mad.

"They won't let you in?" he asked.

She felt instant relief at his words—he sounded surprisingly nice. "No, the lady said she had to do some stuff inside first."

Brady put his face up to the glass door and began peering inside. She noticed the orange helmet on his hoodie and attempted to make small talk. "So you're a Browns fan?"

"Yep, inherited it from my dad, unfortunately."

"Like a disease, huh?" she joked nervously. She really didn't want him to hate her. "I like the Browns, but I'm just not really into football."

He ignored her. "It's almost nine, where is she?"

Vivienne's mind raced as she tried to think of something to say. "Um, do you ever go to any games, Browns games?"

At that he glanced over at her. "I know you feel bad about this, but you really didn't have to come here."

"Well, I—"

Her phone beeped. It was a text from Kendra: *Did you find it?*

Vivienne: *No! Not even open yet.*

Kendra: *Remember to ask about Andrew.*

Vivienne: *Ok!*

Just then Bonnie appeared and unlocked the door from the other side. "Sorry about that, but I've got to turn on some lights and stuff before opening up."

Brady walked in and immediately began surveying the surroundings.

Bonnie eyed him up and down and then turned her attention to Vivienne. "Now, you said your mom brought something in?"

"Yes, it was a backpack—pink, like a little girl's. Around eight o'clock last night. Where would we look for that?"

Luckily, the Fulton Goodwill was one of the smaller stores, not one of those huge Goodwill warehouses. There were probably fifty rows of clothing in the middle, and all of the other stuff was set up in displays along the walls.

Bonnie pointed over to the back of the store. "In the back there you'll see a couple of racks of the purses and bags." Brady was already heading to the back.

"But I would almost guarantee you won't find it there!" she called after him. "If your mom came in last night, it's likely still in drop-off."

Vivienne cringed. "Drop-off?"

"Yes, it's where the stuff goes before we put it out in the store. I'm not really supposed to let you back there, though."

Vivienne's face must have looked pathetic because before she could ask, Bonnie added, "But I guess if you put everything back exactly as you found it, it probably wouldn't do any harm."

Vivienne pushed that thought out of her head and followed Brady to the back. He was rifling through the racks of purses and bags, but it was immediately obvious it wasn't there.

A bright pink backpack with a sequin *V* would have stood out, especially against the mostly brown and black leather. In fact, Vivienne spotted a really decent-looking Kate Spade and decided that when the whole nightmare was over, she might go back there to shop.

Brady looked over his shoulder. "It's not here."

She had to look away. "Well, Bonnie said it might be in drop-off?"

Brady ran his hands through his hair. "You mean all the shit they haven't gone through yet?"

She tried her best to sound optimistic. "I'm sure it won't be too bad."

CHAPTER 15

Brady opened the door to the drop-off room and thought his head might explode right there. He wanted to punch something but opted to take a deep breath instead. "Well Vivienne, do you think *this* classifies as bad?"

She was smart and didn't say a word. He wanted to tell her to just leave, to get far, far, away from him. But now that he'd seen the magnitude of the job in front of him, he knew he'd need her help.

The room was the size of a two-car garage—maybe bigger. Plastic garbage bags filled the room wall to wall, at least knee-high. It looked like a giant ball pit filled with black and white balls of trash.

"Yeah, it's a lot." Goodwill Lady appeared behind them. "Once a month, we ship off most of this to other stores because we just don't have the room. This is almost a full month's worth." She turned to Vivienne. "If your mom would've dropped the backpack off after Tuesday, there would be a lot less here."

Of course there would, thought Brady.

Goodwill Lady went on, "I would start over by that door. But honestly, the guys just throw the bags all over the place in here, so it really could be anywhere."

Of course it could. Brady took another deep breath. His frustration level was reaching a breaking point.

"Oh, and I'm really not supposed to let you back here, so please don't take stuff out of the bags, okay? It's okay if you look through them, just leave 'em the way you found 'em."

"Okay," Vivienne finally said. "Thanks a lot for letting us do this."

Goodwill Lady made her exit, and the first thing Brady did was survey the room. "Well, my guess would be about two hundred bags, give or take." It wasn't really a guess, more of a quick spatial calculation. "There are two of us, say a minute per bag, so if we go straight through, nonstop, it should only take us about an hour and a half—worst-case scenario." But lately, it seemed as if worst-case scenario was the only scenario.

"Brady, I don't even know what to say at this point," she said quietly.

He didn't know what to say either. When he had pulled into the Goodwill parking lot and seen Vivienne standing at the door, he wasn't angry. In fact, he was kind of excited. No matter how stressed out he was about finding the money, or how frustrated he was with her, there was a nagging feeling inside of him that wouldn't leave. And it wasn't a bad feeling.

"Wait, I thought of something." Vivienne was on her cell phone. "Mom—hi—no, not yet—Mom, what did you take the stuff in? Black bag, white bag, what?" A pause. "Okay, thanks."

Brady could tell by the defeated sound of her voice, Vivienne's mom hadn't chosen one of the few ecoconscious brown bags that were mixed into the pit.

"She said they were black bags, no drawstring, the kind you tie by hand."

Of course they were. A red drawstring would be way too much to ask for. "Okay, I'd guess that cuts it down by a third."

"But it's probably at the top, right?" She was trying so hard to sound positive. It was irritating but strangely comforting at the same time.

"Probably," he conceded.

"And at least it's bright pink—it should be easy to spot, right?"

He found himself smiling, ever so slightly. "Right."

They worked near the door first, like Goodwill Lady suggested, wading through the bags of junk in silence. They were basically sitting on bags, opening bags. A new problem became immediately apparent—a lot of the bags were tied tightly, in knots. It made the process way more tedious, and the one-minute-per-bag estimation was completely off. It could take a lot longer than he'd initially thought.

Only five minutes into the search, Vivienne was talking. "So can I ask you something?"

"Maybe."

"Is Andrew really gay?"

Of all the things she could've said, he hadn't expected that. The image of Kendra and Beth standing there, eyes wide and mouths open, flashed in his mind. He laughed. "Yes, he's really gay."

"So that was all part of your plan, right? Get the tall, dark and handsome guy to lure the girls in?"

"Well, it worked, didn't it?" Brady opened another bag—nothing but old towels, not a glimpse of pink.

"What did you think I was gonna do? Run away from you?"

He shrugged. "I didn't know what you were going to do, but Andrew's always a good distraction."

"Yeah, for my friends, I guess. He's not really my type."

Brady looked up at that, immediately intrigued. "Oh, of course—I'm sorry. You like the all-American football player type."

She laughed. "Yeah, and I told you how that worked out."

Another thing became immediately apparent. Vivienne liked to talk.

"To tell you the truth, I didn't like Chad from the very beginning."

Brady shook his head. "See, that's what I don't get. A guy asks you out and you say 'yes' even though you think he's a jerk."

"No, it wasn't like that," she countered. "See, he was dating this girl for two years and then she moved to Arizona, so I didn't know him very well. He just seemed like a nice, quiet guy. But after spending like five minutes with him, I knew it was a big mistake."

Brady wanted to know more. "So how long did you go out?"

"Two months. I only stayed with him that long because, well, he was Chad Sutton. People thinks he's such a great guy. He's got everyone fooled."

"Not everyone—not you."

"Brady." He felt his insides do a twist when she said his name. "I know what I did was incredibly stupid, but I swear I was going to put that envelope in the mailbox after the game. Yesterday was not a good day, and every chance I had to return it, something happened. I hope you believe me."

He looked at Vivienne with her pretty face and perfect smile—she was such a contrast against the chaotic pile of dirty, discarded junk that surrounded her. He had to laugh at the irony of it.

"What's so funny?"

"Nothing." He shook his head. "I believe you." The truth was, he always had. She didn't seem capable of being such an elaborate liar.

He put his head down into another bag. More clothes, more throwaways, more crap.

An hour later, they had gone through over half of it. He had found three backpacks: Thomas the Train, Hello Kitty and Star Wars—no pink one with a big V in sight.

"Hey, Brady, look at this."

He turned around and they were suddenly only an arm's length apart. She smiled, and the weird nagging feeling inside of him got a little weirder.

"Rubik's Cube," she said as she held it up in front of him. "You're supposed to be a genius, right? Here." She handed it to him. "Let's see if you can solve it."

"I'm not a genius." He looked down at the multicolored cube in his palm. He didn't like using his freakish brain for entertainment. People were always so impressed by it, but it never felt like he was doing anything special. It just felt automatic.

But he still had an ego, just like anybody else. "I can solve it—I just think we should look for the backpack."

"Oh, I see, because it might take too long." Her eyes were taunting him. "What was I thinking?" Now he knew exactly what the expression 'under the skin' meant, because Vivienne was definitely getting under his.

"I haven't done one of these since I was like ten." He looked over the rows of jumbled-up colors, the next five moves already in his head.

Vivienne reached for the cube. "Hey if you're worried you won't be able to do it..."

No problem. As if on autopilot, his fingers began twisting and turning the little colored squares. His brain was in control and he watched the sides morph into solid colors. Done.

"Oh my God, Brady! That took you like ten seconds!"

He shrugged. "Probably closer to twenty." Okay, maybe he did enjoy getting a reaction out of some people. "Last year, a speed-cuber at the Nationals in Vegas did it in around seven seconds."

"Speed-cuber?" she asked.

Brady was suddenly embarrassed. "Yeah, they have competitions, like huge tournaments for the Rubik's Cube."

"Really?" She smiled. "Did you ever do one?"

"What, compete?" He shook his head. "No, my friends and I used to compete against each other just for fun." Then he quickly added, "But that was a long time ago."

Vivienne probably thought he was a complete loser. Speed-cubing, astronomy—the Cleveland Browns, for Christ's sake. And she didn't even know about the worst thing—running a gambling business with his dad.

They sifted through more bags, getting closer to the end. They had been there almost two hours. With every bag he searched, and every minute that passed, the knot in Brady's stomach grew bigger and bigger.

He could tell she was getting worried too. He could see it on her face when she tried to make conversation again. "So if you're not from Garfield, where are you from?"

"I'm from right here in Fulton."

"Oh," she said, like they were having a nice conversation over coffee and not standing in the middle of a giant trash pile. "Well, at least you didn't have to drive far to get here."

Yep, she was definitely getting nervous.

And he was way past nervous.

Brady picked up the last black bag. He sifted through the inside—old baby clothes. He dropped it at his feet.

Vivienne avoided his eyes, hands on hips, head down, looking around the room, looking anywhere but at him. "Maybe we missed a bag." She glanced up for only a second. "We could look again real quickly—"

"No," he said calmly.

He looked up at the ceiling and then at her. "Vivienne, we looked through every single bag, even the white ones, even the brown ones. We checked the tie bags and the drawstrings. We separated them, we went slowly, we were methodical. We didn't miss any."

Her eyes were back on the floor. "Maybe it was actually in one of the bags we already checked, like hidden down deep or something, and we overlooked it?"

He couldn't take it. "Really, you think so? A bright pink backpack with fucking sparkles on it is not something we would've overlooked." And then he added, "At least, I wouldn't't've."

Asshole Brady was out in full force, but he couldn't help it. He couldn't believe this was happening. Never in a million years had he thought that he wouldn't get the money back, that he would have to go home and say, "Sorry, Dad, it's gone for good."

"Hey!" Vivienne got that optimistic look on her face again. "My mom said she brought it in around eight last night. Maybe it did get put out in the store. And maybe someone did buy it last night before they closed. That has to be it."

"Did you say something?" he quipped. "Because all I heard was 'maybe, maybe, maybe...'"

She didn't seem daunted by Asshole Brady. "It's a definite possibility."

He couldn't rule it out completely. "Okay, say by chance that happened, how in the hell do we find out who bought it?"

She shrugged. "We can ask Bonnie, maybe she would help us out."

"Ladies and gentlemen, we have another maybe." He sighed. "Do you really think Goodwill Lady is going to give us personal information about the customers? It's not gonna happen, Vivienne."

"We have to try."

"Again the we." He dusted himself off from the grime that had settled all over his clothes. "I've officially given up, Vivienne. I will chalk this one up as a loss, have to pay back my dad for the next ten years, and never—ever—make the mistake of trusting a girl just because she's pretty."

He had to get out of there before he said anything else. He turned to the door and she grabbed him by the arm, pulling him back. "Wait!"

She stood in front of him, only inches away, her eyes pleading. "I'm so sorry I screwed this up so bad, but I have to find that backpack."

Now he was confused. "Vivienne, it's my money, remember? I said I'm done."

"That's the thing." Her eyes hit the floor again. "There was something of mine in the backpack too."

"Oh, I see." So, she wasn't really helping him, she was helping herself. He laughed. "This whole time, I actually thought you felt bad about the money."

"Brady, I did—I do!" She stepped closer. "You probably don't care, but I didn't sleep at all last night because I realized how badly I screwed things up for you."

She had done absolutely nothing to prove she was telling the truth, but when he looked at her, he believed her. He did. As she stood in front of him, so close he could see the little V on the chain around her neck, he felt his anger dissolve away. "So what is it? This *thing* that's so important to you?"

CHAPTER 16

Vivienne didn't know if it was the time or place to go into the whole story, but she had to give him something. "It's a notebook."

"Ahhh..." He smiled. "Like your diary?"

"No," she sighed. "It's not even mine."

His eyebrows rose. "You've got someone else's diary?"

"No." She paused. "And it's not a diary."

"How did you—"

"I didn't steal it!" she answered quickly, before he had a chance to ask the question. "Someone gave it to me."

He eyed her up and down, once again giving her that *Should I believe a word she says?* look. She really wanted him to believe her, and not just because she thought he could help her. The truth was, she didn't want him to leave. "It's just incredibly important to me."

His voice got quiet. "Okay, fine, I guess we could try with Goodwill Lady. Who knows? Maybe we'll get lucky."

She felt her whole body relax in relief and she smiled at him. "Thank you."

In that moment, as they stood across from each other, their eyes met. And this time she didn't look away. She couldn't look away. He suddenly stepped closer until they were only inches apart. He was so close she could see a small scar on his left cheek and she could smell his faint scent of soap and mint. He gave her a crooked grin and put his hand on her shoulder. Her legs suddenly felt hollow, her stomach flip-flopped, and her heart pounded in her chest.

Surrounded by garbage and gunk, knee-high in people's unwanted crap, it was the most romantic moment, in the most unromantic of places. His eyes never leaving hers, his hand moved slowly over her shoulder, around to her back, turning her into a ball of shivers. Oh my God, was he going to kiss her?

He stepped back suddenly, holding up a long fuzzy cobweb. "You had this on your back." He smiled.

Her cheeks were on fire with embarrassment. "Oh, thanks." Holy humiliation.

"Hey!" Bonnie was standing in the doorway with a big grin on her face. "Did you kids have any luck?"

Brady answered first. "No."

"Oh, that's too bad." She gave the room a quick scan. "Well, it looks like you guys put everything back the way it was, so I appreciate that." She held the door open for them and waited.

They followed Bonnie into the store, and Brady pulled Vivienne aside. "Look, I have an idea, but you're going to have to lie to Goodwill Lady."

"Her name is Bonnie, by the way."

"Okay…Bonnie. You're going to have to tell Bonnie some incredibly sad story. The backpack has to be sentimental. Can you think of anything?"

She said the first thing that popped into her head. "Well… I mean, I could tell her it was the last that thing my dad gave to me before he died." That came out way too easily.

"Perfect," he said, and then he stopped, eyes wide. "Oh God, is your dad—"

"No! He's alive and well," she assured him. "But it sounds really sad, right?"

Brady laughed. "This is so messed up."

"Yes, it is."

By the time she finished telling Bonnie the completely fabricated tale, the woman looked like she might burst into tears. "Oh, you poor thing, of course I'll help you."

Vivienne glanced over at Brady. He definitely knew how to act the part, too. His face was full of concern.

"Now, I could get in big trouble for this." Bonnie looked around the empty store and lowered her voice. She leaned in closer. "I can get the receipts from eight to ten last night. If the customer paid by check, you're in luck. With a credit or debit card, I can at least get you a name."

Thank God! Maybe they had a chance of finding it after all. "Thank you so much, Bonnie. I really appreciate it."

Bonnie disappeared into a door behind the register.

"If we just get a name, do you think you could find an address?" Vivienne asked. "I mean, you found me pretty easily."

He smiled. "Yeah, but I knew what city you lived in."

"Oh, right." She had to stay hopeful. "But you're good with computers and stuff, right?"

"I'm okay, but my friend Jay is ridiculous. He can find anyone. But obviously, the more common the name, the longer it will take." Then he added, "Just pray we don't get a Smith."

Vivienne drummed her fingers on the counter. "I feel terrible about lying to her like that," she said quietly.

Brady shrugged. "You're not hurting anyone by it. Sometimes you've got to tell a little lie for the greater good."

"Is that your personal philosophy?" she asked.

"I don't know, is it yours?" he retorted.

Maybe he didn't believe her after all. "What does that mean? I told you the truth about the envelope. You said you believed me."

"I do believe you—about the envelope."

"Well what are you referring to, then?" she asked, probably louder than she should have.

"Shhh...nothing, just drop it."

"No." She lowered her voice. "Tell me."

He turned and looked her directly in the eye. "Okay, Vivienne, when I asked you if Jeff Sutton was your dad, you said yes."

She shook her head. "No—no, see, you said it like, 'Jeff Sutton is your dad, he's a lawyer, right?' and I said 'right.' Technically, that's not really a lie."

Brady rolled his eyes. "You can't be serious."

"Well—"

Just then Bonnie reentered the room with a small piece of paper, all smiles, her eyes sparkling. "These receipts aren't itemized, so I can't tell you what they bought. Goodwill isn't that sophisticated yet. But there were only two. Friday nights are one of the slowest times. Lucky for you."

"You hear that, Vivienne? Bonnie says we're lucky."

She ignored his sarcasm and gave all of her attention to Bonnie, who leaned over the counter, pointing to the yellow paper. "Even luckier, this one paid with a check. The other one a debit card. But"—she paused—"they had to enter their zip code with their pin, so you have that."

"Wow, this is so helpful, Bonnie." Vivienne gave her most sincere smile. "Thank you again—for all your help, really."

Brady took the paper. "Yeah, thanks a lot."

"No trouble at all. I really hope you find it."

They gave her a quick wave and turned to leave when she called out behind them, "You two make a really cute couple!"

Oh God, she did not just say that! Vivienne felt her shoulders tense, but she kept walking.

If Brady was embarrassed, he didn't show it. When they got outside, he was all business. He read the scrap of paper.

"Michelle Malinowski, nice." He got on his phone and began texting Jay with the info. "He'll find her fast."

"That's kind of scary, actually," Vivienne said. "If he can do it, how many other people can?"

"If people realized how many Jays are out there in the cyberworld, they'd be way more careful with their personal information." Brady pointed to the other name on the list. "The check guy is Mark Whitaker, 877 Lincoln Avenue in Bellevue. That's on the east side, I think, maybe half an hour from here."

Vivienne pulled her hands up into her sweater sleeves. It was cold, cloudy, and threatening rain.

Brady's phone beeped. "Malinowski is at 493 Homewood Drive in Rexford."

"Wow, that *was* quick." She smiled. "Tell Jay I said thanks."

He started walking to his car and she followed. What would they do now? Did he want to go on his own? Should she walk over to her car?

"Rexford's a lot closer than Bellevue, so we should probably go there first," he said. "I can drive if you want?"

She felt her stomach do another flip-flop. "Sure." She tried to sound nonchalant.

Just then, her phone beeped. A text from Kendra: *Need update.*

Vivienne: *Still looking. Yes, he's gay.*

Kendra: *Brady or Andrew?*

Vivienne: *Andrew!!!!!!!!!!!*

Kendra: ☹ *Text me later.*

Vivienne got into the passenger side of Brady's car and welcomed the little bit of warmth. The weather outside was getting nastier by the minute. She tried to relax, but the more time she spent around Brady, the harder it was. Wasn't it supposed to be the other way around?

He was digging in his pocket for his keys. "Hey, do you want to stop and pick up some food? I'm going to pass out if I don't get something to eat."

"Yes, definitely." She was hungry too, but even more concerned about peeing her pants.

Brady started the car and they were off.

CHAPTER 17

"Do you like corned beef sandwiches?" *Stupid question, what girl likes corned beef sandwiches?*

"They're okay, but I can just eat some fries or whatever." She was playing around with the buttons on his car stereo. "Can I change the station?"

"Sure," he said, although she'd already changed it at least three times. "What kind of music do you like?" he asked.

"Pretty much anything…except maybe songs with 'baby' or 'babe' in the lyrics."

He laughed. "I'm with you on that one."

"What about you?" she asked.

Sitting in the confined space with her was putting him on edge. "Ever heard of New Dogma? I'm pretty sure they don't have any songs with 'baby' in them."

"Oh yeah, kind of rock alternative," she said. "I like their music."

"Jay and I got to meet them before their concert at the Q."

"Seriously? How was that?"

"It was pretty cool, but it was more like stand in a long line and get an autograph. We didn't really get to hang out and talk to them."

"But that's still awesome." She was definitely a 'glass half-full' kind of person.

"Yeah, it was," he admitted.

Brady drove toward McGuire's, his stomach grumbling so loud he was afraid she'd be able to hear it over the music. "I know this local place that's got really good food. We could just pick up something and take it with us."

"Sure, that sounds good." She pulled down the vanity mirror and began putting her fingers through her hair. "Just want to make sure I don't have any more cobwebs on me." She smiled.

She didn't even realize how distracting that simple gesture was. He quickly pulled out his phone and made a call to Maggie. "Hey Maggie...I'm good, how are you? Hey, I'm only a couple of minutes away—do you think you could make up a couple of burgers with fries to go?" He looked at Vivienne for confirmation.

"Oh no, seriously I just want fries." Then she added, "Maybe a Coke?"

"Okay, Maggie, one burger, two fries, and add a couple of Cokes." Then he felt another hunger pang. "You know what? Make it two burgers...okay, thanks."

"So you're on a first-name basis with Maggie?" Vivienne pulled something out of her little purse-thing she kept around her wrist. It looked like a little pink egg, and she began sliding it over her lips. *Don't stare, dumbass!*

"Oh…yeah, she owns McGuire's Pub," he bumbled. "It's a neighborhood bar I go to once in a while." *And it's also the place where I conduct an illegal gambling business…*

"So you live close by?"

"Uh, yeah, see that street right there?" He pointed to a sign on the corner that read Wilmore. "My house is six down on the right."

Brady parked in front of the red brick building with green-and-white awnings. He figured using the front entrance like a normal customer was more appropriate under the circumstances.

The truth was, McGuire's was the last place he wanted to go. If any of the guys from the Thursday night club happened to be inside, he was screwed. He didn't even want to think of the fresh material this would provide them—Brady coming into McGuire's with a girl.

But he had thought of something else too. What if Vivienne expected him to pay? He figured he should at least be able to offer, but he only had five bucks on him. He couldn't take that chance, and he knew Maggie would be fine with an IOU.

Inside the dimly lit bar, a few people sat at tables and only two guys sat at the bar. Unfortunately for Brady, one of them was Jimmy Rainey. *Shit, shit, shit.*

When he spotted Brady, his eyes got wide and his mouth opened up like he was about to yell something—and then suddenly, he clamped his mouth shut and grinned. Next Thursday was gonna be hell.

Maggie came running over, all smiles. "Well, isn't this a nice surprise! How is my favorite customer?" *Please don't hug me, please don't hug me...*

Her eyes darted over to Vivienne. "Well, hello there!"

Brady spoke quickly. "Uh, Maggie, this is my friend Vivienne."

Maggie stuck out her bony hand. "Well, it is so very nice to meet you, Vivienne."

"Nice to meet you too." They shook hands.

Maggie looked like she was about to burst from excitement overload, but thankfully, she played it cool. "Well, I'll go grab your food."

"Um, excuse me, could you tell me where the ladies' room is?" Vivienne asked.

"Oh, sure, hon." Maggie pointed to the back of the bar. "It's down that little hallway, second door on your right."

"Thank you." Vivienne gave him a quick smile. "Be right back."

Maggie didn't waste any time. "My oh my, Brady, she is beautiful! I especially love the red hair. She must have Irish in her. No doubt about it!"

Brady could feel the embarrassment flooding his face. "We're just friends, Maggie."

She gave him a dismissive wave. "Well, I am going to tell you something, Brady—from the way she looks at you, that girl wants to be more than friends. Women know these things about each other."

That girl wants to be more than friends... The hot feeling in his face traveled down through the rest of his body, and the weird 'good' feeling deep inside of him came back with a vengeance.

"Just saying." She gave him a wink. "I'll go grab that food for ya."

"Hey, Maggie!" He had almost forgotten. "Do you think it could go on my tab?"

"Absolutely not." She frowned. "It's on the house."

"Thanks." Brady had to use the bathroom too, so he made his way to the back. He would have to pass Jimmy Rainey on his way; there was absolutely no way to avoid it. He tried to sound as casual as possible. "Hey, Jimmy."

Jimmy smiled like he had just won a year's worth of free Budweiser. "Brady, you sly devil." He shook his head. "I knew you had it in you. I just knew it."

What had he done? The heckling he would have to endure Thursday night would be unprecedented.

In the restroom, Brady took a piss, washed his hands, splashed cold water on his face, fixed his hair (which meant shaking it), checked his teeth, zipped his sweatshirt, unzipped his sweatshirt.

He went back out to the bar to find Vivienne—*Oh God, no*—talking to Jimmy Rainey. And she was laughing!

"So this was when Brady was just a kid, oh, maybe around eight years old…"

Brady beelined it over to them as fast as he could. "You know, Vivienne, we should really get going."

She bit down on her lip, amusement all over her face. "Yeah, okay." She held out her hand to Jimmy. "Well, it was very nice to meet you, Jimmy."

"The pleasure is all mine, young lady."

Yeah, Brady bet it was. "See ya later, Jimmy."

"Yes, you will," Jimmy goaded. "Looking forward to it!"

Just in time, Maggie was back. "Here you are!" She placed the white paper bags and cans of Coke on the bar. "Vivienne, it was so nice to meet you. I hope you'll come back and visit us again real soon."

Vivienne glanced at Brady with a grin on her face, and he had to look away.

"Thanks again, Maggie." He gave her his customary wave. "I'll see you later."

"Okay, you two have fun!" she called after them.

Brady cringed one more time before they were finally out the door.

CHAPTER 18

After they'd left McGuire's, Vivienne had a bunch of questions she wanted to ask Brady, but he was too busy eating. Anyway, she wanted to see if he would start the conversation for once. She nibbled on her fries and waited for him to say something—anything.

She got nothing. In fact, they were only five minutes from Rexford, and he still hadn't said a word. He just ate his burger and drank his Coke. How did he do that?

The silence was excruciating. She thought at least they could listen to some music, but he had turned off the stereo as soon as she'd gotten into the car. Was that a hint?

They finally entered a quiet residential neighborhood and turned onto a street full of split-level houses. Brady drove slowly as they looked for the address and then put the car in park. "This is it."

He nodded his head across the street, toward a tan house with black shutters. It looked like a Little Tikes factory had exploded on the front lawn. There were plastic toys scattered everywhere, in every color of the rainbow—bright red mini-cars, a blue-and-yellow slide, a green turtle sandbox, an orange basketball hoop. There was also a minivan parked in the garage—it was gray.

Brady unwrapped another burger and took a bite. "Sorry I'm starving."

Any other time she would've ordered a burger, but her stomach was in knots. It had been, ever since she'd woken up that morning and remembered the backpack was lost. "Well, this looks like a definite possibility with all the toys and stuff."

She glanced over at him. He was chewing slowly, with his eyes closed.

"Wow, that must be some burger."

He swallowed and took a sip of his Coke. "You don't know what you're missing."

She watched him crumple up the wrappers and napkins and stuff them into the white paper bag one by one. He glanced over at her. "What?"

Oh my God, she was so staring! She quickly looked away. "Nothing...uh, there's a car in the garage, so hopefully they're home."

"Yeah. Do you think we should both go, or maybe just you?" Brady asked. "I think they might be more willing to help if you're by yourself."

"Because being alone will make me look more pathetic."

"Well, that's what we're going for, right?"

"Right." She went to grab the door handle.

"Wait, hold on." His hand was on her shoulder. "Do you know what you're going to say?"

She turned and smiled at him. "Yes, I'm going to tell the terrible lie."

"Right—but you gotta put on your sad face. That face won't work." Hand still on shoulder.

"Oh, right." She put on her sad, but hopefully somewhat believable face. "Better?"

"Better." Hand squeezing shoulder.

"Here goes nothing." Vivienne jumped out of the car and walked quickly across the street to the tan house. She made her way around the obstacle course of colored plastic, weaving her way up to the front porch.

Before she even knocked on the door, she could hear screaming.

"Jack broke my Lego castle!"

"Did not!" More screaming.

"Mommy!!!"

Baby crying.

Dog barking.

"Dylan, put that down!"

"Mommy!!!"

Holy crap. Vivienne took a deep breath and knocked as loudly as she could.

For a few seconds there was silence, and then a rumble of feet coming to the door. Three little blond boys shoved each other out of the way as they pulled open the door. "I got it, Jack!" "No! I got it, Dylan!" "Mommy!"

The oldest was maybe six, the other two looked like twins, probably around three or four. Big wet eyes stared at her from behind the screen door. "Who are you?" the oldest asked.

"Hi there, is your mommy home?" Vivienne asked in her friendliest voice.

Behind them, a woman, presumably Mommy, came to the door carrying a baby on her hip and a phone on her shoulder. "Hold on, I'll call you back in a sec."

She pushed the boys out of her way—with her leg—and gave a tense smile. "Hi, can I help you?" She had bags under her eyes the size of golf balls.

Vivienne knew she had to get straight to the point. "Hi, my name is Vivienne, and this might sound strange, but something really important to me was dropped off at the Goodwill in Fulton by mistake. I was told you were shopping there last night?"

"How did you know I was shopping there?" Maybe she wasn't as sleep-deprived as she looked.

"Right, see, I happen to have a good friend who works there, and she knew how upset I was—"

Just then a stuffed animal flew through the air and hit Mommy square on the side of the head. She put her finger up. "Could you hold on a sec?"

Then Mommy shut the door. Vivienne could hear what sounded like furniture being tossed around, followed by a piercing wail.

While Vivienne waited, she thought about last year's Family Science class, when she and Kendra had to take care of Owen to learn the hardships of parenting. Owen was their robot baby, or 'infant simulator' in teacher lingo. The thing had cried so much she'd wanted to throw it against a wall. The whole experience was brutal, but she was starting to think a field trip to this house could be way more effective.

The mommy reappeared. "Sorry, what was it—the thing you're looking for?"

"Oh, it's a backpack. It's pink with a V made out of sequins?"

She shook her head. "Sorry, no girls here."

Vivienne's heart sank.

The mommy nodded to the baby boy on her hip, who was now eating her hair. "He's definitely our last one. I was just buying some clothes for the kids. They grow out of them so fast, you know?"

Actually, Vivienne didn't know. She didn't have a frickin' clue. But she did know one thing. There had been two chances left to find the backpack, and one of them had just gone poof.

"Well, thanks for your time anyway," she said quietly. She was afraid to turn around. She knew Brady was watching and she didn't want to face him. She didn't want to disappoint him—again.

Then the mommy asked, "Hey, would you be interested in a babysitting job, by any chance?"

Oh God, no. Just no. "Well, I already have a part-time job, and it keeps me pretty busy."

"Oh." She frowned. "Okay, well good luck with your backpack."

And then the mommy slammed the door shut.

CHAPTER 19

Brady watched Vivienne's body language as the woman closed the door and he could tell it wasn't good news. *Shit.*

She walked back toward him with her head down and her hands empty. Brady put the key in the ignition and started the car back up. "No luck?" he asked when she got in.

"No," she said in a voice barely above a whisper.

No backpack, no money, and only one place left to check. If it wasn't there—he didn't want to think about if it wasn't there.

Nothing more was said as they drove to Bellevue. He wanted to stay positive, to say something reassuring, but the truth was he wasn't feeling very optimistic. Given the fact that Vivienne wasn't talking, he thought she probably felt the same way.

Bellevue was an older suburb on the east side of Cleveland, in the University district. It was a culturally diverse area, home to museums, botanical gardens and the orchestra. It was also home to a wide spectrum of socioeconomic classes. The wealthy residents lived near the artistic center of activity, in stately houses rich with architectural history. And the not-so-wealthy residents lived on the edges of city limits, in public housing.

When they got to the home of Mark Whitaker, Brady was surprised. It was in the wealthy area, near Severance Hall, an imposing Tudor-style house with a steeply pitched roof and stained glass windows. The yard was well manicured and there were no cars in the long brick driveway. It definitely didn't look like the home of a Goodwill shopper.

"I hope this is the right address," he said as he pulled the car over to the curb and parked across the street. He checked the piece of paper again. Yep, it was the right address, which was not good for them.

The house seemed so intimidating, and he began feeling strangely protective over Vivienne. "Maybe I should go with you this time. I don't think it's going to make a big difference if I'm there. I mean, they either have it or they don't."

He glanced over at Vivienne, who was slumped to the side, her head resting against the passenger window. Raindrops began pelting the glass, and she traced them with her finger.

It was weird seeing her like that, not a good weird. "Vivienne?"

"Brady," she started, her eyes fixated on the window. "I can't believe how nice you're being about all this."

He wasn't going to make her feel any worse than she already did. "You know what?" He shrugged and repeated what his dad had told him many times over. "It is what it is."

She turned and smiled at him. That was better.

He smiled back. "You know shit happens, I guess."

As if on cue, the rain started falling harder, building into a steady downpour. "Yep, crap definitely happens," she said.

"It's shit. Shit happens."

"I prefer crap."

"Here." He began pulling his arms out of his sleeves. "You need this more than I do." He handed her his Browns hoodie.

"No! Brady, you're wearing a t-shirt!" She shook her head. "I'm fine, seriously."

"Vivienne, you already look cold and we haven't even gone out into it yet. I'll dry off quickly, but that thing will be soaked. It'll never dry."

She looked down at her heavy sweater. "Are you sure?"

He nodded and watched as she put the sweatshirt on, zipped it over her sweater, and pulled up the hood. She yanked both of ends of the drawstrings down until only the middle of her face was peeking out. "Good?"

"Yes, good." He liked how she looked in his Cleveland Browns hoodie. A lot. "Okay, we'll have to make a run for it. Ready?"

"Ready."

They both jumped out and sprinted toward the driveway. The wind picked up and the rain came down in sheets. Giant puddles mottled the brick driveway, and he felt the water soak right through his shoes. They ran along a cobblestone pathway that led up to the front of the house. A stone archway covered the entranceway, protecting a massive wood door that looked like it came straight out of medieval times. By the time they got under cover, they were both drenched.

Brady knocked, but it barely made a sound against the girth of the door. He knocked again, hard enough to cause a stinger in his knuckles, but no answer. "How in the hell's anyone supposed to hear that?" He began searching for a doorbell.

Vivienne was looking too. "There!" She pointed up to a black iron chain hanging from the side of the archway. "I think maybe you're supposed to pull it?"

"Seriously?" He reached over and gave it a tug. Loud chimes reverberated from inside. "Never seen that before."

They waited—no answer.

One more pull of the chain. Chimes. More waiting. No answer.

"I guess nobody's home." Vivienne was looking at the ground.

"Nothing can be easy, huh?" He was freezing his ass off. "Let's go back to the car."

They ran back through the rain that was quickly turning into a wintry mix, and as soon as they got into the car, Brady cranked up the heat as high as it would go. He closed his eyes and put his head back, pushing his dripping-wet hair away from his face.

"Can you stay for a while?" he asked. "Or do you need to get back?"

"I can stay if you can," she answered.

The rain pelted the rooftop noisily but it was oddly soothing. As they sat in silence, an icy slush pile began accumulating at the bottom of the windshield. He couldn't believe all that had happened to him in the last twenty-four hours. He glanced at Vivienne, who looked as defeated as he felt. Why couldn't they have met under different circumstances?

"I'm sure your dad is pretty mad at you?" she asked. "About the money, I mean."

"A little."

"So, Mr. Sutton was your dad's lawyer?"

He had thought she might ask about that at some point. She obviously knew it was strange to pay someone nine hundred dollars in cash. Maybe he should just say his dad didn't believe in banks.

Or maybe he should tell her the truth. That was his internal debate. For whatever reason, he didn't want to lie to her. And maybe if she knew what the money was really for, it would lessen her guilt a little. But could he trust her?

He looked at her. "Well…"

She pulled the hood down, away from her face, and her wet hair framed her pale skin perfectly. For the first time, he noticed how green her eyes were. All rational thought disappeared and any debate going on in his head ended. "Vivienne, I kind of lied to you about the money."

CHAPTER 20

"Okay…" Vivienne said.

"I'm going to tell you something, but you need to promise me you won't repeat it to anyone. I mean, seriously. Only a handful of people know."

At that, her face perked up. "Absolutely, I promise." She was hanging on his every word.

"Well, as you probably already guessed, the money wasn't for legal fees." He paused. "The money was Mr. Sutton's winnings for the week."

"Winnings?"

"My dad is a bookie." He paused to let it sink in. "You know, he takes bets on football games."

"Oh…" Her eyebrows rose in realization. "So the money in the envelope was gambling money?"

Brady nodded. "Yeah. I was supposed to meet Sutton—Mr. Sutton—at McGuire's on Thursday night and he didn't show. That was the night of the New Dogma concert."

She quickly interjected, "And you needed to get there early for the meet-and-greet."

"Yes, and so when Sutton didn't show—"

"You went to his house to put it in his mailbox," she finished for him.

"Yep."

"And we know what happened after that." She sighed and looked away.

"Yeah, but I wanted you to know the truth. The money was gambling money, not legal fees or anything like that."

"But your dad still had to pay Mr. Sutton, right?"

He shrugged. "Yeah, but he can cover it. He's got money set aside, you know. He just takes it as another loss." Brady's loss, actually—a loss that he'd be paying back forever if they didn't find the damn backpack.

"So, do you help your dad with the bets and stuff, since you're so good with numbers?"

"We're actually like business partners." He had told her the truth so far; he might as well keep it going. "There's actually a lot of work that goes into it. My dad takes all the bets on the phone and stuff, and I meet the customers at McGuire's every Thursday and do the money exchanges."

She was watching him intently, and he suddenly felt self-conscious, which wasn't something he felt very often. He diverted his eyes to the foggy glass in front of him. "See, my dad was in a bad accident a few years back, and it's not easy for him to get out of the house. So I meet the guys for him."

"Oh."

"The guys who bet with him are mostly just old coworkers my dad knew from the steel plant, and then there's some old guys who don't like to do the online betting. Remember Jimmy back at McGuire's?"

She smiled. "How could I forget?"

"Well, he bets with my dad, mostly just twenty on the Browns each week, but he's one of our customers."

She seemed amused more than anything else. "Our customers?" Now she had a big smile on her face. "Wow, Brady the gambling man."

"No," he needed to clarify. "I don't gamble at all. I take other people's bets, I don't make the bets."

"Oh my God, Brady, that is totally the same thing!"

"No, it's really not." A flicker of irritation came to the surface and he felt the need to defend himself. "We're just providing a service. You can't really win at gambling in the long run. The bookie always has an advantage because of the juice. We do it for the juice—that's it."

"What the heck is the juice?"

"It's the service fee, usually ten percent. So if the bookie has a bunch of winners and a bunch of losers, over time, he comes out ahead because of the juice."

"Hmm…interesting."

He gave her a few seconds to mull it over and then asked, "So what do you think of that little revelation?" He said it in a joking way, but he'd be able to gauge what she really thought by her answer.

She smiled. "It sounds pretty exciting, actually."

"Yep, it definitely can be." He felt a sense of relief but went a little further. "Some people think it's shady. I mean, technically it's illegal."

"Well, that's dumb. I mean, people do it online all the time," she said matter-of-factly. "God, if I have to watch one more commercial for those fantasy football leagues, I'll puke."

Brady laughed. "The thing is, it's huge for my dad. It gives him something to do when he's stuck at home."

"So it's just you and your dad at home?"

Talking to her was getting easier. "Yeah, my parents are divorced. My mom lives on the other side of Fulton. Things have been really tough for my dad since the accident, and when my mom—well, dropped the bombshell that she wanted a divorce, I just knew I wanted to live with him."

"So you didn't expect it—the divorce, I mean?"

"No," he said. "Not at all. They never fought or anything."

"Crap, that sucks." Then she added, "You know what? My parents seem fine, but I don't think I'd have a clue one way or the other. I mean, we're all so busy, it's hard to tell."

"Exactly, and parents are masters of façade, Vivienne."

She laughed. "That's a new one."

"I had this friend when I was younger—" He suddenly realized he had been talking a lot. "Sorry, should I shut up?"

"No!" She pulled her legs up onto the seat and turned toward him, sitting Indian-style. "Tell me the story."

"Well, I had this friend named Donny Bart. He lived in the nicest house on our street, and he was the kid who got the all the cool toys before anyone else did. So we'd always hang out at his house on the weekends."

Brady shook his head, remembering. "Mr. and Mrs. Bart were ridiculous. They couldn't keep their hands off of each other, seriously. I mean, it was like they were the happiest couple in the world—always major PDA, and right in front of us too. They didn't care."

"No!"

"Yes. Of course Donny was mortified, but we all thought it was hilarious." Then Brady added, "Just to give you a visual, the Barts were big people, like really big."

"Oh God," she laughed. "So, what happened?"

"Masters of façade, that's what parents are."

"Tell me!"

"Okay, okay, so one day the Barts just moved, like packed up in the middle of the night and left town. And I never saw Donny again."

She frowned. "Where'd they go?"

"Well, one night, maybe a year later, I'm on Xbox and I see Donny's avatar pop up on the screen. So I get on the headset and I'm like, 'Dude, what happened, why didn't you say goodbye?' and Donny tells me out of the blue he has a new baby brother, and I'm like, 'Oh, that's cool' and he's like, 'No, not cool.'"

Vivienne let out an "Oh no."

"Apparently, Mr. Bart was bangin' one of the tellers at his bank."

"And she got pregnant?"

"Yep. She got pregnant. I guess she was only like twenty-five."

"Oh my God, that's terrible." Vivienne sounded genuinely sad. "I feel so bad for Mrs. Bart."

Brady shrugged. "Well, it just goes to show, even when things seem great on the surface, you never really know."

"Yeah, I guess not," she said quietly.

That was a stupid story to tell to someone whose parents aren't divorced, dumbass!

"But I'm sure your parents are fine," he quickly added.

"No, it's not that." She shook her head. "I just keep imagining Mrs. Bart finding out."

"Well, don't think about that." He had thought the story was pretty funny but Vivienne obviously had a different take on it. "I heard the Barts got back together," he lied.

"Really?"

He sighed. "Can we just change the subject? Can I ask you something?"

"Sure." She smiled.

Sitting so close to her, with only the center console between them, the icy rain spattering down, the windows fogged up from their body heat, he suddenly felt like he was going to combust.

"Do you care if I turn this down a little?" He reached for the heater knob and turned it to the lowest setting.

"That's what you wanted to ask me?"

"No." He paused. He didn't want to upset her, but he was dying to know. It had been in the back of his brain, pestering him, ever since they left the Goodwill.

He looked at her cautiously. "Will you tell me who the notebook belongs to?"

And he watched her face fall.

CHAPTER 21

"Will you tell me who the notebook belongs to?" Brady asked.

It wasn't the question she was expecting. She didn't know what she was expecting, but it wasn't that. "Oh, the notebook..."

"You know what? Sorry. Never mind. It was a dumb thing to ask."

"No, it's okay, really." She would've told him anything at that point. Literally, anything.

Sitting in that confined space with him had stirred up feelings inside of her she'd never felt before—ever. As he talked, she couldn't look away.

His damp, messy hair, curled up on the ends, hung slightly over to the side. When he smiled, his light brown eyes sparkled and little creases formed around his perfect mouth. She admired the smooth lines of his neck leading down to his surprisingly broad shoulders and chest, now exposed by the thin, wet t-shirt that clung to him. Unlike her pale and freckly skin, he had the kind of skin that tanned dark—his arms still had color from the summer. And his Brady-soap-scent, whatever the hell it was, permeated the air inside the small space they shared. She would bottle it up and take it with her if she could.

Yep, she would tell him anything.

"The notebook belonged to someone named Mike. It's kind of a long story."

There was a hint of surprise in his face. "I'm listening."

"Well, I'm not sure if I mentioned to you that I work at Shady Oaks? It's a nursing home."

"No." He paused for a second. "I don't think so."

"Well, it's a part-time job. My mom's a nurse and she worked there a long time ago, so she got me the job. It's just a couple of days a week, after school. I was actually working there yesterday and I had to stay late. That was part of the reason I couldn't drop off the envelope in Chad's mailbox."

"Okay…"

"Anyway, my job is to help prepare dinners and then deliver them to the residents. And I met this resident named Gloria."

At that moment, her phone beeped with a text message. Probably Kendra wanting an update. She pulled her phone out and glanced at the screen. Her stomach turned when she saw who it was from.

Brady picked up on her reaction. "Bad news?"

She shook her head. "It's nothing."

"Okay." He didn't push. No questions asked.

Which was why she wanted to tell him. "It was Chad."

"Well, you better see what he wants."

She clicked on the text: *Vivs, I am so sorry about the other day. PLEASE call me so I can apologize, I know we can work things out.*

She stuck the phone back into her pocket.

"What did he want?"

"He wants to talk, but that is not going to happen."

Oh God, like Brady even cares? She quickly turned the attention onto him. "So what about you?"

"What about me?"

"You know, do you have any crazy ex-girlfriends texting you?"

"No," he laughed.

And then suddenly a thought came to her, something she'd never even considered. *What if Brady had a girlfriend?!* She bit her lip. Screw it. "Any current girlfriends?"

"No." His face flushed ever so slightly. "No current girlfriends either."

"Oh." She tried to sound casual and hide the relief she felt, but she knew she was failing miserably. Then awkward silence.

"You said something about a resident named Gloria?" he quickly asked.

"Yeah." Vivienne took a deep breath. "See, Shady Oaks is a really depressing place. Like, most of the people there are super old and super miserable—and most of them never get any visitors." She stopped. "Are you sure you want to hear about this?"

"Only if you want to tell me." His voice was so comforting. "I mean, we're just sitting here in the rain, waiting for these assholes to come home. Tell me your story."

"Okay." She had never really talked to anyone about Gloria, but now she wanted to. Even though she barely knew him, she felt like she could tell Brady anything. "It was last St. Patrick's Day…"

CHAPTER 22

"Vivienne, can you come and help me with these?" Janet yelled from across the kitchen.

Vivienne stopped wrapping her silverware and walked over to the serving counter. Rows and rows of little plastic bowls filled with green Jell-O waited for their finishing touches.

"Before you take the trays, you need to put a dollop of Cool Whip on these, and some sprinkles, okay?" There was a container full of green and white sprinkles in the shape of tiny shamrocks.

"Aww, that's cute, Janet."

Vivienne started spooning out the Cool Whip. "Do you think any of them even realize it's St. Patrick's Day?"

Janet rushed back and forth from one duty to the next. "Well, the Irish ones do. The residents appreciate things like that—more than you'd think."

Janet was the main cook at Shady Oaks and had been there for over twenty years. With the help of Vivienne and two other aides, she was responsible for feeding all sixty-five of the residents in B wing. But even as busy as she was, Janet still always found time to do something special for the holidays.

Vivienne started loading the trays onto the trolley. Tonight's dinner: chipped beef, mashed potatoes and peas with a soft roll. Shamrock Jell-O for dessert. All the food made her stomach turn, not because Janet was a bad cook, but because everything had to be made soft and runny. Not to mention that the aromas of the food, mixed with the everyday smells of bodily fluids, made for a very unappetizing combination.

She knocked on Mr. Gorman's door. "Hello, Mr. Gorman?" The door was opened a crack and she pushed it in further. "I've got your dinner for you."

Mr. Gorman sat in his chair in front of the TV, the only light in the dim room. He was watching *Wheel of Fortune*, which he was actually pretty good at. He was one of the more lucid residents. "Hello, Vivienne. You look lovely today."

"Thank you, Mr. Gorman." She smiled and positioned the tray on a small table in front of him. She took a napkin and tucked it into his collar. The first time she'd delivered his dinner, he'd asked her if she wouldn't mind doing it. His wife Donna had always done that for him before a meal.

Working at Shady Oaks was not easy. It was emotionally draining. The residents needed a lot of care. Many were frail and disabled, and many were slowly losing their minds. Most of them were sick, but not sick enough to die. And they wanted to die, she knew that for certain, because she heard it every day. "Oh, Vivienne, I just wish the good Lord would take me." Yep, that was the theme of the day, every day: *I want to die.*

And the fact that no one ever came to visit these people made Vivienne sick. Janet had told her that family visitors were rare—for any of the residents. A few lucky ones received obligatory visits on Mother's Day or Father's Day, but that was pretty much it. Most of them even spent Christmas alone, and that's why Janet always tried to do something special for the holidays, however small or simple it was.

But, Vivienne slowly got used to the environment and even looked forward to it some days. She enjoyed talking to the residents, especially Mrs. Marsh, or Gloria, as she liked to be called. Vivienne would purposely deliver her dinner last so that they could spend a few extra minutes together.

Gloria was a burst of sunshine in the dismal place. Her eyes would light up when Vivienne came into the room and they never lost their sparkle. She always wore pink lipstick and beautiful flowered nightgowns. She tied colorful silk scarves over her thinning gray hair. She was always happy—always.

Gloria had an amazing memory for her age, which Vivienne would guess to be pushing ninety. She loved to talk about her late husband George and all their travels across the globe. She described in detail the incredible adventures they took, like their safari in the Serengeti, and their hot air balloon ride over the Napa Valley. Gloria was one of those people that seemed to have lived life to the fullest, with no regrets.

She'd never mentioned any children, and Vivienne had just assumed she didn't have any. But when she was outside Gloria's door that day, St. Patrick's Day, getting her dinner tray from the bottom of the trolley, she heard Gloria talking to someone.

Vivienne peeked into the room and saw her sitting on the edge of the bed holding what looked like a small photograph in front of her. "I will see you soon, my darling, I can feel it," she said. "It won't be long, and we will be together. I love you so very much."

Then Gloria looked up and saw Vivienne. "Oh, hello, dear." She put the photo into a drawer in the side table and waved Vivienne into the room. "Come in, come in."

Vivienne rolled the cart into the room. "Hi, Gloria," she said, putting on her biggest smile, pretending she hadn't heard a thing.

"Dear, I'm not very hungry right now. Put that over on the table and come sit with me." She patted the spot on the bed next to her.

Vivienne walked over and sat next to Gloria.

"I want to show you something." She reached into the drawer and pulled out an old pocket notebook, about the size of a postcard. It had a worn leather cover, cracked and coming loose at the binding, feebly protecting tattered pages of yellowing paper. A photograph peeked out from inside.

Gloria carefully pulled it out. The photo was faded and frayed on the edges. A young soldier in uniform stood proudly in front of a sprawling white house. At the bottom, along a thin white border, it read Michael James Marsh.

"Wasn't he handsome? He was only a little older than you in that picture."

Vivienne's heart sank.

Gloria held it with both hands and sighed. "You're probably wondering why I never mentioned Michael to you." She smiled, a tight-lipped, pained smile. "He wanted to be a doctor, you know."

The sadness in Gloria's voice was so foreign and so unbelievably heartbreaking, Vivienne immediately felt tears welling up in her eyes.

"December seventh, 1969—do you know what happened that day, Vivienne?"

Vivienne shook her head no.

"Well, it was the day that my life changed forever. It was draft day, the first one held since World War Two. And did you know how those boys were selected?"

Another shake of the head.

"Well, it was pretty simple. They just picked a random date out of a barrel, and if you were born on that date, you were drafted first, and so on. And guess what that very first date was?"

She flipped over the photograph, where there were two lines of writing in elegant cursive:

My Hero
September 14, 1950 – June 14, 1970

Gloria pointed to the first date. "September fourteenth."

Vivienne felt a lone tear escape and fall down her cheek. She quickly wiped it away.

Gloria laughed, a horrible laugh filled with anguish. "He thought it was a sign, my Michael did. I tried everything to change his mind. I begged him to get a deferment. He could've gotten it, you know." A bittersweet smile crossed her face. "But he said he wanted to serve his country, and once Michael's mind was made up, there was no changing it." She looked at Vivienne with tormented eyes. "That's the irony. You try so hard as a parent to raise a child of high moral character, and in the end, that's what killed him."

"Oh God, Gloria, I'm so sorry." Vivienne felt an ache in her chest like never before.

Gloria went on, almost apologetic in her tone, "I never mention him because the sorrow runs so deep inside of me that I fear it will swallow me up. And that wouldn't do me any good, now would it?" She put her hand inside Vivienne's and squeezed. "The truth is, Vivienne, every night before I go to bed, I pray that I will see my Michael again, very soon. And of course my George too!"

Tears were rolling down Vivienne's cheeks and she didn't bother wiping them away. "I just wish there was something I could say..."

"You don't need to say anything, dear. You don't need to say a word. Your presence means everything. It means more to me than you will ever know." Gloria reached over to the box of Kleenex and handed one to Vivienne. "Here, dear, now I don't want to see you upset about this."

Vivienne wiped her face with the tissue and attempted a smile.

"That's better!" Gloria's eyes sparkled again. "Now listen to me, Vivienne. Don't ever underestimate how much you are doing for the residents here. For some of us, seeing your young and cheerful face is the only thing that makes life bearable here."

Vivienne took a deep breath. "Well, I better get going." She nodded over to the tray of cold food. "Don't forget about your dinner."

"I won't, I promise," Gloria said lightheartedly, trying to go back to her old persona, the happy, vibrant Gloria of old. The only problem was, Vivienne knew it was all an act, a sad attempt to mask her sorrow.

As Vivienne left the room, she gave Gloria her cheerful face, a mask of her own. Inside, it felt like her heart had been torn into a million pieces.

***

"Wow, Vivienne."

"I know."

"I don't think it can get any more depressing than that."

"Well"—Vivienne paused—"a couple of weeks later, I go into work and Janet tells me that Gloria died—she died in her sleep."

"I stand corrected." Brady exhaled loudly.

"And then Janet tells me that Gloria left something for me, and she hands me the notebook. It turned out to be a notebook her son Michael kept with him in Vietnam. I flipped to somewhere in the middle and he was writing about how alone he felt, and how scared he was, and I got so upset I almost had to leave work."

"Jesus," Brady sighed.

She didn't realize how much pent-up guilt she had been carrying around since losing the notebook. She felt her body relax, like someone had been stretching a tight rubber band across her chest and it had suddenly been cut loose. She felt like crying but held it back.

"Shit, now the money seems so trivial." He gave her a weak smile.

"Everything seems trivial." In that moment, all she wanted to do was lay her head on Brady's chest, close her eyes and have him promise her that they would find the backpack. But she didn't move. She rested her head on the back of the seat and he did the same.

And then, she saw something flash through the rain-streaked glass. Lights.

A black sedan was pulling into the driveway of 877 Lincoln Avenue.

CHAPTER 23

Brady watched the black BMW drive up the long driveway and disappear into the garage, the door lowering slowly behind it.

He glanced over at Vivienne. "We should give them a couple of minutes."

She nodded, staring out the window. She looked scared.

Brady's heart thudded against his chest as they waited. Now that he knew the story about the notebook, he was even more nervous about finding the backpack. "You ready?" he finally asked.

"Yep," she said quietly. This time the sad face wasn't going to be a problem for her at all.

They got out and ran to the front door for the second time. The rain hadn't slowed very much and the air was icy and saturated. Under the archway, Brady could see his breath blowing out in white clouds. He quickly grabbed the chain and pulled.

The chimes did their thing, and a few seconds later the door opened. A tall woman with short black hair and a long, gaunt face stood on the other side. She wore a black dress and a frown.

"Can I help you?" Her eyebrows rose—high, black arches that looked like they were painted on with a sharpie. She looked them up and down with obvious disapproval.

"Hi, my name is Vivienne." She sounded panicky. "I was hoping you might have a minute to talk to us. I—"

"I'm not interested, but thank you." She began shutting the door.

"Wait!" The desperation in Vivienne's voice surprised even Brady.

The woman paused and waited, her arches coming together like a big 'M' in the middle of her boney forehead.

"Ma'am, I'm really sorry about bothering you, but we just wanted to know if you shopped at the Goodwill last night. The Goodwill in Fulton?"

Vivienne looked pathetic by any standards. Brady's water-logged hoodie hung off her tiny frame, and she was visibly shivering. He was wearing a t-shirt, for Christ's sake. If the lady had any heart at all she'd hear them out.

Her arches lifted apart. "Oh, my husband stopped there last night." She stepped back and opened the door wider. "Come in, come in out of the rain."

Thank God.

They stepped inside, and Brady immediately shot a look at Vivienne. "Wow," he mouthed.

He'd never seen anything like it. Soaring ceilings planked with wood beams, giant chandeliers hanging by iron chains, ornate paintings spanning the length of the walls, oriental rugs scattered across stone floors. It smelled rich and woody and exotic.

"Mark, dear!" the lady called to the back of the house, her voice echoing over the classical music playing in the background. "Could you come here a minute?"

Then she reached out and offered her hand. "I'm Ruth Whitaker."

"Vivienne," a shake. "Brady," a shake.

Mark Whitaker was pretty much in character with Ruth—slicked-back hair, black angular glasses, a freshly starched button-down shirt and shiny black shoes. He walked confidently with his hands in his pockets.

"Mark, this young lady and gentleman wanted to talk to you about your trip to Goodwill," she said with a touch of cynicism.

"Why, yes, I shopped at the Goodwill store last night," he announced with a plastic smile. He proceeded to tell them how the Whitakers were art and antique collectors, always on the lookout for hidden treasures. They frequented art distributors, vintage shops, auction houses and estate sales. But every once in a while, a gem could be found in a pawn shop, at a yard sale, or, yes, even inside a Goodwill store.

"Why do you ask?" He smiled as he rocked back and forth on his heels.

Vivienne sighed. "Well, this is obviously a long shot, but did you purchase a pink backpack by any chance?"

The couple looked at her curiously. "A pink backpack?" asked Ruth, as if a backpack was something she'd never heard of.

"Oh, I'm very sorry. No backpack," Mark said quietly.

That was it. Their last chance. Brady didn't move as the realization settled in.

"But I did find that!" Mark proclaimed loudly as he pointed to a small table in the foyer. "A Puffy Pairpoint lamp. It's a reproduction, of course, but one of the best ones I've seen. It's quite charming, don't you think?"

Was this guy for real? At that moment, Brady wanted nothing more than to shove that Puffy Pairpoint lamp straight up Mark Whitaker's ass.

"Would you two like some tea?" Ruth asked. "It's so dreary out there."

Vivienne politely refused, and Brady turned away without saying a word. He was out the door and back inside his car in a matter of seconds.

No backpack. "No backpack," he said it out loud to himself.

Brady had been so sure he would be able to get the money back. All he had to do was find Vivienne Burke and all would be right with the world. How could this have happened? How in the hell was he going to face his dad?

Vivienne came running down the driveway—looking wet, frozen, and dejected. When she got into the car, Brady started it up and began driving without saying a word. It felt like he had been punched in the head a few times, and he just wanted to go home, tell his dad the bad news—just get it over with.

"I don't get it." Vivienne finally broke the silence ten minutes into the drive. "I mean, how could it disappear? Maybe we missed it at the Goodwill..."

"Vivienne, we picked that place apart. It's not there."

She pulled out her phone. "Hey, Mom," she began. "No... are you absolutely sure it was the Goodwill in Fulton? Okay...in a black bag? I know...did you search the minivan again? Okay...okay...no, it's okay...I know...I gotta go, Mom. Okay...love you too. Okay...bye...bye."

Silence.

And more silence.

And even more silence.

The silence was good for his head, but by the time Brady pulled into the Goodwill lot, he felt numb and exhausted. He didn't know what to say to Vivienne as he parked his car next to hers.

Luckily, she said something first. "Brady, can you give me your cell number, just in case?"

He had wanted to ask the same thing from her—but that was before. When he'd thought there was still a chance to find the backpack, and still a chance to put the whole mess behind them.

Now he wasn't sure what he wanted. "Yeah." He read it off.

"Thanks. I'll call you if something comes up." She gave him a quick smile, a forced smile.

"Yeah, okay." He watched her get into her car and pull away.

Vivienne drove off to Richmond, and Brady drove in the opposite direction.

CHAPTER 24

"Oh my God! What happened to you?!" Kendra grabbed her arm and pulled her into the house.

Vivienne could only imagine how she must look. She looked over Kendra's shoulder and saw Nancy hovering. "Can we go in your room?"

"C'mon."

She followed Kendra up the winding stairs, but they only made it halfway before Nancy called out from below, "Hello, Vivienne!" and came scurrying over.

"Hi, Nancy!" she yelled back without turning around.

Kendra's mom insisted on being called Nancy. "Mrs. Lindford makes me feel so old," she said. Nancy also loved to listen in on their conversations and get the latest 'drama' as she called it. "My life is so boring—c'mon, give me some gossip."

Well, there was no way in hell Vivienne was going to give her the news of the day. Not today.

Nancy called out again, in her overly cheery voice, "You girls want me to bring you up some snacks?"

"No, thanks!" Kendra slammed her bedroom door and turned the lock. "What happened? Why didn't you text me?" she asked, her eyes wide.

Vivienne flopped back onto Kendra's queen-sized poster bed, donned with eight-hundred-thread-count sheets and European goose down pillows. Nothing but the best in Fancy Nancy's home.

She buried her face into the sateen bliss—she knew Kendra wouldn't mind. Her head hurt and she didn't know where to begin.

"No offense, Vivienne, but you look, like, really bad." Kendra sunk down into her giant furry beanbag. "C'mon, tell me what happened."

Vivienne sat up and propped a pillow behind her head. "I don't know where to start."

Kendra smiled. "Well, why don't you start with that thing you're wearing? I'm dying to know where you got that attractive…uh…Cleveland Browns sweatshirt?"

She'd forgotten to give Brady his sweatshirt back! She looked down at the wet hoodie. She'd never taken it off. "It's Brady's. I guess I forgot to give it back to him."

Kendra broke out into a huge grin. "Oh, Vivienne, that is the oldest trick in the book. Take something with you, and then you have an excuse to call. Am I right?"

"No, you're not right, Kendra!" All the emotions that had been buried inside her all day came bubbling to the surface. "I seriously forgot I was wearing it!" she yelled. And she had forgotten.

Kendra put her hands up. "Okay, chill, I'm just teasing." She walked over, sat on the edge of the bed and reached for Vivienne's feet. She began untying her shoes. "Well, let's at least take these off."

"Sorry."

"Okay, tell me everything, from the very beginning. I want to know every—single—detail."

Vivienne took a deep breath. "Well, I got to the Goodwill first—"

"Wait!" Kendra grabbed her in midsentence. "I need to know one thing first. Are you absolutely sure—"

"Yes Kendra, for the love of God, I'm sure Andrew is gay."

Kendra didn't skip a beat. "What about the other one—Jay?"

"Um…not that I'm aware of."

"Okay, okay. Start again."

And so Vivienne told Kendra the story, but not the entire story. She left out the part about Brady's dad being a bookie, like she'd promised.

"Wow," Kendra said quietly. "Seems like you really like this guy, Vivienne."

"What?" Vivienne looked up. "What do you mean?"

"Are you actually going to play dumb with me? I'm your best friend." Kendra's eyes sparkled. "And even if I wasn't, it would be obvious. I mean, the way your face changes when you say his name—"

"Okay!" She suddenly couldn't contain herself. "I like him!" Despite how miserable she felt, she broke out into a smile. "I like him a lot."

Kendra did a mini-clapping gesture. "Yay!"

"But"—Vivienne came to her senses—"only one problem. He hates me."

"Somehow I doubt that."

"Trust me on this one, Kendra."

But Kendra was not deterred. "So you've got to give him his sweatshirt back, right?"

Vivienne had no idea what she was going to do next. The bed was so comfortable, and at that moment all she wanted to do was sleep. "I got his number. I guess I could text him."

"You are definitely going to text him. Maybe even call him," Kendra sighed. "But first…" And then she stopped.

Vivienne waited. Something was wrong.

"First we need to talk about Chad."

What? "You're kidding me, right?"

Kendra did one of her cringe faces. "Well, he was asking about you at the party last night, and I told him you went home because you felt sick."

"Right…"

"Well, he called me about an hour ago and—"

"He called you?" Vivienne felt anger stirring inside.

"I want you to know I never would've answered if I knew it was him, but the number came up 'unknown,' which I thought was strange, so—"

"What did he say, Kendra?"

"Okay, so he starts off with 'It's Chad. You lied to me, Kendra.' No 'Hi, how are you?'" Kendra got up from the bed and began pacing. "And I'm like, 'What do you mean?' and he's like, 'Kirby told me Vivs left with some guy last night. Some guy he doesn't know.' And then Chad waits, just silence on the other end, and my mind is blank. Totally blank, Vivienne."

"What is his problem? We broke up—I can do whatever I want."

"I know, Vivienne, but I'm telling you, he sounded scary. His voice was so calm—totally messed up. I told him I didn't know what he was talking about, and then he's like, 'Cut the bullshit, Kendra.' And then I got pissed and I'm like, 'It's none of your business, Chad' and I hung up on him. I didn't know what else to do! I just hung up."

Vivienne put her hands on her head. She wanted to hit something. Like Chad's stupid face. "I'm sorry you had to deal with that."

"Oh my God, I don't care." Kendra sat back down on the bed. "I just can't believe he's such a freak. Everyone thinks he's this great guy."

"I told you," Vivienne said. "He's got everyone completely fooled."

"So what are you gonna do?"

"About Chad?"

"Oh, screw Chad!" Kendra reached over and grabbed the end of the tattered Browns hoodie. "About this!"

Vivienne pulled the sweatshirt tighter around herself and then buried her face into the Brady-scented softness. "I don't want to give this up."

Kendra laughed. "You better text him!"

"Of course I'm going to text him." Vivienne smiled, an energized smile, a hopeful smile. "As much as I love this hoodie, I'd much rather have the real thing."

CHAPTER 25

Brady closed the door quietly behind him, which was dumb because he was just trying to delay the inevitable. He had to face his dad and tell him the bad news, there was no escaping it.

Ever since the accident, Brady swore he would never hurt his dad again. He made a vow to himself that he would do everything in his power to make his dad happy—Brady owed him at least that much. And now he was breaking that vow.

His footsteps were heavy as he made his way to his dad's office. When he got there, his dad didn't even turn around. "No luck, huh?"

"Dad, I am so sorry. We looked everywhere. We started at—"

"Stop," his dad cut him off. "Before you say another word, let me talk, okay?"

Brady sat down in the La-Z-Boy and waited. He couldn't remember ever feeling like a bigger piece of shit.

His dad turned in his chair and rolled over so they were eye to eye. "Brady, I am the one who is sorry. I feel sick about what I've put you through. You made a mistake, but I never should've put you in that position in the first place."

"Dad…"

"I'm your father," he went on. "Getting you involved in this business was so selfish. I just wanted to do something—anything. Not being able to work…it just seemed like the perfect idea, you know?"

Brady nodded. "Yes, I know, Dad. Don't start blaming yourself for my screw-up." He was starting to feel sick.

"Let me finish, Brady," his dad sighed. "I never considered for a minute that you are a child. Genius or not, you are the child and I am the parent."

"Jesus Christ, Dad! I'm seventeen, I'm not a baby."

"Look, I've made a decision."

Brady's heart sank. "What?"

"I can't have you involved in the business anymore. From now on, I will go to McGuire's and do the exchanges."

"What?! Are you serious?" He was furious. "Because I screwed up?"

"Brady, it's not like that. I am doing this for your own good."

"Oh, please, I'm not a frickin' two-year-old!" He stood up and ran his hands through his hair. "I can handle it, Dad, I promise."

"Brady, I know you can, but you're missing the point! I'm not doing this to punish you—I'm doing it because I love you."

Brady couldn't remember the last time his dad had told him that he loved him. They just didn't say those kind of things to each other.

"Would you sit back down, please?" His dad's voice was quiet and surprisingly fatherly.

Brady slumped back down into his chair and waited.

"Look, you can still tag along when I go to McGuire's. I want you to tag along. I just don't want you to be carrying the responsibility. That's my job. I'm a big boy and it's about time I quit worrying about a stupid bum leg and go pay my buddies a visit."

Brady saw a change in his dad's eyes, and it was a good change. More than anything else in the world, he wanted his dad to be happy. He wanted his dad to get out and do things, see people. It was all he'd ever wanted.

"Well, I'm sure they'll be happy to see you. They ask about you all the time."

His dad smiled. "So, we're good?"

Brady nodded. "Yeah, we're good."

"Now that we've got that out of the way, have you talked to that girl?"

"What girl?"

Dad laughed, a real laugh, like one Brady hadn't heard—maybe ever. "Oh, Brady, Brady, Brady." He shook his head. "The girl? Violet? Vivienne?"

At breakfast Brady had given his dad the abbreviated version of what had happened the night before. The game, the party, Vivienne's house, the lost backpack...

Brady shifted uncomfortably in his chair. "Yeah, she actually showed up at the Goodwill."

Dad raised his eyebrows. "And?"

"What do you want to know?" Brady shrugged as casually as possible, but knew his dad could see right through him. "I mean, I know she feels really bad about everything. She must've said sorry like five hundred times."

"We all make mistakes, Brady."

"I know, Dad." Like he needed to be reminded.

"And it sounds like she was put into a scary situation with Sutton's jackass son. I guess the apple doesn't fall far from the tree."

"What do you know about Sutton?" Brady asked.

Dad sat back in his chair and crossed his arms in front of him. "Remember when I told you Sutton likes to bullshit when he calls—that's how I knew he didn't have a daughter?"

"Yeah."

"Well, one day, out of the blue, he asks me if I'm married. I told him I was divorced, and I guess he automatically thought we had some kind of common bond or something because he starts telling me all this really messed-up shit."

"Like?"

"Sutton said when he got divorced, he knew how to manipulate the system, him being a lawyer and all. He had friends in high places, if you know what I mean. Got custody of their only child—that would be Golden Boy."

Dad shook his head. "And this is the kicker, Sutton convinced Golden Boy—he was just a little kid at the time—that his mom was a big druggie, when she wasn't. And that she didn't want him, when she did. Turned him totally against her.

"What did you say to that?"

"I'm not sure how he thought I would respond, but I just said, 'Wow Sutton, that's a really shitty thing to do.' He ignored it, there was some silence on the other end, and then he put his bets in. We never made small talk again. I would tell the asshole not to call anymore, but up until last week, he was losing his ass, and it was too much fun taking his money."

"What a bastard." No wonder Chad had issues.

Dad rolled back to his desk. "So, anyway, your mom stopped over with dinner—lasagna, it might still be warm. She made a salad too. It's in the fridge."

Mom came over with dinner once a week. Brady could never imagine not having a relationship with her because of his parents' divorce. Of course he had put most of the blame on her in the beginning, but after talking with his dad a few times, he was starting to think maybe it wasn't as one-sided as he had thought.

Brady made his way to the kitchen and cut himself a big slice of lasagna. He got a glass of milk and went back to the office, where Dad was putting things away for the night.

"So, Dad, can I ask you something?"

"Sure."

"You said that you and Mom were talking about divorce before the accident, that you guys both wanted to go your separate ways. Right?"

"It's getting late. Eat your dinner."

Dad didn't want to talk about it, but Brady had to know. "I just don't get it. I don't remember you guys fighting or anything."

Dad sighed. "Brady, you know how adults always say, 'It's complicated'? Well, it is."

"That's it? Sounds like a cop-out to me."

"I don't know what to tell ya, kid. It's the truth. Marriage is complicated, women are complicated, shit happens—in no particular order." He glanced at his watch and stood up. "Maybe someday we can talk more about it, but right now I'm whipped. I'm heading to bed."

That was all Brady was going to get—conversation over. "Night, Dad."

He took another huge bite of lasagna, savored the homemade goodness and contemplated what his dad had said. Maybe it wasn't a cop-out. Brady obviously didn't have any experience in the marriage department, but he did have a little experience in the woman department.

And if his experience with Vivienne Burke was any indication, then 'complicated' might not be a strong enough word.

CHAPTER 26

Vivienne's eyes kept wandering over to the clock on the wall. She watched the red second hand, tick, tick, tick. Eighth period was almost over and she couldn't wait to get home.

She had texted Brady on Sunday: *Hey, I have your Browns hoodie. If you give me your address, I can drop it off.*

Brady (five minutes later): *Hey Vivienne. I can come by your house and get it. Today is really busy, how about tomorrow?*

Vivienne: *Is 7 ok?*

Brady: *See you then.*

The bell finally rang and she practically ran to her locker. As she approached it, her heart skipped a beat. Chad was leaning against it—wearing his psycho smile.

Chills ran down her spine, but she put on her best poker face. She didn't want him to think for a second that he could get to her.

"Hey, Vivs." He moved away from the door as she approached. "How are you?" His voice was nice enough, but she could still hear the icy edge.

"I'm fine, Chad."

She opened her locker door and rummaged through some books and binders longer than she had to, hoping he would take the hint and leave. But of course he didn't move. He was waiting for her to face him.

She finally turned around and he stepped closer, only inches between them. She concentrated on the stitching around the collar of his shirt, refusing to look up at his face. "Do you need something, Chad?"

She flinched as he put his hands on her shoulders. "Vivienne, I want you to give me another chance." He seemed sincere, but she knew all too well what was hidden underneath.

Vivienne was at a loss. She didn't know what else she could say. She finally mustered up the courage to look him in the face. "Chad, it's over. I don't feel the way you do, and no matter what you say or do, that won't change."

Other than a slight flicker in his eyes, his expression didn't falter.

"Okay?" She pulled herself away from his hold and tried to move around him.

He quickly stepped in front of her, blocking her again. "It's because of him, isn't it?"

At this she looked up. "Who?"

Chad smirked. "You know. Your new boyfriend, of course."

"I don't have a boyfriend, Chad." She pushed herself past him.

"Brady!" he shouted from behind.

Vivienne stopped dead in her tracks.

"That's his name, right?"

That didn't take him long to figure out. Probably Beth. She almost turned around—almost. Instead she put her shoulders back and walked away as fast as she could.

***

At 6:45 p.m., Brady texted and said he would be over in fifteen minutes. Vivienne did a last-minute check in the mirror. She reapplied her lip gloss and smoothed down her hair for the hundredth time. She had washed and dried his sweatshirt, after sleeping with it for the last two nights, and it sat neatly folded on the bed next to her.

"Knock, knock!" Mom opened her door a crack. "I'm heading out to Target. You need anything?"

She didn't hesitate. "Yes, conditioner, please. Morgan uses way too much. You need to tell her that her hair looks greasy."

Mom laughed. "Be nice..." She paused. "Vivienne, you know how sorry I am about that backpack. I had no idea you had something so special in there."

Vivienne had finally told her mom about the notebook. She hadn't had a choice. Her mom knew something was going on when Vivienne acted so crazy about finding it. "Mom, I know. It's okay."

However, Vivienne hadn't said anything about the envelope full of money. She had always been pretty open and honest with her mom, because she'd never really felt like she had anything to hide. But this was different—this was complicated, this was messy.

Looking out her bedroom window, she saw her mom pulling out of the driveway into the darkness. Another car pulled in front of the curb, just as her mom left—Brady.

Vivienne watched him get out of the car and start walking up the driveway. He was wearing a black coat and jeans. Flip-flop went her stomach. It didn't take much.

She grabbed her phone off the dresser and glanced at the time. Seven o'clock on the dot.

CHAPTER 27

In the Goodwill parking lot, Brady had realized Vivienne was still wearing his Browns hoodie. He'd let her take it. First off, he felt dumb asking for it, and secondly, although he didn't want to admit it, a part of him wanted to see her again. And it was the perfect excuse if he needed it. But he hadn't needed it, because she'd texted him first. Even better.

Of course he was pissed they hadn't found the money, but any frustration he'd felt with Vivienne had faded away, replaced by that weird 'good' feeling. And in the last two days, the feeling had only intensified.

It was Monday at 6:38 p.m. He'd told her in the text he would come by at seven. He had changed his t-shirt three times and tried on two different flannels. His dad caught a glance of him through the bedroom door and laughed. "I like the brown one! It brings out the color in your eyes."

"Shut up!" he yelled back.

Brady wasn't acting like himself—at all. He went to the bathroom and examined his face again. Nothing in glaring need of attention except for a little patch of stubble under the left side of his chin. He grabbed a razor and cleaned it up and then put on a dab of aftershave.

"Dad, I'm leaving!" He grabbed his keys off the kitchen table and was out the door.

At 6:52, he turned onto Sycamore Avenue and parked down the block, under a tree. The days were quickly growing shorter, and by that time it was already dark. He popped a piece of gum in his mouth. "Hey, Vivienne...hi, Vivienne...hey, how are you?" he muttered to himself as he watched the minutes tick away on his phone. At exactly 7:00 p.m., he pulled along the curb in front of her house. The porch light was on but the rest of the house looked quiet.

Brady took a deep breath and wiped his hands on his jeans. He got out, walked to the front door, knocked once, and waited.

When she opened the door, he felt a rush of blood go straight to his head. She had on jeans, a black sweater, and a smile. "Hey."

"Hey." *Be casual...*

"You want to come in, and I'll go grab it?"

"Uh, yeah, sure."

He stepped inside and looked around the small foyer. The lighting was dim and a television played quietly somewhere in the background. No little sister this time.

"I have your sweatshirt upstairs." She pointed up the staircase. "Be right back."

She jogged up the stairs, and as soon as she disappeared into the hallway, Brady heard a knock on the door behind him. "Uh, should I get that, Vivienne?" he called upstairs.

She didn't answer. Another knock came—this one louder.

Brady turned and opened the door to see a face he vaguely recognized. "Hey, Brady," said the stranger. And then it hit him—it was Chad Sutton. What the hell?

Chad didn't wait for an invitation and pushed past Brady into the house. How in the hell did Chad know who he was?

Vivienne came down the stairs and her face fell. "Chad, what are you doing here?"

"I thought maybe we could go get a bite to eat," he said cheerily, acting as if Brady wasn't standing right between them.

Vivienne's eyes quickly turned to Brady, desperation all over her face. "I don't think so, Chad. Brady and I are going out." She began putting one arm through the sleeve of his Browns sweatshirt. "I'm ready."

What? Brady let her words sink in for a second.

Mr. All-American was immediately in Brady's face. Chad had at least a couple of inches on him and looked more than capable of kicking his ass. His eyes were full of warning. "Oh, really?"

Brady's voice was calm and steady, but inside he was shitting bricks. "You have a problem with that, Chad?"

Vivienne rushed to Brady's side and put her arm through his. "We really have to go."

Chad's eyes darted back and forth between them, and he settled them on Vivienne. "I thought you said he wasn't your boyfriend."

So Vivienne had talked to Chad about him?

"Yeah, well, I lied." Not letting go of Brady's arm, Vivienne began pulling him toward the front door. "We're gonna be late for the movie."

They stood there waiting for Chad to make his exit. He looked Brady up and down with a sarcastic smile plastered across his big face. "Well, you kids be safe now."

What an asshole. They were halfway down the driveway when she said under her breath, "I am so sorry. I just want him to leave."

Brady looked back to see Chad finally getting into his car, but he wasn't going anywhere. Was he waiting for them?

Brady opened the passenger door for Vivienne. Might as well make it look as believable as possible. He started the car and pulled away—to where, he had no idea. He glanced in the rearview mirror to see Chad following them. "Looks like he's coming along for the ride."

Vivienne looked back. "Oh my God, I am so sorry! He is such a freak!"

"Seriously, what is his problem?" When Brady checked the rearview mirror again, Chad was turning off onto a side street. "I think he's finally leaving."

Vivienne dropped her head into her hands. "I am so sorry, Brady." She sounded like she was going to cry.

"Please stop apologizing. That guys a piece of work."

She sighed. "He just doesn't get it. He has this warped idea that I'm going to go out with him again. He was at my locker today doing the same thing."

Brady kept driving—still having no idea where the hell he was going. "How did he know who I was?" he had to ask.

"I guess Kirby told him I left the party with a guy, and I think my friend Beth must've told him about you. She's got a big mouth."

"Well, how did he know I'd be at your house just now?"

"That's what's really scary, I have no idea. For all I know he could've just been sitting outside my house, doing whatever psychos like him do, and then you showed up."

Chad definitely sounded like stalker material. "Maybe you should tell your parents or something."

"No! Oh my God, they would flip out. I think it would just make it worse." Vivienne pointed to the intersection up ahead. "You can just take a right up here and we can turn around."

Brady didn't want to take her home yet. Before he could think too much about it, the words spilled out. "Hey, do you want to get something to eat? I mean, since we're already out."

Had he just said that? He kept his eyes on the road.

"Sure."

"Any ideas where to go? I don't really know the area."

"Umm…SweetBrews is just a couple of blocks from here. At the next intersection take a left."

"What's SweetBrews?"

"It's a coffee shop. They have these pumpkin spice lattes that are my absolute favorite."

"Okay, SweetBrews it is."

For once in his life, he wasn't hungry. He was nervous. But when they got to the coffee shop, he ordered a chocolate chip cookie with his hot chocolate. There was no way he was touching the pumpkin drink, no matter how great Vivienne thought it was.

They sat down across from each other in a booth in a back corner. It was quiet and private and nice. They both took sips of their drinks, and then Vivienne smiled and blurted out, "What's three hundred eighty-four times nine hundred seventy-six?"

His brain went on autopilot. "Three hundred seventy-four thousand, seven hundred eighty-four."

She took out her phone and began typing in the numbers.

"Don't. It's right."

She had to check. Everyone always checked. She shook her head. "That's just crazy."

"Not really." He shrugged. "It would be like me asking you 'what's two plus two?' My brain just stores a lot more crap, I guess—it's automatic."

He watched her sip her pumpkin drink and lick the whipped cream off her lips. He bit into his cookie and looked away.

"So were you just born with it—Rain Man?" she asked teasingly.

Did he want to go there? A sick feeling started swimming around in his stomach with his hot chocolate.

That was the one story he didn't talk about. In fact, that was the one story he tried not to even think about.

But when he looked at her sitting across from him, he wanted to tell her. He just did.

"Do you remember how I told you my dad was in an accident?" He watched her face.

Her smile disappeared. "Oh...sorry, Brady, you don't have to tell me, really."

"No, it's okay." Brady smiled reassuringly. "I want to tell you about it."

And so he did.

CHAPTER 28

Eight Years Before...

Today Brady had Nurse Gina, one of the day nurses in the ICU. She had been working in the pediatric trauma unit for sixteen years and she had a son named Diego. He knew all of this because Gina liked to talk—a lot.

"How are you doing, Mr. Brady?" she asked in her upbeat, singsong voice.

Not good, Gina, not good at all.

"That's good." She fluffed his pillows, and he could feel her hot cigarette breath on his face. "It's beautiful outside today. It looks like summer is in full swing."

That's great, Gina, thanks for the weather update, but obviously I don't give a turd.

Brady shouldn't be so hard on Gina. She was one of only two people who actually talked to him—Mom being the other. No one thought he could hear them, but he could. He could hear everything.

And he heard a lot of things he probably wasn't supposed to hear.

Like how if he was in this coma for more than three weeks, the chances of him coming out weren't good. And how the contusions on his cerebellum would likely cause cognitive complications—the C words were all over the place. And how when he woke up—if he woke up—he probably wouldn't remember anything that had happened.

But he did remember. He remembered everything.

Visiting hours would begin soon and that's when Mom would come. She stayed all day long until they pretty much kicked her out. She begged and pleaded to sleep in his room overnight, but the doctors wouldn't allow it until he was released from the ICU.

It was funny how Mom would sit with him and mumble things like, "Those dumbass bastards won't let me sleep here with you...dumbass hospitals and their dumbass rules. It's ridiculous."

She swore a lot in front of him, which she had never done before. Which made him think—that she was thinking—he couldn't really hear her at all.

Mom also liked to tell him about things she'd bought for him, maybe thinking he needed some extra incentive. "Brady, I found that Lego spaceship you wanted, the one with the limited-edition alien minifig, and it's here waiting for you when you wake up."

God, he wished he could wake up. And he didn't need the motivation of Legos or anything else Mom promised.

He had the crying. Holy crap, the crying. Like nonstop. Every time someone new came to visit, more crying. The crying was the worst part of the whole thing.

Except for Dad—that was the worst. Brady knew his dad was in pretty bad shape too. Brady heard the nurses talking about the accident. "Just heartbreaking…they say his dad might never walk again."

Just like everything else, it seemed, Brady remembered the accident clearly. They were late for baseball practice. Dad was sitting in the kitchen eating a sandwich. "You can be a couple minutes late, Brady. This is Little League, for Christ's sake." Dad had just gotten home from his job at the steel plant, and he was in a bad mood. Brady knew he would probably rather be at McGuire's with his work buddies, but Mom was held up at work, so Dad had to take him.

Brady didn't want to be late. None of the other kids were ever late. "Dad, can we go now?" he whined.

Dad gave him a warning look. "Do you have your glove and cleats?"

"Yes, they're in the car."

Dad took another bite of his sandwich. "Pain in my ass, can I finish eating? Get in the car, I'll be there in a minute."

Just as Brady got to the car, Jen came running up behind him and pushed her way in front. "Move it, dipwad." She grabbed for the front passenger door. "Dad's dropping me off at Mackenzie's first."

"No!" They couldn't afford any stops. "Jen, I'm going to be late as it is!"

She ignored him and Brady got into the back. There was no point in arguing. Jen was older and a girl—she always got her way.

By the time they pulled out of the driveway, he was already three minutes late. By the time they dropped Jen off, Brady was eight minutes late and jumping out of his skin. "Can you go a little faster, Dad?" Another warning look.

As they approached the busiest intersection in Fulton—three lanes in each direction—the light went from green to yellow. "Dad! Run it!"

Instead, Dad hit the brakes. "Would you shut the hell up, Brady? I mean it!"

"Sorry." They stopped and waited. And waited. The light was taking forever.

"Hey, Dad, can you pass me my glove?" he asked.

Dad threw it in the backseat.

"And my cleats?"

Dad sighed. "They're on the floor, I can't reach 'em. Wait 'til we get there."

"But, Dad, I need to put them on now!"

"Jesus Christ, Brady!" His dad was reaching down in the front seat. "Here's your damn—"

But he never finished his sentence, because that's when it happened.

The engine revved loudly. The car jerked forward. A horn blared. Tires screeched. Rubber burned. Brady screamed. The truck hit. The car crumpled. Everything changed. Forever.

***

Brady looked down into his mug of hot chocolate and avoided her eyes. "So what it comes down to is, I caused the accident. I got a new and improved brain, and my dad got a permanent disability. My dad is limping around because of me."

"C'mon, Brady, you can't think like that."

He looked up. "Why not? I was the one who wouldn't shut the hell up. I had to have those cleats, I just couldn't wait."

"You were like eight!"

"Nine." He knew he was being petty, but he didn't want her trying to minimize his guilt. It was his fault, end of story.

"Well, how long were you in the coma?" she asked, not deterred.

"Twelve days."

"So when you woke up, you just had this new ability? The number thing?"

"No. When I woke up, I couldn't think straight at all. That's when all the pain started. They were pumping me so full of morphine, I honestly don't remember a lot of that time. But when I started feeling better, I noticed things were different."

"Like how?" She leaned forward over the table with her hands folded in front of her.

"It's hard to explain. I guess after a brain injury, or brain damage—as Jay always likes to remind me—some people can do really crazy things. Like there was this guy who dove into a shallow pool at a party and messed up his head pretty bad. Then one day he's at a friend's house and he sees a piano. He sits down and starts playing all these awesome melodies—like he's a professional. Thing is, he never had a lesson in his life."

She shook her head. "That is so wild."

"It's called 'acquired savant syndrome.' Less than a hundred people in the world have been documented with it."

"Wow," Vivienne said. "So, is that why you don't like doing the number thing? Because of the accident?"

"Maybe a little, and because honestly, I'm not really doing anything."

"Oh, right," she teased. "Your freakish brain does all the work."

Brady smiled. "Well, yeah."

"You do realize your brain is a part of you. You are kind of one and the same."

He paused. "Yeah, Vivienne, I get that, but it really doesn't feel that way."

She shrugged. "I don't think you should feel bad about it. If I could do that, I'd show it off. Why not?"

Brady laughed. "Oh my God, you sound like Jay. Every time we go somewhere, he has to bring it up in front of girls"—a pause—"people, to get attention." *How embarrassing.*

"A real chick magnet, huh?"

Brady's face flushed. "Uh…no, but Jay likes to think so."

Vivienne took a sip from her drink and then smiled. "I think Jay might be right."

Okay, she was flirting with him, right? He was pretty clueless about girls, but it seemed like she was flirting. How should he respond to that? His brain went into overdrive but was coming up empty. Everything in his head was chaos. Why couldn't he have any coherent thoughts around her? Why couldn't he come back with something witty or clever?

But Vivienne couldn't stay quiet for more than ten seconds, so he didn't have to. "So, have you ever asked your dad what he remembers about the accident?"

"No." Brady had never talked with his dad about the accident—ever. He wanted to, God, he wanted to. Just so he could finally tell his dad how sorry he was for, well, for ruining his life. But he never got the courage to bring it up.

She tilted her head to one side and smiled, a reassuring smile. "Maybe you should."

It had been only five days since they had first met, but Brady felt like he'd known Vivienne for five years. He cared about what she thought. "I don't know, do you think so?"

"Sure, I think it's always good to put things out there."

He had to admit, it did feel good to finally tell someone about the accident. It was like he could physically feel some of the burden floating away. Or maybe it was just being around Vivienne that made him feel better. Whatever it was, as he looked at her sitting across from him with her freckled face and smiling green eyes, he knew what he had to do.

And just as he was about to do it, she said, "Well, I should probably be getting back now."

"Oh, yeah." He put his mug of lukewarm hot chocolate on the table. "It's getting late."

They put on their coats and made their exit from SweetBrews.

It would have to wait.

CHAPTER 29

Vivienne was reeling. Something was happening to her, something new, something exciting. Just being near Brady made her head spin and her insides turn to jelly, made her knees weak and her heart aflutter. What other cheesy clichés could she come up with?

They were only a couple of blocks away from her house, and he would be dropping her off soon. All she knew was that she didn't want to say goodbye, not yet.

Say something, Vivienne—think!

But he said something first. "So, do you work a lot of hours at the nursing home?"

"Oh, usually just Tuesdays and Fridays for a couple hours after school, and then sometimes on Sundays. It's not too bad."

More silence. *Say something else!*

But before she could think of anything, Brady was already pulling in front of her house. "Here we are." He put the car in park.

"Here we are," she repeated like an idiot. Then she suddenly realized she was still wearing his sweatshirt, for the second time. "Oh, I almost forgot." She unzipped the hoodie and quickly began pulling her arms out of the sleeves.

"No"—he put his hand on her arm—"you keep it."

Flip-flop went her stomach. "No, no..." She began wiggling out of it. "I'm sure it's one of your favorites." She wanted that sweatshirt more than anything, but she tried to act casual.

"No, seriously, I want you to have it. Take it."

A horrible realization suddenly hit her. Oh my God, he was saying goodbye. It was a frickin' parting gift! All the fluttering and flip-flopping came to a screeching halt.

"Oh, well, thanks." She attempted a convincing smile and reached for the door.

"Wait." His hand was on her arm again. She turned toward him and he gave her that shy-Brady look. Flip-flop.

He grinned. "The reason I was asking about your job is because I was wondering if you were maybe free on Friday night? I thought maybe we could hang out."

She blinked. "Oh, Friday?" *Be casual...* "Yeah, I'm free. I mean, I work til seven, but after that, yeah, I'm free. Yep." She was a stuttering idiot!

"Cool, how about I pick you up at eight? Would that work?"

"Yeah, that would work," she said nonchalantly. She had a feeling she was failing miserably at hiding her excitement. She opened the car door.

"Hey, Vivienne."

She felt her breath catch in her throat. "Yeah?"

He nodded at the sweatshirt. "It looks better on you."

***

Vivienne watched Brady drive away and she pulled his hoodie—now her hoodie—tighter around herself. They were going out Friday night!

She was giddy with happiness and found herself almost skipping up the driveway. Halfway up, she heard a shout behind her. "Hey!"

Her stomach dropped—Chad. All her excitement instantaneously evaporated. When was this crap going to stop?

She turned around to find Chad standing at the end of the driveway, arms crossed in front of him, sneering at her. "Wow, Vivienne, don't you look positively glowing! That must've been some date."

Her anger and frustration came to a boiling point. "Oh my God, Chad!"

She walked toward him with newfound confidence. She wasn't sure if it was being around Brady or just being pushed so far that she'd finally fallen off the edge, but she wanted to chew Chad out like never before.

"What is wrong with you?" she yelled. "Have you been out here the whole night?!"

"What?" His face transformed into a look of mock surprise. "No. I just came back here to apologize about earlier."

She took a deep breath. "Okay, Chad, you do realize this is stalking, right?"

He rolled his eyes. "Don't be so dramatic, Vivienne."

That was it. She bit her tongue and turned to leave.

"Wait! I'm sorry. Please, Vivienne!"

Oh. My. God. Next to her unruly curiosity, her tendency to be a sympathetic pushover was probably her next biggest flaw. "What?"

"Give me another chance—one night. Just go out with me one night." He smiled, his face full of excitement. "I promise if you don't change your mind about us, I'll never bring it up again."

Chad was obviously delusional, and she had to make it as clear as she possibly could. "Chad." She looked him directly in the eye. "It will never work between us. I'm sorry. My answer isn't going to change."

The excitement in his face fell and he looked away. Then his eyes turned dark and piercing. "Brady O'Connell—you actually like that guy?"

Now Chad had a last name.

"Beth told me about him." He shook his head in disgust.

Frickin' Beth.

"As you well know, he's from white-trash Fulton, and I kept thinking, how did Vivienne meet a guy like that? And his last name—I just knew I'd seen that name somewhere before. It was really bugging me, and then it was like a lightbulb went on. I looked in my dad's phone and sure enough, there it was: *O'Connell-bookie*. And then I remembered the night at our house, the bullshit about the cat. Something wasn't right about it."

He paused and smiled, obviously pleased with himself. "And it all came together. Brady came to see my dad that night and you saw the asshole outside, didn't you?"

Vivienne was frozen, her mouth wouldn't move. She quickly looked away, and that said it all.

"That's it! You met him that night at my house!"

She turned to leave, and Chad grabbed her arm from behind.

"Let go of me, Chad!" Her heart was hammering in her chest.

"Brady is complete trash." Chad's face was menacing. "His dad's a lowlife collecting disability. I mean, he's my dad's bookie, for Christ's sake. You do realize that, right?"

"Yes, Chad, I know about his dad's business."

She could see a flicker of surprise in his eyes. "Ha! His business—that's funny." He wouldn't let go of her arm. "My dad has a business, Vivienne. Brady's dad is a criminal."

She ripped her arm away. "I'm done talking to you." As she turned and ran up the house, she could hear Chad laughing behind her.

"Sweet dreams, Vivienne!" he yelled.

She slammed the door behind her and turned the deadbolt. Her whole body was trembling so badly, she had to grab the banister. Why wouldn't he leave her alone? What was she going to do?

When she got into her room she immediately collapsed onto her bed. What she wanted to do more than anything was call Brady—to hear his calming voice. But what would she say to him? 'Hi, Brady, yeah…so psycho Chad showed up at my house again and wanted to tell me that you're trash and your dad's a criminal.' Probably not a good idea.

She called Kendra instead, and the minute she heard her friend's voice, Vivienne could feel the words catch in her throat. "Kendra, can you come over? It's an emergency."

CHAPTER 30

"Yo! A little help here, Brady!" Jay yelled from below.

"Shit, sorry." Brady grabbed the barbell from Jay and set it in the stand above the bench.

"Dude, what is with you? This was your idea, remember?"

"I know. Sorry."

Jay sat up on the weight bench. "Screw this. Let's go home and play *Halo*."

"Jay, we're supposed to be working out every day." They both played baseball for Fulton High. Brady was shortstop and Jay played left field. Coach expected them to work out in the off-season, but fall was the time of year they slacked off, so Brady had suggested they go.

"I'm calling bullshit. This is about the girl—Vivienne."

"What?"

"Dude, you never want to work out until like January— why now?" Jay looked way too amused.

Brady ignored him. He picked up a curling bar and started doing reps.

"And you're acting all different—all distracted." Jay stood with his hands on his hips and stepped in front of Brady. "You like that girl, Vivi—ennnnnnne."

"Shut up, asshole." Brady concentrated on counting out his reps.

"Oh my God!" He gave Brady a playful punch. "You totally do!"

Brady switched arms. "Whatever."

Jay moved over to the leg press. "She's definitely hot. She has that whole Emma Stone vibe going on."

"You think she looks like Emma Stone?" Brady didn't see it. To him, Vivienne just looked like Vivienne. There wasn't anyone like her.

"Well, maybe Emma Stone with a lot of freckles."

"I actually saw her Monday night," Brady said.

"Who, Emma Stone?"

Brady gave him his 'you're not funny' look.

"So is Vivienne like your bae now?" Jay laughed.

"Whatever, asshole."

"Okay, seriously, why didn't you tell me?"

"Maybe because I knew you'd act like this. It was no big deal. She wanted to return my sweatshirt, so I went by her house to pick it up."

"And?"

"And that douchebag Chad showed up."

"Chad, the ex-boyfriend?"

"Yeah, she didn't invite him or anything. He just showed up. And holy shit, what a tool—acted like I wasn't even there." Brady dropped the curling bar and picked up a towel. "Then Vivienne tells him that we're going out to a movie. And he looks at me like he's going to kill me."

"Sorry, but I've got news for you, bro. This whole working out thing—it's a little too little, a little too late. You know what I'm saying?"

Jay went on, "I saw that guy at the game—he's a beast, legit. He could seriously kick your ass."

Brady shrugged. "Yeah, probably."

"Well, what happened with Vivienne?"

"We just went and got coffee." He regretted it as soon as he said it.

Jay busted out laughing. "Coffee, are you serious? You don't drink coffee!"

"Hot chocolate—whatever." Brady picked up his sweatshirt and water bottle.

"So what now?"

He had to tell Jay about the date—he was going to find out sooner or later. "Well…we're gonna go out Friday night."

Jay shook his head. "Asshole, when were you going to tell me? You can't keep this stuff from me!"

"It's not a big deal, Jay," Brady lied.

"Uh, are you kidding me? Yes, it is!" Jay shot back. "So where are you gonna take her?"

"I don't know—I mean, I haven't really decided yet." But Brady had decided. "I have an idea, but it's a little— unusual."

"Well, I would expect nothing less, Rain Man."

"Ha-ha."

***

Brady was starving after the workout so he headed straight for the kitchen. Dad was making himself a salami sandwich.

"Hey, Dad, can you leave the stuff out? I'm gonna make one too."

"Sure thing." His dad hobbled into the living room and sat in front of the flat-screen. "The Cavs opener is coming on in a little bit!" he called out.

"Okay!" Brady called back.

"And there's some pasta salad in the fridge, I made it myself."

What? Brady opened the fridge to see a glass bowl full of bow tie pasta, swimming in what appeared to be Italian salad dressing. But there were cherry tomatoes, cut-up celery, black olives and little cubes of cheese.

"You seriously made this?"

"Yep, aren't you impressed?"

"Very!" He was impressed, and surprised as well. A simple pasta salad might not be a big deal to most, but for his dad it was totally out of character, in a good way.

Brady filled his plate with two sandwiches and a heaping pile of pasta salad and took a seat next to his dad. They watched the Cavs pregame for a few minutes, eating in silence. For some reason, his mind kept going back to the conversation he'd had with Vivienne, about the accident. *Maybe you should ask him.*

"Dad, can I ask you something?"

"Sure."

"Do you remember anything…about the accident?" He could barely get it out.

Dad stopped mid-chew and put his plate on the table. "A little bit." He took a long swig of his milk. "I remember driving you to baseball practice. And then, I guess the next thing I remember was waking up in the hospital."

Brady picked at his pasta salad and contemplated what he would say next. "Dad, the thing is, the accident was my fault." Brady kept his eyes on the flat-screen, but he could feel his dad watching him.

"Brady, what are you talking about? According to police reports, and eyewitnesses, I drove into that intersection. If it's anybody's fault, it's mine."

"Do you know why you drove into that intersection?"

Dad shrugged. "I don't know. I was probably distracted."

Brady's voice was shaking. "Dad, I remember it all, but I never told anybody. Well, I told one person…but the point is, I remember." He paused and took a deep breath. "I distracted you. I wanted my cleats, and you said no and I told you I had to have them, and then you reached down to get them."

Brady felt his voice catching in his throat, but he had to get it out. "You must've hit the gas, because the car jolted, and then I looked over and saw the truck coming."

He finally turned to face his dad. "So it was my fault, Dad. Your bad leg, your limping, all of it—everything was my fault, and I am so sorry."

His dad looked horrified. "Oh God, Brady—you can't blame yourself for this, you can't!"

"I just wanted you to know how sorry I am..." The tears were welling up in his eyes and he had to look away.

But his dad wouldn't let him. "Look at me, Brady. Son, look at me."

So Brady quickly wiped his eyes on his shirt sleeves and looked at his dad. He suddenly felt like he was nine years old all over again.

"Now I want you to listen to me. This accident was not your fault. Period. One thing I can tell you, after living on this earth for forty-nine years, is that shit happens. It does—any place, anytime, anywhere. That's life, Brady, and when shit rolls our way, we've just got to make the most of it. We've got to keep going. Right?"

Brady nodded.

Dad went on, "Do you want to know what I *do* remember?" He held his salami sandwich in the air and turned it around as if he was examining it. "I do remember we were running late and I insisted on finishing my goddamn sandwich. That I do remember. Do you remember?"

"Yeah." Brady nodded again.

"And if I would've just put the goddamn sandwich down, we wouldn't have been rushing, and things would've turned out completely different. You see, Brady? Me, you"—he waved his sandwich through the air—"the goddamn phases of the moon, it doesn't matter. You can't blame the accident on any one thing. It's a lot of little things that come together in the perfect storm, so to speak."

Brady sighed, "And then shit happens."

"Exactly!" Dad laughed. "Now you're learning, boy genius!" Dad put his arm around Brady and pulled him closer. "Now I don't want you thinking like that anymore, got it?"

"Got it."

"So, are we good—again?"

Brady nodded. "We're good." But he was better than good. He felt like a new person.

An indescribable feeling of peace came over him as he leaned back onto the couch. Brady didn't care that he was seventeen years old; he still felt like he was nine years old, and he rested his head on his dad's shoulder.

His dad patted him on the head. "Now, let's watch the Cavs whip some Raptor ass."

CHAPTER 31

Vivienne squirted another swirl of whipped cream on another piece of apple pie and continued down the row. Janet had just finished setting out the last of the plates. "Remember to give Mr. Gorman the cherry piece over there. He's not a fan of apple."

Vivienne was so distracted she didn't respond.

"Vivienne—earth to Vivienne!" Janet called out, snapping her fingers in front of her face.

"Sorry, what'd you say?"

"I said make sure Mr. Gorman gets the cherry pie." She pointed over to the lone piece sitting off to the side.

"Oh, okay." Vivienne hadn't been herself since Brady had dropped her off Monday. She couldn't stop thinking about him. Every time she got a text from him, her heart skipped a beat.

Some made her laugh: *I'm thinking about buying a Puffy Pairpoint lamp for my room. I found one on EBay—only $38,000*

Others were just sweet and simple: *Night, Vivienne* ☺

But texting wasn't enough for her. She wanted to see him, be near him, touch him…kiss him. And hopefully in a couple of hours, she would be doing just that.

"Is something wrong, hon?" Janet was now standing next to her, concern on her face.

"No! No, nothing's wrong," Vivienne said, and then she smiled. "Sorry, I kind of just met this boy, and I guess I'm not thinking straight."

"Oooohh." Janet's eyes lit up. "Well, why didn't you say something?! C'mon, I want the goods. Tell me everything!"

"Well, his name is Brady and we met…" For the first time, she realized she would never be able to tell the real story about how they met. "At a football game."

"And?"

"And he goes to Fulton High—he's a junior like me. And he's really smart, super nice, and cute." She could feel her face burning up as she talked about him.

"So is he a good kisser?" Janet raised her eyebrows up and down.

"Oh my God!" At that, Vivienne's cringed in embarrassment. "Well, we haven't kissed yet." And then she added, "But we are going out tonight."

"Where are you going?"

"I don't know. He said it was a surprise." She couldn't contain herself.

"Oooohh, he definitely sounds intriguing!"

"He is. He's really different, but in a really good way."

Janet eyed her. "I haven't known you that long, Vivienne, but I've never seen you like this. You like this boy a lot, don't you?"

"I guess I do. Is it that obvious?"

Janet held her thumb and index finger together. "Just a wee bit. But I'm happy for you, girl."

"Thanks. I'll let you know how the date goes next week."

"You better." Janet walked back to the kitchen and started filling more trays. "You know what the key to any good relationship is, right?"

Janet had been married to her husband Bob for like thirty years. She'd told Vivienne they'd met at a Whitesnake concert, and Janet was appalled when Vivienne said she'd never heard of them.

"Okay, I'm going to go with the obvious, although I have a feeling its wrong. Love?"

"Nope."

"Trust?"

"Keep guessing."

"Hmm…respect?"

Janet shook her head. "All good guesses, but keep trying."

"A sense of humor?"

"No, but that's definitely helpful."

"C'mon, I give up."

"The key to a successful relationship is empathy."

"Empathy?"

"It comes down to this: the longer you live in this world, the more you learn that it's not all some big fairy tale. Shit happens, plain and simple."

Vivienne laughed. "That's exactly what Brady said!"

"Already like the kid."

Janet stopped filling the plates and pointed a spoonful of mashed potatoes at her. "Sometimes you'll feel unloved, sometimes you'll feel disrespected, sometimes you'll feel your trust is broken. And sometimes, you sure as hell won't feel like laughing. That's just the way it is. So the most important thing is *empathy*. Always, always put yourself in the other person's shoes. Always."

Vivienne nodded her head. "Always."

"Alright, we're running late, so you better get moving."

Vivienne loaded the final trays into the cart and began rolling it out of the kitchen when Janet called over, "Hey, I forgot to mention, don't deliver to Mrs. Perez. She, uh, passed yesterday."

Vivienne felt a twinge in her chest. "How?" Mrs. Perez couldn't have been older than seventy, and she hadn't been that sick either.

"In her sleep. I guess it was just her time to go." Then Janet went back to filling plates and Vivienne heard her mumble under her breath. "Shit happens."

CHAPTER 32

Vivienne came out of the house in jeans and a long winter coat, carrying a hat and gloves. Brady had told her to dress warm; it was getting down to thirty-six degrees tonight.

He had debated about where to take her on their first date. Obviously he wanted to do something special—but there was a thin line between special and weird, and so he was doubly nervous.

"Hey." She got into the passenger seat, and the faint scent of Vivienne—sort of fruity vanilla—surrounded him.

He tried to sound as casual as possible. "Hey."

Luckily, Vivienne wasn't one to hold back on conversation, and before he even pulled out of the driveway, she was asking questions. "So what's the big surprise?"

He smiled. "I'm not telling yet." Brady had told her they would be outside, hence the warm attire, but that was about it. "First question, are you hungry?"

"Not really," she said, and then she quickly added, "Oh, unless I'm supposed to be. I mean, if it's all part of your plan, then sure."

"No," he laughed. "I just wanted to make the offer. We could pick up some food and take it to eat on the way."

"On the way? How far are we going?"

"About a thirty-minute drive. Maybe thirty-five."

"Really?" Her eyebrows lifted. "A little road trip?"

"Yes, just a little one. Is that okay?"

"Sure, it sounds fun. But we don't need to stop. I mean—unless you're hungry."

"No, I'm good." He had already eaten, but he'd wanted to leave the option open for her. He could always eat more if he had to—his stomach was a bottomless pit.

The date had barely begun and his heart was already pounding. "What time do you have to be back?"

"My parents are pretty cool. They go to bed early and they trust me, so whenever." Then she added, "But probably no later than midnight."

He nodded. Was she as nervous as he was? She didn't sound like it. He headed toward the highway and got on I-71 South.

She began playing with the radio. "What do you want to listen to?"

"Whatever's fine." Another attempt at sounding casual. He had already spent hours alone with Vivienne, but this felt different. They were on a *real date*, and the anticipation was brutal. What if she thought his idea was totally lame?

She settled on something he didn't recognize, maybe Maroon Five, and turned the volume down low. "Do you ever think about where it could be? I mean, where the backpack could be?"

He had thought about it many times, like every day for the last week. He shrugged his shoulders. "Sometimes."

"Where do you think is the most likely place?"

"Well, if your mom is absolutely positive she dropped it off at the Goodwill—"

"Brady, she did. Trust me, we went over it a million times. She went straight from our house to the Goodwill in Fulton and she put the bags in the drop-off area at around eight o'clock. Oh, and we searched the minivan too, just in case."

"I know, I'm sorry. Just trying to narrow down the possible scenarios."

"Well, what's your best guess?"

"You know what? Why are we even talking about it?" He didn't want anything putting tension between them. The backpack was gone, move on.

But Vivienne didn't want to. "It still bothers me, a lot. And I'm not going to apologize again, because you told me not to, but I really care about what you think."

He hated hearing her voice like that—the sad, dejected Vivienne voice. "Okay, you really want to know?"

She smiled. "Yes, I really want to know."

"Well, there are three possible scenarios. One, somebody came to drop stuff off at the Goodwill, looked through your mom's bags, and took the backpack. Two, one of the Goodwill employees saw it and snagged it. Or three…" He trailed off.

"What's three?"

"Well, what kind of shape was it in—the backpack?"

Vivienne shrugged. "It was a little beat up."

"Well, it might've gotten thrown out. And if that's the case, then it's out in the middle of a garbage dump somewhere, covered in fly shit and scavenger birds. Birds like shiny objects, you know?" he laughed.

"Nice." She wasn't laughing, but she was smiling.

"Sorry, I'm just being realistic."

"Well, do you want to know what I like to think?" she asked.

"Of course, do tell."

"Okay, I'm going to go with scenario number one. I imagine there's a single mom somewhere, you know—working her butt off and going to school, trying to make a better life for herself and her daughter. She makes a stop at the local Goodwill on Friday night to see what's new, and as she walks by the drop-off, she decides to take a peek. She sees the backpack with the big V and thinks, 'Perfect!' See, because her daughter's name is Victoria."

"Of course it is." Brady grins.

"And so the next morning before school, she is putting—"

"Wait, it would be Saturday morning, so she wouldn't have school."

A pause.

"Brady, are you kidding me right now?" She sighed. "I'm sorry, it's *Monday* morning and she's putting Victoria's lunch in the backpack, when she notices a little bulge inside the zipper pocket…Oh, and I forgot to mention she's behind on the rent, her car is broken and Victoria's birthday is coming up."

"Of course it is."

The excitement was building in Vivienne's voice. "So she pulls out the envelope and begins counting out the bills and freaks out…she's jumping up and down for joy…and she tells Victoria she's going to give her the best birthday ever!" Even in the dim light of the car he could see the sparkle in her eyes.

"Wow, that's a pretty good story," he said. And it was.

"Well, just trying to think of something positive—you know, look for a silver lining and all that."

Then a thought came to Brady. "Sutton's name is on the envelope. I wrote 'Jeff Sutton, attorney-at-law' on the envelope. You don't think anyone would actually return the money to him, do you?"

"No way." Vivienne shook her head. "I mean, I don't think so. Most people think lawyers are rich anyway. Someone using an old backpack would probably figure they needed it a lot more."

"You're right. And if by some one-in-a-million chance, someone actually did return it, it's not like Sutton would ever tell my dad. He'd just pocket it."

Vivienne's voice got quiet. "I do think most people would want to return the notebook, though."

"Maybe," Brady agreed, "but the money and the notebook kind of go hand in hand, you know? People aren't going to return a notebook and not the money." *Shit, be quiet, stupid.*

"Yeah, unless they do it anonymously…like maybe put it in a mailbox." He heard a hint of hope in her voice, so he kept his next thought to himself.

But then Vivienne said exactly what he was thinking. "But my name isn't anywhere on the notebook. They'd think it was Mr. Sutton's and they'd put it in his mailbox."

"You know what?" Brady needed to get it out there once and for all. "I know how much the notebook meant to you, and that's the only reason I'm upset about losing the backpack. But truthfully, I don't give a shit about the money anymore. Really, Vivienne."

He paused because he wasn't sure if he should say what he was about to say. *Screw it.* "That lost backpack is the reason we got to know each other. That's my silver lining in the whole thing."

Silence.

He glanced over at her and she was smiling.

Just when things had gotten quiet between them, they reached their exit. Logan Township, State Route 273. He turned off the highway ramp and came to a lone stop sign. No traffic lights, no gas stations, nothing but vast darkness. The headlights illuminated a green sign that read Logan – 2 miles, with an arrow pointing west, and Greenfield – 4 miles with an arrow pointing east.

"Uh, Brady? Where are we going?"

He took a right and began heading west. "Can't give it away now," he said teasingly.

The country road cut through an expanse of cornfields, shaved down from the recent harvest. He put on his brights and let the yellow center line guide them. "I know, it's a little creepy, but it's an adventure, right?"

"C'mon! Give me a hint!" she pleaded.

Patches of trees began popping up on the sides of the road. "It's not far." Soon they were in a wooded area, and Brady slowed the car.

"Okay...you're really freaking me out right now!" Vivienne was practically jumping out of her seat.

He kept his eyes peeled to the sides of the road. Occasionally a mailbox would appear, marking a gravel driveway that led into more darkness. He was looking for one mailbox in particular. "We're almost there..."

And then he saw it. The mallard duck—sitting atop a white mailbox. Faded black numbers scrawled across the side read 4183. Brady quickly killed the lights as he pulled into the gravel drive. He steered his black Focus into a small clearing, in between a cluster of trees, and shut off the engine.

"Brady! What are we doing here?!" Vivienne asked in an urgent whisper.

Now that the car was finally stopped, he was able to get a good look at her. She looked back at him with eyes wide and a smile to match. The weird 'good' feeling came over him in a wave and he quickly looked away. "You see that?" He pointed through the trees.

She quickly buried her face in her hands and crouched down in her seat, so low she was almost under the dashboard. "What is it?"

He laughed. "It's okay, seriously."

"Just tell me. You're really freaking me out right now."

"It's just a house, Vivienne."

She slowly pulled herself up and uncovered her face. "See?"

Set far back from the road, at the end of the gravel drive, was a clearing. A large white farmhouse sat in the middle of it, a couple of windows glowing with orange light.

"Who lives there?" she asked.

Brady shrugged and smiled. "Honestly, I have no idea."

CHAPTER 33

Not exactly how she had envisioned their first date, but it was definitely exciting. She looked at the farmhouse in the distance. "Brady, this is super creepy."

Brady looked at her with that easy smile of his. "You will be perfectly safe with me. I promise."

"Sorry." She shook her head. "I'm not getting out til you tell me more."

He laughed. "Okay, I do know who used to live here. I used to come here a lot when I was little. It was my Aunt Julie and Uncle Kevin's house."

"And..." She waited.

"And see, my Uncle Kevin was a prepper—"

"A what?" she interrupted.

"He was one of those antigovernment extremists, you know, getting ready for the end of the world. After 9/11 he became convinced that the US was headed for societal collapse. He was obsessed with prepping for the end of days—he started collecting guns and filling the basement with shelves and shelves of food and water. We would go down there to play and just count the cans—there were like thousands."

"Please tell me we aren't sneaking into the basement."

"No, I promise." Brady laughed again. "So, my uncle was also convinced that all the nonbelievers would descend upon his house and raid all his supplies. So, he built this amazing lookout platform." He paused and frowned. "Maybe I should've asked you if you were afraid of heights first."

"Wait—we're going up on it—this platform?"

"It's not really a platform. It's more like a tower. The thing is huge, has stairs going up and everything. It's definitely sturdy."

She wasn't afraid of heights, but she was little freaked out. What if they got caught? "I don't know, Brady. I'm not afraid of heights, but isn't this like trespassing?"

He smiled, that easy smile again. "I came out here the other night. The tower is really far back from the house and hidden by the trees. I sat up there for like an hour, no problem."

"You came out here already?"

"Well, yeah, after I got the idea, I wanted to make sure the thing was still here."

She couldn't believe the amount of trouble he had gone through just for their date. "Okay, I'm game."

"Just make sure to shut your phone off. Can't have any lights at all." He reached into the backseat and grabbed a flannel blanket.

Flip-flop. Any hesitation or doubts instantly vanished as she imagined the two of them lying on the blanket together, or even better, under the blanket.

"Ready?" he asked, his voice sounding excited, eager.

She nodded. Oh my God, at that moment, she would follow him anywhere. Seriously anywhere.

"Okay, just stay right behind me. The ground's a little bumpy."

They carefully got out of the car and quietly began the trek through the trees. Vivienne could see her breath making white clouds in the frigid air. She followed on his heels as he methodically made his way through the rough path.

"Careful," he whispered and stopped. A giant tree root was jutting out into their path.

She stepped around it. When she glanced over to the farmhouse, it was behind them now.

"It's only a little bit further. Sorry, I don't remember it being so muddy."

She trudged through the wet leaves and mud, not even bothered by the fact that she was probably ruining her Uggs. Not bothered one bit.

When she glanced back to the house the next time, the orange lights in the windows looked tiny through the trees. The tower was definitely far back, which made her feel better about the whole thing. Finally the path seemed to widen, and suddenly they were standing in a clearing of high grass and weeds.

"This is it," Brady said.

In front of them stood a huge structure, four giant beams rising up, flanked by support beams in a crisscross pattern up the sides. Instead of a simple ladder, a small staircase zigzagged upward. Her eyes followed the stairs up to a large square platform that was enclosed by wood railings.

Brady was watching for her reaction. "What do ya think?"

"Wow, how high is it?"

"I would guess around twenty-five or thirty feet," he said casually. Then he stepped closer to her. "You still up for it?"

"Yep." She smiled. She didn't care if it was a hundred feet.

"I brought you here because I wanted to show you something. Follow me."

And so she did. Up the small staircase, one step at a time, holding the railing, she followed.

"See, the Orionids shower is at its peak tonight, and the conditions are perfect because it's a new moon."

What did he just say? "God, you make me feel like an idiot sometimes."

"Sorry, I'm into astronomy a little. Have you ever heard of Halley's Comet?"

"Well, I'm not that much of an idiot." Of course she had heard of it, everybody had heard of it. That didn't mean she had any clue what it actually was. "But you can refresh my memory."

He glanced back at her, and she could see a flash of his smile in the darkness. "Well, Halley's Comet is made of ice and rock and space dust, like a giant dirty snowball. It only comes by Earth every seventy-five years. The last time we could see it was in 1986, before we were born, obviously, and the next time will be in 2061."

"Bummer. We'll be old."

He laughed. "Yes, but the good news is that it does leave a lot of debris in its orbit. And this debris we can see twice a year—in May and October."

"Debris?"

Brady laughed. "Yeah, the dirty ice and rock that's left behind burns up in the atmosphere and becomes meteors. It's a meteor shower. And tonight is the peak viewing time for the Orionids meteor shower—the one in October."

They reached the top of the stairs where there was an opening in the floor. Brady helped her up through it so they were both standing in the middle of the square platform. She instinctively grabbed onto his arm. "Holy crap, this is high."

Thankfully, the platform was much larger than it looked from the ground—it could easily fit ten people, and waist-high wood railings surrounded the entire perimeter.

She looked out at the fields of blackness and could see the highway out in the distance, the tiny white and red lights of cars whizzing by. Even the highway looked surprisingly beautiful.

"Here." Brady laid out the blanket and sat down.

She sat next to him. Flip-flop.

"Okay, you've got to lay down to get the full effect."

Flip-flop, flip-flop.

She lay back next to him as her eyes adjusted to the sight in front of her. It was truly incredible and she felt her breath catch in her chest. The black sky was smattered with sparkles, like someone had thrown a bunch of glitter into the air and it had stuck. She had never seen anything like it. For some reason, she felt like she was going to cry. A good cry.

Without thinking, she reached over and grabbed Brady's hand in hers. She squeezed it tightly. "Wow."

People say there are moments in life you will never forget. Moments where you feel something so unexpected, so beautiful, so perfect, it actually hurts. It aches down to your core, and you know you are changed forever.

Vivienne was having one of those moments, and she didn't ever want it to end.

CHAPTER 34

Brady felt Vivienne's hand on his and his heart started racing even faster. Everything had turned out perfect so far—well, except for maybe the mud. And he knew the sky would be amazing.

"It's so—I don't even have words," she said quietly.

He turned to look at her. "I know. It kind of takes your breath away."

He could see her smile in the darkness.

"What were you saying about the moon? I don't see it."

"Right, 'cause it's a new moon—like the opposite of a full moon. And because it's dark, everything else is easier to see."

"Got it."

"Just let your eyes relax and try not to look at any spot in particular. This way, you'll notice any movement easier. You don't really want to look for meteors, if that makes sense."

"So this isn't a bunch at once?" she asked.

"No, 'meteor shower' isn't really the best name. They're just sporadic. But we might get one every couple of minutes tonight, which is a lot." He had seen a couple of meteor showers before, and even in less than ideal conditions, they had blown him away.

But his thoughts weren't really on meteor showers; they were somewhere else entirely. While she looked for her first meteor, he contemplated his first move. Should he just lean over? How long should he wait? What if he came on too strong?

"So does it look like a shooting star?" she asked.

He paused, not wanting to sound condescending. "Well, these are shooting stars, actually. Shooting stars aren't really stars. They're meteors."

She looked at him and he could see the frown forming. "Really?"

"Yep, they're really just the debris from the comet burning up in the atmosphere."

"Well, that's just great." She paused. "So you're telling me that wishing on a shooting star is really just wishing on dirty space debris?"

He had never really thought about it that way. "Sorry?"

"It's okay." She smiled, her eyes still fixated on the sky. "I'm going to think of them as stars anyway."

He tried to relax his eyes, but it was impossible to relax any part of his body while she was lying next to him.

"Oh!" she said loudly, and then quickly caught herself. She grabbed onto his arm and shook him. "I saw one, Brady! Over there! That was so cool!"

"See? Did I tell you?" He looked toward the northeast and saw a flash in the sky. Chills ran down his spine; it never got old. Only a few seconds later, another flash, longer this time.

"Oh! Did you see that?" Vivienne shrieked.

"Shhh!" he laughed. He watched her profile, her eyes sparkling, anticipating the next burst of light. He felt like *he* was gonna burst.

"How many stars do you think there are out there?" she asked.

He turned back to the sky. "Scientists say around one hundred octillion."

"How much is an octillion?"

"Well, there are ten trillion galaxies, and over a hundred billion stars in the Milky Way galaxy alone, so using that estimate, it comes out to one hundred octillion stars in the universe. Or, a one with twenty-nine zeros after it."

"Wow, my mind is officially blown."

"Yep, even my freakish brain can't comprehend that one."

He could just prop himself up on his elbow and lean over and...

"I wonder if Gloria is up there," she said quietly.

He wasn't expecting that. "It's possible."

"Do you believe in Heaven—in an afterlife?"

What was with the heavy questions? He hadn't prepared himself for the 'meaning of life' discussion. But Vivienne wasn't one to hold back. She was always full of questions, always curious. That was one of the things he liked most about her.

Now he could feel her eyes on him. He scanned the expanse of black sky littered with stars. "Do you?"

She shrugged. "I'm not sure. I mean, I want to." He could sense the uncertainty in her voice. "Gloria definitely believed. All of the residents at Shady Oaks believe. They have rosaries and Bibles and pictures of Jesus on the walls. They all talk about the good Lord taking them to Heaven and stuff like that. But what else do they have?"

"Well, I guess Heaven is definitely in the realm of possibilities."

She was still looking at him, not the sky. "The realm of possibilities."

"Sure." He hesitated. "I mean, can you imagine the possibilities? Just look at this, Vivienne." He waved his arm in the air. "We're so busy every day with our faces glued to our phones, and we never really pay attention to what's out there."

"So you think there's a God up there?"

He sighed. "I think there are possibilities up there."

"Okay…but what's your best guess?"

He looked at her. "You're not going to quit, are you?"

She smiled. "I value your opinion."

"Okay, I'll tell you what I know." He paused. "A life force made all of this—the whole universe, the whole octillion of stars, you, me, everything. And everything in the universe is pulsing with energy—like every single thing."

A doubtful look came over her face and she pulled off her knit hat. She held it up with her finger. "So, you're telling me this hat has energy?"

"Yep. Think about what happens when you burn it."

She studied the hat for a second. "Interesting..." she said.

"And we all share the energy. It connects all of us together." He propped himself up on his elbow and faced her. "And the best part?"

"What?" she asked softly.

"This is straight from Einstein himself—energy never dies."

She smiled. "I like that theory."

I like you, he thought, *a lot.*

The energy was palpable in the small space between them. As she looked at him, and he looked at her, he knew they were done talking.

So he leaned in closer.

And then he kissed her.

CHAPTER 35

And then he kissed her.

Warm lips on hers, soft and slow, the heat from his mouth melting into hers, the cold tip of his nose brushing against hers, his hands on the sides of her face and then moving through her hair.

His body shifted carefully over the length of hers and the kiss grew deeper, the warmth spreading from him to her, filling her with a yearning she had never felt before. She wrapped her arms around his back, pulling him in even closer. The way her body responded to his touch was so unfamiliar, it almost scared her. Almost. Call it hormones, stupidity, lapse of judgment...whatever, at that moment, she was completely lost.

In the cold, crisp autumn air, under an octillion of stars, Vivienne felt like the only girl in the world. And Brady was the only boy, and this was the only kiss. And she didn't want it to stop. Ever.

But then it did. Brady pulled away. He seemed flustered and let out a nervous laugh. "I'm sorry, I just—"

"Don't be." She felt every inch of her body ache. "Really."

His gaze held hers as he smiled down at her. She hoped he could see it in her eyes, how she was feeling inside. She wanted to kiss him again, to kiss him in a way that said 'I'm not sorry.' To kiss him in a way that said 'No regrets.' And just as she reached up to pull him closer, he flinched.

"Shit." He hovered over her, motionless.

"What?" *No, no, no.*

"Did you hear that?" His face looked panic-stricken.

"What?" All she could hear was the voice in her head that was screaming, *Kiss him!*

He quickly moved over to the side, and she slowly turned over onto her stomach. They peered through the railing, and then through the trees, toward the house. Sure enough, two beams of light shone brightly in the darkness—it looked like a pickup truck had pulled into the driveway.

Now she was panicked. "What should we do?"

"It's fine. Hopefully they'll just go in the house."

But as soon the truck door slammed, they heard something else. A sound that instantly sent fear into the pit of her stomach—a dog. And it was barking frantically.

"Skeeter!" an old man's voice bellowed in the darkness. "Come, boy!"

But it was no use. Skeeter had other plans. The dog was heading straight toward the tower, howling wildly as he went.

"Let's go!" Brady shuffled to his feet and grabbed her hand before she knew what was happening. Her body immediately went into crisis mode, her adrenaline surging as she flew down the narrow steps faster than she thought possible. She didn't think—she just moved.

They made it to the bottom in a matter of seconds, but as soon as they came into the clearing they halted.

Skeeter was waiting for them.

A huge German shepherd stood across from them in an attack stance, ready to pounce. Vivienne didn't think the name Skeeter really suited him. He looked more like a Butch or a Spike or a Killer. He growled viciously, showing his teeth and daring them to make a run for it.

"Don't move," Brady said under his breath. As if she wasn't already completely petrified.

"Skeeter! Damn it, boy, what are you going on about?!" The old man came into view and stopped abruptly when he saw them. "What the—?"

Skeeter's barking started up again, and the old man grabbed the dog's collar. "Heel, boy!" And just like that, Skeeter was quiet.

"What are you two doing all the way out here?" the old man asked, his long gray beard moving up and down as he talked. "Don't you know this is private property?"

He wore a black knit cap pulled down to his eyes, a ragged flannel coat, and baggy old jeans held up by suspenders. He was also carrying a rifle.

"Uh, sir…" She had never heard Brady sound so nervous. "My aunt and uncle used to live in this house, and I just wanted to show my girlfriend the lookout tower—there's a meteor shower tonight."

As terrified as she was, the words *my girlfriend* were not lost on her, and she felt her heart swell a little bit more in her chest.

The old man broke out into a nasty grin, a big black hole in the middle of his jagged teeth. "I see. So you went up there for some hanky-panky?" he teased.

She felt her face flush with embarrassment, thankful that it was at least dark. Neither of them said a word.

"Well, I could call the cops, you know." He lifted the rifle up and rested it on his shoulder. "But I'll make you a deal."

Vivienne did not like the sound of that, and she moved closer to Brady. She wondered if the old man even realized how scared they both were.

"Do either of you know anything about gardening?"

They looked at each other questioningly. Gardening hadn't exactly been a hot topic of conversation between them.

"I know a little bit," Vivienne said carefully, her eyes still focused on the rifle.

"Well, I garden for my food. It's better than anything you can find at those so-called supermarkets. Their tomatoes are like plastic." The old man shook his head. "Anyway, I've got to prepare the ground for next spring. It shouldn't take long with three of us."

Brady cleared his throat. "Sir, um, we really have to be getting back."

The old man ignored him. "It won't take long. C'mon. Follow me." He turned and started toward the house, with Skeeter at his heels.

Brady whispered. "I think we better just do what he says."

She nodded. What other choice did they have? Her heart pounded against her chest as they walked through the trees in shadowy darkness.

"The name's Carter, by the way," the old man yelled over his shoulder.

Brady quickly replied, "I'm Brady."

"Vivienne!" she called out.

As they got closer to the house, her anxiety grew and she began babbling. "You know how you watch those cheesy horror movies and the teenager's always doing something really stupid and you want to yell and scream at them through the TV?"

"I'm guessing we're the stupid teenagers?"

"Yep."

Brady said calmly, in his rational, logical voice, "Just because Carter lives in the middle of nowhere doesn't mean he's an axe murderer. Now if he asks us to go down into his basement…"

She glanced sideways at him and could see he was smiling. Did he think this was funny? She grabbed onto his arm and squeezed hard. "Stop it! I'm seriously freaking out right now, Brady."

He stopped and looked down at her, and all the feelings from up on the tower came flooding back. "Vivienne, it will be okay. We've just got to help the old guy out, and then we're out of here."

When he looked at her that way, she couldn't help but trust him completely. If he said it would be okay, she believed him. "Okay," she said, and then added, "But if he does anything weird, we take off and run straight for the car, okay?"

"Agreed."

They followed Carter until the trees thinned and they reached the backyard. As they got closer, Vivienne's stomach lurched. They continued over to his truck—an old light blue pickup, covered in rust patches.

Carter reached into the back of the truck and emerged with two shovels. He tossed one to Brady and then a smaller one to her. "C'mon, now, don't be shy."

Vivienne couldn't move—she knew what they had to do. She knew it as soon as they came out of the trees.

Brady walked to the back of the truck, his head down, and she followed. She could feel her gag reflex coming on. A green tarp covered the entire truck bed.

Carter pulled the tailgate down. "I was going to do this tomorrow, but now that I've got two able-bodied young people, the job should go a lot faster." The old man took something out of his pocket. "Here, this helps." He opened the small blue jar—Vicks VapoRub—stuck his finger in it, and then rubbed a big gob of clear goo into the hair under his nose.

Then Carter ripped off the green tarp, revealing the truck's contents.

Brady and Vivienne both took a step back and then looked at each other. Brady's eyes were full of apology, hers were full of tears—from the rancid fumes.

She couldn't believe that only minutes before, it had been just the two of them—holding each other as they gazed at a sky full of stars.

And now it was just the two of them—holding their shovels as they gazed at a steaming mountain of shit.

Not crap—shit.

CHAPTER 36

"Holy shit!" Jay laughed. "No pun intended. Man, what an epic fail."

"Yep, that it was." They were talking over headsets on Xbox, and Brady had just filled his best friend in on the disastrous end to his date the night before.

What really got to him was the fact that he had spent so much time planning the 'perfect' date and he'd never even considered a dog. It was a huge oversight, and it had ruined everything. Fucking Skeeter.

He and Vivienne had only lasted three or four shovelfuls until Carter finally had some mercy on them and let them leave. On the drive home, Vivienne didn't act like she was bothered by it, but how could Brady really know? He had debated over and over whether he should kiss her goodbye, and he'd chickened out at the last second. He was convinced he still smelled like cow shit, or horseshit, or whatever kind of shit it was.

When he'd texted her in morning, she'd seemed fine:

Brady: *Hey, was wondering if you had plans tonight?*

Vivienne: *No plans, I'm free* ☺

Brady: *Can I call you later?*

Vivienne: *Sure, ttyl…*

But when he'd called her later in the day, something just hadn't seemed right:

"Hey, Vivienne."

"Hey."

"How's your day going?"

Long pause. "Good…kind of long, but good." She sounded tired.

"Well, I was thinking tonight maybe we could do something more conventional, like go see a movie?" he had asked.

"Oh…Brady, I completely forgot about this family dinner thing that I have tonight, and I really can't get out of it. Would it be okay if we got together tomorrow?"

His heart sank. "Oh…yeah, no problem."

Actually, big problem. She was definitely blowing him off.

Jay thought he was overreacting. "Bro, you're making too big a deal out of this. She said she wanted to go out tomorrow. You need to chill."

Brady couldn't help it. When it came to Vivienne, there was no "chilling." She stirred everything up inside. "But, it just seemed like—I don't know. It seemed like she was lying—about the family thing."

"Dude! I can't believe how much you like this girl!" Jay's avatar, with the game tag *AintNoMockingJay*, was in a heated battle. "Please don't tell me you're going to turn into one of those pathetic losers who follows their girlfriend around like a puppy dog and has coffee with her at Starbucks." He paused. "Oh, wait—you already did that."

"You're hysterical, Jay." Brady began shooting everything in sight, taking out his frustration on the game.

"Okay, okay, I'm sorry. Do you want me to come pick you up? I think Connor's having people over. His parents are out of town."

Brady ignored him. "I keep thinking about something. Do you remember when we were at that party, that Beth girl said something about a big Halloween party? She said that stoner Kirby has one at his house every year."

"Brady, how do you remember shit like that?" He paused. "Never mind, I forgot who I was talking to for a second. Do you think the party's tonight?"

"I don't know. I mean, Halloween's next weekend, but it still could be."

"You think she's blowing you off for a party?"

"Maybe?"

"Well, then, we'll just have to crash it!" Jay shouted through the headset.

"But, Jay, if she is there, and she sees me, she'll think I'm a complete stalker for showing up."

"Well, you kind of are being a stalker, but that's beside the point. Hold on."

Brady saw Jay's avatar disappear from the screen, and his phone immediately began to buzz—a Facetime from Jay.

Brady picked it up and flinched. The entire screen was filled by a deformed pig face. Then a deformed horse face. Then a grinning Jay face. "Which one do you want to be?"

***

From inside the car, Brady could hear "Thriller" booming from Kirby's house. "I knew it."

The stoner had obviously gone all out for his Halloween party. The old house was covered in stretchy gray spiderwebs and little orange lights. There were fake tombstones scattered in the yard and a fog machine blew white clouds across the grass. The Grim Reaper hung from a branch in a big oak tree, and a mummy wrapped in toilet paper sat on the front porch.

"She might not even be in there." Jay tossed him the pig mask. "Here."

"What the hell? Why do you get to be the horse?"

"Jesus, I didn't know you had a preference." Jay took back the mask.

Brady suddenly felt unsure about the plan. What if Vivienne was in there? What if she just wasn't that into him, and was blowing him off? "You know what, maybe we should just forget about this."

"Oh my God, Brady, will you grow a pair?" Jay shouted. "It's just a party. There's a shitload of people in there—no one's going to pay attention to us."

It was a big party. Cars were parked up and down the street and partygoers in costumes roamed around outside the house. Brady also spotted a bonfire out back with a huge crowd around it. "Okay, but please don't do anything stupid."

"Bro! I'm offended. All I care about is finding some hot girls. And with this mask"—Jay pulled the ridiculous pig mask over his head—"I can't go wrong."

Brady put on the horse mask and reluctantly got out of the car. As they walked toward the house, a trio of witches wearing really tall hats, and really short skirts, came barreling toward them. "Hey, piggy, piggy, piggy!" they laughed.

Jay turned to follow them and Brady grabbed him by the arm. "Let's go."

They headed into the house and were immediately hit with a gust of hot air. The room had definitely surpassed maximum occupancy and the crowded space smelled of sweat and stale beer. Brady started feeling claustrophobic under his mask. He pushed his way through the clusters of costumes, trying to get looks at their faces. No Vivienne yet.

They made it to the kitchen, where a very realistic Freddy Krueger was manning the keg, his knife fingers resting on the tap. Luckily he didn't seem to care who they were, and moved his hand away so they could pour themselves a beer.

Brady poured himself one and handed a cup to Jay.

Jay lifted up his mask. "Dude, I got my mom's car. If she smells even a hint of beer, I'll be grounded 'til next summer. I think she has her own breathalyzer, swear to God."

Knowing Jay's mom, he wasn't exaggerating.

"Do you see Vivienne anywhere?" Brady took a quick drink.

"No." Jay scanned the room. "It's so hard to tell with all these costumes, and this mask is so fucking hot, I'm like dripping sweat already." He wiped his sleeve on his forehead. "Maybe we should try out back."

"Yeah."

As soon as Brady walked out onto the back deck, he felt the welcome relief of cold air. Some people sat in groups on the deck, one group playing beer pong, another group passing around a joint. But most of the people had gathered around the bonfire in the backyard. A quick spatial estimate said about fifty people. From up on the deck, Brady had a good vantage point, and he began searching the crowd.

Jay pointed to a girl in a red cape. "Isn't that her friend—that Kendra chick?"

Brady's eyes darted over to the girl. It was definitely Kendra—he didn't forget faces. Kendra was Vivienne's best friend. Not a good sign.

"Yeah, that's her." He scanned the faces of everyone around her.

"What do you think she's supposed to be?"

Brady looked at Jay and his dumb pig face. "I don't know, Red Riding Hood? Who the hell cares?"

Jay shrugged. "But she's not carrying a basket or anything. Maybe she's a vampire."

"Really, Jay?" Brady was at a loss. "Will you please help me here?"

"I don't see her, bro. She probably actually had a family thing. Now can we go mingle?"

"It's too hard to see with all these costumes, I need to get closer." Brady made his way down the deck steps and toward the bonfire.

Just then he heard a guy's voice shout, "It's over, I told you."

In a split second, the entire crowd got quiet. All of the attention turned to the guy, a pirate, who appeared to be fighting with Cleopatra.

Cleopatra yelled back, "I told you I'm sorry! What do I need to do?!"

They were causing a spectacle, and the crowd was hanging on their every word.

Pirate ignored her pleas and walked away, heading straight for Brady. Cleopatra chased after him, all eyes in the crowd following them. She stumbled and dropped her drink in the grass—she looked slightly intoxicated.

The couple stopped directly in front of Brady as he watched through his mask.

"I made a mistake! Can't you give me another chance?" Cleopatra pleaded.

"No, I can't!" the pirate yelled, so loudly that people in the house were starting to come out and watch.

Brady couldn't move. Shock, confusion, anger, hurt—they hit him all at once.

Cleopatra, her red hair peeking out from beneath the black wig, gave one final plea. "Chad, please."

Pirate turned to walk away for good, but not before telling her one last time, "I said it's over, Vivienne."

CHAPTER 37

Brady paced back and forth in his room with thoughts that wouldn't quit. It was 1:41 a.m., and sleep was impossible. It felt like his head was going to explode.

Heartbreak—that's what he must be feeling. He literally felt sick, and now he knew what it truly meant. His heart actually hurt—it felt like someone had punched him square in the middle of his chest.

Why did he care so much? He'd only known her for nine days and six hours, not that he was counting. What was wrong with him? Like Jay said, she was just a girl. And like Jay also said, how well did Brady really know her?

When he looked back on things, it seemed more and more likely he didn't know the real Vivienne at all. If he put feelings aside and looked at it logically, it was so obvious. She lied about being Sutton's daughter, she took—no, she stole—the envelope, she claimed she was going to return it but somehow never had the time. And only after she was caught, did she fess up, and then the envelope mysteriously disappeared!

But then other things didn't make sense. Why would she go to the Goodwill? Why would she return his sweatshirt? Why would she go out with him on a date?

Maybe so you would believe her! Maybe so you would stop looking for the money, dumbass!

He just needed to stop thinking about her. Just stop thinking about her face, her smell, her kiss…her lies…her fucking lies! Brady flopped down on his bed and stared at his phone.

Vivienne had texted and called, but he hadn't responded:

Text one: (10:42 p.m., twenty minutes after he left the party): *Hey, my dinner thing is over, you want to meet up?*

Liar.

Text two: (11:23 p.m.): *What's up, Brady? Text me back.*

No chance in hell.

Phone call and voicemail: (11:46 p.m.): *Hey, just wondering where you are…just wanted to know if maybe you'd want to meet up…I guess it's getting kind of late…just call me when you get this, okay?*

No, not okay, Vivienne.

Text three: (12:08 a.m.): *I'm hoping you just lost your phone…text me back when you get this* ☺.

Nope, phone's right here. But I'm sure as shit never going to use it to call you again.

He picked up a pillow and launched it across the room, hitting the game tower and sending it crashing to the ground, all the plastic game cases flying out in the process.

Seconds later, his bedroom door flew open. "Jesus Christ, Brady! What the hell's going on? All I can hear is you pacing back and forth."

Brady shot up in his bed. "Sorry, but I'm losing it, Dad!" He ran his fingers through his hair. "I'm seriously losing it."

His dad's face quickly went from anger to concern. "What is it?"

Brady fell back down on his bed and covered his face with a pillow. "I'm an idiot. I'm a complete idiot." It came out muffled and incoherent.

His dad sat next to him on the bed. "What's going on?"

"It's nothing." Brady turned on his side, away from his dad. "I'm sorry about waking you up."

"Girl trouble?"

God, he was pathetic. "Is it that obvious?"

"Well, such a strong reaction out of a man can only be attributed to one thing." Dad sighed. "You want to tell me about it?"

"I just don't get how I could be so wrong about someone. And I don't know why I care so much. I just wish I could turn it off—this feeling—whatever the hell it is." He turned back to his dad. "You know?"

"Oh yeah, unfortunately I know all too well." Dad smiled.

Brady felt a pang of guilt. If he felt this bad about a girl he'd only known a few days, he couldn't imagine what his dad had been through. "I'm sorry things didn't work out with you and Mom. Not just for my own reasons, you know?"

"I know." Then he said something that completely took Brady by surprise. "But it was a lot different with your mother and me because we never did the traditional dating thing."

"What do you mean?"

"Scoot over." Dad pulled his legs up on the bed and squeezed in next to Brady. "See, on Christmas Eve she came into McGuire's to get Uncle Marty out of the bar. He was late for the big dinner at your Grandma and Grandpa Kenny's."

"Yeah, I vaguely remember the story. You helped her get Uncle Marty into the car, and then you asked her out. Love at first sight, that kind of thing."

"Well, not exactly," Dad sighed. "See, I had a few drinks in me and I said it half-joking, expecting her to turn me down flat. But to my surprise she said, 'Sure.' So we went out and I took her to a movie. One of those—what do they call 'em, chick flicks?"

Brady nodded.

"Anyway, the truth was she just didn't seem into the date and I remember thinking the whole thing was a big mistake. She was a college girl, smart and so pretty. And I was a steel worker who liked to spend my free time in a bar. And she was a lot younger too—I was twenty-nine and your mother was only twenty-two.

"So after the movie, I was just going to drive her home, and she says she doesn't want to go home. And then she starts blubbering about this guy she was dating since high school, and how he was at some other college and how he wanted to take a break."

Dad paused, as if he was contemplating whether or not he wanted to say what was coming next. "She was so upset, and she was crying, and I was consoling her and, well, one thing led to another—"

No, just no.

Brady put his hands over his ears. "Stop! Stop right there! Don't say anything else!"

"Okay, okay...sorry," Dad laughed. "Well, she went back to Ohio State for her last semester of college. We talked a couple of times and then it just kind of fizzled out." Dad stopped.

"And then?"

"And then one day I'm sitting in McGuire's and Uncle Marty barges in, walks right up to me and punches me in the face—thought he broke my nose. He starts screaming at me."

Brady knew where the story was headed. "Because Mom was pregnant."

"Yes." Dad let out a long sigh. "And apparently she and Tony hadn't been, uh...intimate, you know, around that time, so there wasn't any question it—"

"Wait," Brady interrupted. "Tony? Not the same Tony she's with now?"

"Yep." Dad nodded. "One and the same."

Brady couldn't believe it. Had his mom been in love with Tony this whole time? Had she ever loved Dad? Had he ever loved her?

"So you guys just got married? Without even knowing each other?"

"I know, sounds crazy, right? But you know how traditional your mother's family is, and I just wanted to do good by her, so I asked her. It just seemed like the right thing to do. Plus, I didn't want your Uncle Marty to kill me."

Brady didn't know what to say.

"But we do love each other, Brady, it's just a different kind of love. I mean, we've raised two wonderful kids together, and we went through the accident together. I never could've gotten through that without your mother. We'll always be connected." Then he added, "And as strange as it sounds, I'm actually happy for her and Tony."

The truth was sad, but it was the truth, and the divorce suddenly made a lot more sense. "I bet there's somebody out there for you too, Dad."

Dad smiled. "Maybe." He shrugged. "I have noticed one or two nice-looking ladies at McGuire's since I've been back."

That made Brady happier than anything else he could've said.

Dad nudged him with his shoulder. "So you want to talk about the girl?"

Brady was suddenly exhausted. "Not now. I'm finally feeling tired."

"Good, then, I did my job." He got up and stopped at the door. "Brady, if it's meant to be, whatever troubles you have will work themselves out." He flipped off the light. "Goodnight."

"Night, Dad." Brady lay in the dark and thought about Cleopatra and her pleas. "But no, it's definitely not meant to be."

CHAPTER 38

It was a cloudy and damp Sunday, and the weather matched Vivienne's mood. She had worn her favorite navy cardigan with jeans and leather riding boots. Her hair was curled into loose waves and she had spent way too much time on her makeup, but she wanted to look her best.

She wasn't going to bother texting or calling anymore. It was 1:30 p.m., and she was driving to Brady's house. She knew Sundays were football days and he would be home helping his dad with the business. If she could just see him in person, she could figure out what the hell was going on.

No return texts, no return calls—nothing. He was completely blowing her off.

Different reasons ran through her mind repeatedly: maybe he'd lost his phone, maybe he'd broken his phone, maybe his dad had taken his phone away, maybe he was really sick, maybe he was in the hospital, maybe he had been abducted by aliens... And she would rather believe any of those reasons than the one reason that lingered in the back of her mind: *Maybe he found out about Chad.*

When she reached McGuire's Pub, she saw the sign for Wilmore up ahead. She remembered Brady had said six houses down on the right. She turned down the street lined with endless brick bungalows, tapping her hand nervously on the steering wheel. When she reached house number six, she pulled the car over to the curb and parked.

She quickly pulled down the visor and took one last glance at herself. A pale, freckled face with worried eyes stared back at her. She took a deep breath. "Okay, Vivienne, you can do this."

She headed for the front door and avoided looking at a large bay window as she walked by it. She stepped onto the concrete porch and spotted a small doorbell button. She pushed it and she waited. And waited. No one answered.

A tiny square window in the wood door tempted her, but she couldn't bring herself to peek inside. She balled up her fist and gave the door a hard knocking. A flash of a face appeared in the window—Brady.

He opened the door, his face expressionless, blank. He didn't look surprised to see her, but he didn't look happy either. Vivienne felt her heart sink.

"Hey, I just wanted to stop by to make sure everything was okay." She searched his eyes for some kind of emotion, anything.

"Everything's fine." A vacant stare. This was not the Brady she knew. This was a complete stranger, and everything was not fine.

She tried again. "Well, why didn't your return any of my calls, or texts? Did you get my messages last night?"

Brady looked down and let out a heavy sigh. When he looked back up at her, his eyes were so full of contempt she literally took a step back. He moved toward her, and then closed the door behind him.

He walked right past her and down the driveway, toward her car. He leaned up against it, arms crossed, waiting for her.

"Did I do something wrong?" she asked as she approached him, her insides tied in knots. It wasn't possible, was it? Could he know about Chad?

He shook his head. "Vivienne, I need to—" Then he stopped as if he was unsure of what to say next.

She stood in front of him, waiting. Her heart felt like it was going to beat right out of her chest. "What's going on, Brady?"

"Was the whole pink backpack story just bullshit?"

The question was so unexpected and out there, at first she didn't understand what he was talking about. "The backpack? What do you mean?"

"Do you have the money, Vivienne?"

The realization of what Brady was implying hit her like a blow to her chest, and she could actually feel the air being sucked out of her lungs. She practically gasped as she responded in the only way she knew how. "You can't be serious!"

She searched his face as if it was all some cruel joke, and he was going to bust out laughing at any second. But he wasn't laughing—not even close.

She could feel the tears welling up behind her eyes and she swallowed hard. "You think I have the backpack—the money?" How could he possibly think that?

He shrugged. "I don't know what to believe anymore, Vivienne. But I do know one thing—I'm not going to be some second choice you can just fall back on."

"What the hell, Brady?" She stepped closer to him. "What are you talking about?"

He put his hands up. "Don't." His eyes bored into her. "I was there."

Her mind raced as the implications of what he said sank in. He had been there last night, and he had seen her with Chad. She had no idea how the hell it could've happened, but he knew. And she completely panicked. "Where?"

"Last night," he said calmly. "The party."

She played dumb. "The party?" She cringed in anticipation of what he would say next.

"Oh my God, Vivienne—or should I say Cleopatra— stop. I was there. I saw you with Chad. I saw you begging him to take you back."

She felt her legs go weak; she couldn't think straight.

He mocked her voice. "'Please, Chad, I'm so sorry, Chad.' It was pathetic, actually. Not your best look."

He waited for an explanation, his face indignant.

"Brady, that wasn't what it looked like."

"Well then you could've won a god-damn Academy Award, because it looked pretty real to me."

She had to choose her words carefully. "It's a little complicated. Could we maybe go somewhere and—"

"Wow," he cut her off. "You're stalling. You really didn't think I'd find out, did you?"

"No! I mean, no, that's not it." He needed to know the truth. "Chad came to see me yesterday and—"

Just then the front door to Brady's house swung open. "Hey, Brady! Do you—?" A girl leaned out. She was petite, blonde, and absolutely stunning. She looked at Vivienne and frowned. "Oh, sorry." Then she quickly disappeared back into the house.

Who the hell is she?! Vivienne felt a lurch in her stomach. "Who's that?"

He shrugged casually. "It doesn't matter."

"Well, it matters to me. Who is she?" She was shouting and she didn't care.

Brady stepped closer to Vivienne and nodded toward the house. "You want to know who she is?" A hint of a smile appeared on his face. "She's an old friend."

"An old friend?" The nauseating warmth in her gut began spreading.

"Yeah, kind of like how you and Chad are old friends."

She stared back at him, looking desperately for the Brady from two nights ago, but he was gone. She could feel the tears coming. "Wow, you didn't waste any time, did you?"

"What?!" he scoffed. "Me? Really?" Then he stepped even closer, so close that she could see the gold flecks in his brown eyes. "Vivienne, this whole thing, with us"—he pointed between them—"it never had a chance, because it all started from a lie."

She stood motionless for a second, too stunned to say anything.

Brady brushed past her and she heard the door slam behind her.

She didn't think, she just moved. She got into her car, gripped the wheel, and slowly drove away. Two blocks ahead, she spotted an empty playground and pulled into the deserted parking lot. A dirty yellow slide and an old swing set sat alone on a slab of asphalt, surrounded by matted-down, dying grass.

Then the tears came, and they came fast, rolling down her cheeks like rain on a windowpane. She wiped them away on her sleeves, trying to compose herself. She couldn't believe what had just happened.

That girl—she couldn't get the image out of her head. She was sickeningly perfect, her blond hair pulled up into a high ponytail, her red sweater hugging her perfectly proportioned body, her perfect white smile—that had disappeared the moment she saw Vivienne.

Was she an old girlfriend? Why hadn't Brady mentioned her before? Wait—why would he mention her?

And it almost seemed like an afterthought now, but how could he think she'd actually kept the money?! Did he think she'd made up the story about Gloria too? Did he think she was capable of that kind of deception?

Vivienne should've known things would end badly. Brady was right. Whatever was between them, however perfect and real it had felt, was built on her screw-up. And now, she had ruined it for good with her latest screw-up.

But what Brady didn't know was that Vivienne had done it all for him.

CHAPTER 39

"Yo, Rain Man, you're doing it again," Jay said.

"Huh?"

Jay shook his head. "Jesus, I asked who the money was on." He nodded toward the flat-screen hanging over the bar.

"Um...Browns, I think." Brady took another bite of his corned beef.

Three weeks had passed since he had last spoken to Vivienne, and he was in some kind of funk. He couldn't get out of it, no matter how hard he tried. He had asked Jay and Andrew to meet up at McGuire's to watch the game, thinking it might help. But his mind kept traveling back to the night under the stars, pre-shit-shoveling, when things were perfect...and the stars were perfect...and kissing her was perfect.

"What's the spread?" Andrew asked.

Brady hesitated. "Um…Browns are getting three and a half."

"Actually, they're giving three and a half," a voice said quietly. It was Eagle Ears Bob. He was sitting on the other side of Brady, living up to his nickname. "Browns are the favorite."

"Those are two words you don't hear in the same sentence very often," Andrew quipped.

Jay was suddenly in Brady's face, a piece of sauerkraut hanging from his chin. "Dude, you're getting numbers mixed up—on the Browns?"

Contrary to the laws of the universe, the Cleveland Browns were having a winning season, and they were actually in contention for a playoff spot. Even when they were the usual Cleveland Clowns, Brady could recite back any statistic imaginable, like it was his address or his birth date.

Jay put down his sandwich and sighed. "Are you ever gonna snap out of it?"

That was the million-dollar question. He wished he could snap out of it. He wished his freakish brain would just think of something—anything—that would fix him. He couldn't stop thinking about her; it was impossible.

"Jay, I don't know what your problem is, but I'm fine," he lied.

"Dude, you seem to keep forgetting that the girl screwed you over—like, royally. She can't be trusted."

Andrew chimed in, "Doesn't seem like he really cares about that."

"It's a travesty." Jay shook his head.

Andrew liked to give brotherly advice to Brady too. "Look, I don't know shit about girls, but I do know something about love, and don't freak out when I say this, but it sounds like you might be——"

"Stop," Brady interrupted quickly. "Don't go there."

"Alrighty, then." Andrew smiled at Jay.

Maggie came scurrying over. "Can I get you boys a refill?" She began taking their glasses and looked directly at Jay's face when she said, "I'll bring ya more napkins too."

"Thanks, Maggie." Brady poured more vinegar on his fries and methodically ate them one by one, keeping his eyes on the game. The Browns were up by fourteen, and under normal circumstances he would be jumping around, giving high-fives. But that was then...

Jay, however, was his usual self and couldn't keep his mouth shut. "Can I at least tell Andrew the Jen story?"

"Seriously, Jay? You didn't tell him?" That was a genuine shocker.

"What's the Jen story?" Andrew quickly asked.

Jay turned to his brother, visibly excited. "Okay, so after the epic scene at the Halloween party, Brady wisely blows off Vivienne and she can't understand why. See, she doesn't know that Brady knows—you follow?"

"Yes, I follow." Andrew rolled his eyes.

"So she shows up at his house the next day, and they're out front fighting or whatever, and then all of a sudden Jen yells something out the front door to Brady, and Vivienne thinks she's like an old girlfriend or something!"

Andrew turned to Brady. "And I'm guessing you didn't mention that the gorgeous blonde was your sister?"

"Hell no, he didn't!" Jay laughed. "She totally thought she'd been replaced!"

Andrew shook his head. "Does Vivienne even know you have a sister?"

"I think I mentioned her once, I'm not sure."

Jen had come home from college for fall break, and on her way back to school, she'd stopped by the house to say hi. When she'd popped her head out the door, the look on Vivienne's face had said it all, and Brady had just decided to go with it. Why the hell not?

"Wow, that is disturbing on so many levels. So what was Vivienne's explanation for the Halloween party?" Andrew asked.

Brady shrugged. "She never gave me an explanation. When I told her I was at the party, it was like she couldn't come up with lies fast enough. She kept stalling, and then Jen interrupted, and that was it."

"Wait—so all this time, you've never heard her side of the story?"

Jay answered for him. "What's there to hear, Andrew? She threw herself at the douchebag—we both saw it, right in front of us."

Andrew almost jumped out of his stool. "Are you shitting me, Brady? Did you ever consider that the douchebag made her do that? You said he was a psycho."

"No, Vivienne said he was a psycho. I only met him once and yeah, he seemed like a tool, but she could've exaggerated it."

Andrew shook his head. "Don't you think it's possible that he threatened her or scared her into it somehow?"

Brady had thought about it. "Okay, why didn't she come to me, then? Or, when I confronted her…why didn't she say something to me, right there? Why did she stall?"

Andrew shrugged. "I don't know, but—"

"Look," Brady sighed, "the bottom line is, she looked guilty as hell. If you could've seen her face when I told her I was at the party. I mean honestly, I just don't want to think about it anymore."

Jay was quick to agree. "Yeah, I bet she had the envelope the whole time. Shit, she probably went on a shopping spree with the money. The girl cannot be trusted, legit."

Andrew wasn't swayed. "I still think you should call her."

"You know she hasn't called or texted me either."

"And why do you think that is?" Andrew asked. "Does the name 'Jen' ring any bells?"

Or, thought Brady, it could be the fact that he'd accused her of keeping the money. Or it could be the fact that he'd told her they'd never had a chance. It could be lots of reasons.

Brady had almost pushed the 'send' button on too many texts to count. But then he would see goddamn Cleopatra and her goddamn tears, and the anger would come rushing back. And then all of the doubts would come rushing back.

Just then, the crowd at McGuire's erupted into cheers as the Browns ran it in for a touchdown in the final seconds of a dominant win.

Jimmy Rainey yelled across the bar to Maggie. "I'm buying a round for the house!" Then he pointed at Brady and company. "Even sodas for those little boys over there!"

Everyone laughed, patted each other on the back, fist-bumped, even hugged. Brady joined in the celebration, and for the first time in a while, he felt a little bit like his old self. Maybe the fog was finally lifting. Maybe he was snapping out of it.

Maybe he was getting over Vivienne Burke, once and for all.

CHAPTER 40

As she stacked the dinners on the cart, Vivienne wore a pilgrim hat and a black dress with a white apron. She looked completely ridiculous, but it wasn't like she was going to run into anyone she knew at Shady Oaks. Besides, the residents loved it. Janet was dressed like an Indian, and although she spent most of her time in the kitchen, she always made rounds and said hello.

"Hey! I've been meaning to ask, did anything happen with that Brady boy you were telling me about?" Janet yelled across the kitchen.

Vivienne's heart sank. "Uh, no, we kind of—I don't know, we really don't talk anymore."

"Really?" Janet hesitated as if she was contemplating about what she'd say next. "I'm sorry to hear that, hon."

Vivienne shrugged. "Yeah, well, crap happens, right?"

Janet laughed. "That it does, that it does."

Vivienne rolled the card down the hallway, and as she passed by Gloria's old room, she felt a pang of sadness. She looked at the small table next to the bed, where Gloria had kept the notebook tucked away—the treasured notebook that she'd entrusted to Vivienne—the notebook that Vivienne had lost.

The notebook. When she thought back to her last conversation with Brady, the part that hurt the worst was the accusation that she'd lied about the money. How could he possibly think she would keep it? And did that mean he thought the whole notebook story was a lie too?

And she couldn't stop thinking about the girl, either, the sickeningly perfect blond who Vivienne could never compete with. Brady had made it abundantly clear that he had moved on.

His words still stung. *This whole thing…with us…it never had a chance.*

But then she remembered what Janet had told her. Empathy is the key—always put yourself in the other person's shoes. And when Vivienne put herself in Brady's shoes, she could totally get why he did what he did.

"Brady." She said his name out loud without even realizing it. No matter how hard she tried, she couldn't stop thinking about him. She wanted to, but she couldn't.

Vivienne came to Mr. Gorman's partially open door and knocked. "Hello! Dinner here!"

Mr. Gorman's eyes lit up when she entered the room. "Well, don't you look festive! I love it, Miss Vivienne!"

She placed the tray on the small table in front of him and noticed a new picture on his wall—Jesus holding a lamb in his arms. She immediately thought of when she'd asked Brady about heaven. *I guess it's in the realm of possibilities*, he had said. It seemed like everything reminded her of Brady these days.

She put on her fake cheery face. "And how are you doing today, Mr. Gorman?"

"Oh, I'm okay. How about you?"

"I'm good," she lied.

"You doing anything special for Thanksgiving?"

"Tomorrow we leave for Boston. We fly out there very year to my grandparents' house. Some of my cousins fly in from Chicago, so it's pretty nice to see everyone." As soon as she said the words, she wanted to kick herself, but Mr. Gorman just looked happy to hear her talk.

"When I come back, I'll show you some pictures." She pulled her iPhone out of her pocket and held it up.

"A phone that takes pictures." He shook his head. "What will they think of next?"

She shrugged her shoulders. "You'll just have to wait and see."

"Oh Lord, no!" He put his hands out toward the new picture on his wall. "Take me now, Lord Jesus!" He said it with a laugh, but she had a feeling he probably meant it.

Vivienne gave him a hug. "Well, I hope you're around for a while. You behave yourself, okay?"

"No promises, Miss Vivienne. No promises."

***

Vivienne peeled her hands away from the steering wheel. She had white-knuckled it the whole way home from Shady Oaks. A lake-effect snowstorm had moved off Lake Erie in a hurry. Thanksgiving was always a funny time of year weatherwise. It could be in the fifties with sunshine or in the twenties with snow. This year it was the latter.

She ran straight up the steps to her room, ripped off her pilgrim apron and black tights and flopped down on her bed. She checked her phone again—no new texts. She had a ridiculous notion that somehow they would magically appear without an alert.

She closed her eyes and tried not to think of *him*. Then her phone rang, and a jolt of excitement went through her, as it always did, until she looked at it.

It was Kendra. "Hey."

"Hey."

"I don't know how to tell you this…"

Vivienne's heart sank. Kendra never started a conversation that way. "What?"

"Well, I just talked to Beth, and you know how she and Chad have been hanging out."

Just the mention of the asshole's name made Vivienne's insides cringe. She had been ecstatic to see Chad and Beth together. Surprisingly, he had kept up his end of the bargain since the Halloween party and had left Vivienne alone.

But this didn't sound good. "And?"

"Well, they aren't hanging out anymore." Kendra paused. "Apparently, the entire time they were together, all he did was talk about you."

Vivienne felt her breath catch in her throat. "What do you mean?"

"He was completely using Beth to keep tabs on you. He would be really nice to her, but she said somehow their conversations always led to you."

Vivienne's heart began thudding in her chest. "Well, what the hell did they talk about?"

"Basically, he wanted to know if you were with Brady. And…" Another pause.

"He told Beth all about Brady's dad—about his business."

"Oh my God."

"And"—Kendra led out a long sigh—"There's more."

Vivienne closed her eyes. "What?"

"Chad told Beth that he still has every intention of calling the cops and telling them a bunch of lies about Brady's dad. He's just waiting until the timing is right."

"That asshole promised!" Vivienne put her face into her pillow and screamed. Regardless of what happened between her and Brady, she still cared about him. And *cared* wasn't really a strong enough word. "Why won't he leave me alone, Kendra?"

Kendra's voice picked up. "Well, I do have some good news. Beth finally told Chad she'd had enough of the Vivienne talk, and apparently he went psycho on her and said some really cruel things. Like, Beth was bawling when she was telling me about it."

"I'm waiting for the good news," Vivienne said.

"So Beth is beyond pissed and she's hating on Chad pretty bad right now, and she said she had an idea. She wouldn't tell me what it was, but she promised she wouldn't do anything without letting me know first."

"Oh, great, now I feel much better."

Kendra sighed. "Well, maybe she'll come through for once. Hell hath no fury like a woman scorned."

"What?"

"I learned it in Brit Lit. Pretty awesome quote, don't you think?"

Vivienne shook her head, which hurt like hell. "Every day I want to kick myself for ever saying yes to Chad that day at the beach. If I would've said no, then someone else would have to deal with the psycho."

"Or," Kendra said, "maybe he wouldn't have taken no for an answer."

"Huh...never thought of it that way. You're probably right."

"Yep."

Vivienne glanced at the time on her phone. 10:48 p.m. "Crap, I've got to get my butt moving. I still haven't even packed for tomorrow. Gotta love the flight at seven thirty in the morning."

"Why are you guys leaving on Thanksgiving Day anyway? That's kinda bizarre."

"I know, right?" Vivienne yawned. "My mom had to work today. She always works a double so she can get Thanksgiving off."

"That would suck to work holidays. Just one reason I wouldn't want to be a nurse. That, and pretty much everything else about the job. I don't know how you work in that nursing home. Not to be mean, but that place kind of smells, don't you think?"

"Yeah, but you get used to it." The smell was one of the easier things to adjust to.

"Okay, well I'll let you know what Beth says."

"Thanks, Kendra. Seriously."

"No worries. Get some sleep."

Vivienne opened a dresser drawer and began pulling out some sweats and tees. She grabbed a pair of jeans and some underwear. She only needed to bring one nice outfit for Thanksgiving dinner, so she pulled her corduroy skirt off a hanger.

She didn't really mind the Boston trip every year. Actually, it was a forty-five-minute drive outside of Boston, where Grandma and Grandpa Burke lived in a big old house on a lot of land. They had a "no electronics" rule on Thanksgiving Day, where everyone had to hand over their phones, iPads, laptops, whatever they had, and wait until bedtime to retrieve them. After the big dinner, they played charades and board games, which surprisingly always ended up being a blast.

Vivienne began searching the shelves in her closet for her navy sweater—gone. She glanced around the room but it was nowhere to be found. *Morgan...*

When she entered Morgan's room, she found her sister sprawled out on the bed, eyes closed, headphones in her ears. Vivienne quickly scanned the room, which was much smaller than hers—and much messier. Clothes were strewn all over the floor with shoes, jewelry, makeup, and things Vivienne couldn't identify. A papasan chair sat in the corner of the room, overflowing with stuffed animals and more junk. Every inch of dresser space was filled. Vivienne's sweater could be anywhere.

She started kicking the clothes around and Morgan immediately opened her eyes. She ripped off her headphones. "What are you doing in here? Get out!"

Vivienne ignored her, got down on her hands and knees, and began picking through the crap. "Morgan! This is like hoarder status! I can't believe Mom hasn't gotten on you about this."

"Vivienne, I mean it, get out!"

Vivienne ignored her. "Do you have my navy cardigan?" She flipped up the dust ruffle and searched under the bed. Piles of more crap. Her eyes scanned the dark space and she saw a glint of something sparkling. She reached her hand as far as it would go and grabbed the shiny thing, pulling it out into the light.

She held it up and examined it. Her heart skipped a beat. It was a sequin V, attached to the front of a pink vinyl backpack.

CHAPTER 41

After Vivienne looked inside the zipper pocket and found the envelope of cash and the notebook exactly as she had left them, tucked away safe and sound, she jumped around the room squealing with happiness.

Then the realization struck her. The backpack had been right under her nose, in the room next to hers, the entire time. And that's when she laid into Morgan.

She hit her sister so hard with the backpack that she jumped up from the bed screaming, "Oh my God, Vivienne! What the heck?!"

"Shut up, Morgan," Vivienne hissed at her. "Where did you get this?"

"What? That thing?"

Vivienne waved the backpack in her face. "Yes, this thing."

"Are you serious?" Morgan laughed. "Why do you care? That thing's from like third grade."

"Where—did—you—get—it?" Vivienne repeated, stepping closer.

Her little sister's eyes got wide. "Okay! I'm trying to remember, stop pressuring me!"

Morgan looked lost and then her face suddenly lit up. "Oh, I remember! Olivia was picking me up for a sleepover and she texted me at the last second and told me to bring snacks. See, Olivia's mom is kind of a freak about junk food, like she's vegan and only eats organic—"

"Morgan, shut up!" Vivienne was about to lose it. "Keep going."

"Sorry…and so I was in the kitchen and I saw the backpack and just grabbed it."

"Wait—where was it?"

"It was on the kitchen table." Then she paused. "Actually, it was in a garbage bag, but I saw it peeking out. The whole table was full of garbage bags—remember? I talked to you that night. Mom was on one of her crazy cleaning binges. So I took it and loaded it up, and we ate a whole package of Oreos, just the two of us. If Olivia's mom would've—"

"Morgan!" Vivienne cut her off again. "So then Mom never knew you took it out of the bag?"

She shrugged. "I guess not."

"And this backpack's been in your room ever since?"

"Yeah. I mean, what's the big deal?" Morgan rolled her eyes. "God, that thing is so old and ugly. I don't get why you care."

She wanted to grab Morgan by the hair, yank her right off the bed, and force her to clean up the rest of the crap in her room, but she had more urgent things to take care of.

"Just forget it." Vivienne practically tripped over her own feet rushing to her bedroom. She slammed the door behind her and immediately called Kendra. "You're not going to believe this."

"What?"

"I found the backpack."

"Are you serious? Oh my God, that's awesome! Where was it?"

"Under Morgan's bed."

"No!"

"Yes, apparently she needed it for a sleepover and she took it out of one of the Goodwill bags without my mom knowing."

Kendra gasped. "So you are telling me it was like right there this whole time?"

"That's what I'm telling you."

"Holy crap."

"Yep, holy crap."

They were both silent for a couple of seconds. Vivienne knew Kendra was contemplating what the next move should be.

"So what do you think I should do?" Vivienne asked.

"Well, obviously you have to call him."

"Duh…but when?" Vivienne glanced at her phone—11:18 p.m. "Crap, it's late, but I really don't want to keep this money one second longer. Do you think I should just call him now?"

"Absolutely," Kendra assured her. "This is too important."

"Yeah, okay." Her heart was racing. "God, I'm nervous."

"It'll be fine. No matter what, he should be totally pumped about the money, right?"

"Right." He should also feel like an asshole for accusing her of keeping it.

"Text me immediately after—I don't care how late."

"Okay." Vivienne took a deep breath and began pacing her room. She practiced what she would say. "Hey, Brady, you're not going to believe this...hey, Brady, I know it's late, but...hey Brady, I'm only calling because..."

Screw it. She would just say whatever came into her head.

CHAPTER 42

It was the day before Thanksgiving. For most people, that meant getting a day off work and doing happy-horseshit family stuff. But for Dad's business, Thanksgiving was a busy workday, with three football games throughout the day.

Dad was slowly doing more and more of it on his own. Brady had been teaching him the ins and outs of the computer program, and now Dad had it pretty much down pat.

Dad was also doing the money exchanges every week. Although Brady hadn't liked the idea at first, he had to admit it was the best thing for his dad. Going to McGuire's and getting out of the house had made a huge difference in his mood. He just seemed happier, more energetic.

Brady wandered into the kitchen and opened the fridge. He didn't know why, because there had been nothing to eat ten minutes ago. "Dad, we have to go shopping!" he yelled into the other room.

"I know! But I figured we're going to get all that food tomorrow!" he yelled back. "I think there's microwave popcorn!"

Brady opened the cabinet, looked over the canned vegetables they never ate, and found one lone pack of Pop Secret Extra Butter in the back. He threw it in the microwave.

Thanksgiving Day was pretty much the same every year. Dad would take the bets on the games, the one o'clock Detroit and four o'clock Dallas, and then the Thursday night game. They would watch the Detroit game together and then Brady would head over to Mom's for dinner.

Jen would be there, of course—and Tony. Aunt Rachel, Uncle Brett and their five kids, all under the age of ten, came in from Columbus, which made it—well, loud.

Grandma Kenny hovered over Mom in the kitchen, giving her "suggestions" on her cooking, while Uncle Marty passed out tasty pumpkin shots with nonalcoholic versions for the kids. Last year he'd snuck Brady an alcoholic one when Mom wasn't looking.

Tony's two kids, from his first marriage, would stop by later. They were about the same age as Brady, which made it awkward for all of them. Luckily they had the same idea Brady had—bury their faces in their phones and avoid excruciating small talk.

When it was all said and done, the house filled up with over twenty people. Mom was an awesome cook; that was probably the one thing he missed most about not living with her. Thanksgiving was no exception. She put on a feast: turkey, stuffing, mashed potatoes with gravy, green bean casserole, cranberry sauce, pumpkin pie—every dish made from scratch.

And to top it off, she would always make extra for Brady to take home. She would fill a large cardboard box with Rubbermaid containers full of food. Every container had instructions taped to the top: *Reheat at 350 degrees for 15 minutes. Don't be lazy and microwave – it won't taste the same* ☺.

Brady would never tell her, but he and Dad never followed the directions. Heating up an oven took way too much time. It tasted just fine in the microwave.

Thinking of all of the food just made him hungrier. He shoveled another handful of popcorn into his mouth and took a sip of the last remaining Sprite. When he was finished eating, he passed by his dad, lying on the couch. "Well, I'm heading to bed."

"Night, son."

"Night, Dad."

After a quick stop at the bathroom to wash up, Brady headed for bed. He plugged his phone into the charger, shut off the light, got under the covers, and stared at the ceiling.

As he did every night, he thought about Vivienne. He wondered what she was doing for Thanksgiving. Brady imagined her coming to his mom's house with him. He would introduce her to everyone as his girlfriend, because he couldn't just say, "This is my friend Vivienne," could he? Or maybe he would just say, "Vivienne" alone— nothing attached.

Oh my God, do you hear yourself? Stop it!

They would sit next to each other at dinner and he would squeeze her hand under the table when somebody said something stupid, which would be a lot. Maybe afterwards he'd sneak an extra pumpkin shot and they would go out on the back porch and hide from everyone. Then he would finish what he'd started on the tower under the stars. He would hold her, and kiss her, and touch her soft skin...

Wait! Maybe he could use Thanksgiving as a reason to text her. Without thinking another second about it, he grabbed his phone and started a text: *Just wanted to say I hope you have a great Thanksgiving.*

Brady stared at the 'send' button. And stared more. And then he deleted it.

You're pathetic. What in the hell is wrong with you?

There were millions of girls out there...billions, actually. What was so special about Vivienne? He had to stop. He had to get her out of his brain for good. It was over. Over. Over. Over.

He pulled the covers up and declared out loud into the darkness, "This time I mean it. I'm done thinking about you, Vivienne Burke."

There.

He closed his eyes and cleared his head, and then it happened. His phone lit up, he looked at the screen, and a jolt shot through him. It was Vivienne.

CHAPTER 43

The conversation was short and awkward.

Brady: Hello?

Vivienne: Hi... uh, I know it's late, but I wanted to let you know...I found the backpack.

Brady: (Pause) Wow, are you serious? Where was it?

Vivienne: Well, I guess it was on our kitchen table with all the other junk my mom was taking to Goodwill. My sister grabbed it on her way out to a sleepover and my mom never knew.

Brady: So your sister had it the whole time?

Vivienne: Yeah, but it was buried pretty deep under her bed. I just happened to be looking for something, and I found it.

Brady: Oh.

Vivienne: So I'm leaving really early in the morning, so I thought maybe you'd want to come over and pick it up?

Brady: Where are you going?

Vivienne: Oh, we go to Boston every year for Thanksgiving.

Brady: Oh…well, yeah, I'll come and get it. I'll be there in like fifteen?

Vivienne: Okay—oh, but don't come to the door since it's so late. I'll come out and give it to you.

Brady: Okay.

Vivienne: Okay, bye.

Oh. My. God. She almost collapsed onto her bed. Just hearing his voice had turned her insides into jelly. She immediately texted Kendra: *He's coming over to get it—I'll text u after.*

Then Vivienne jumped off the bed and proceeded to the bathroom as quietly as possible. She applied a fresh dusting of mineral powder to her naked face, trying to camouflage her freckles the best she could. She brushed her teeth vigorously and popped a piece of gum into her mouth. She sprayed a tiny squirt of body spray in front of her and stepped into it, to get just the right amount.

She glanced at her phone: 11:33 p.m. She grabbed the backpack and tiptoed down the stairs. She put on her wool coat and peeked out the small window by the front door.

As soon as she saw his car pull up in front of her house, her heart starting racing and her adrenaline went into overdrive. She pulled on her Uggs and smoothed down her hair. *Deep breath in, deep breath out.*

Although she was only giving him the envelope, she wanted him to see the backpack. She wanted to show him that, yes, the bright pink backpack with the sequin V existed. Regardless of what happened with Brady, she wasn't going to let him get away with calling her a liar. And if it made him feel a little crappy—good.

She stepped out into the cold and trudged down the snowy lawn, feeling strangely warm all over. As she approached his car, her heart was beating so hard, she thought it must be visible through her thick layers.

Get a grip, Vivienne! He's probably still with the blonde. Have some pride and just make your point. Give him the backpack and tell him he can keep it as a souvenir, then...

But before she could finish the thought, the car window rolled down and Brady leaned over the passenger side. "C'mon," he yelled. "Get in!"

Okay, then...

Vivienne opened the door and slid into the passenger seat, holding the backpack on her lap. The car was warm and smelled like Brady. She glanced sideways for just a second, but it was enough. *My God, that smile...that adorable, comforting, confident smile. Wait—remember the blonde, remember the accusation, remember the heartache!*

He broke the silence. "So...it was in your sister's room the whole time?"

"Yeah, right in the next room." She was surprised at how calm she sounded. She dug into the backpack and pulled out the familiar white envelope with the red scribble. She handed it to him. "Here," she said, and then she added, "It's all there."

He sighed. "Vivienne, I'm sorry about what I said—about you keeping the money. I didn't mean it. It was a shitty thing to say."

"Yeah, it was."

"I guess I was just pissed, you know."

She turned to him. "I totally get that, but Brady, you never gave me a chance to explain anything. I can't believe you thought I'd want to be with Chad."

"What am I supposed to believe, Vivienne? I mean, I was there. And what I saw looked pretty real to me." He put his hands through his hair. "And when I asked you about it at my house, you were stalling."

"I was trying to figure out the best way to tell you, and I never got the chance." She could feel her emotions starting to swell.

"Well, why didn't you call me or text me, then?"

She could feel the anger rise up in her, fast and furious. "Are you serious Brady?" She rolled her eyes. "You had another girl at your house! It looked to me like you had no problem moving on, and so I figured, what's the point?" She lowered her voice. "Plus I didn't find much encouragement in the words, 'This whole thing never had a chance.' I think that's what you said?"

He began shifting in his seat, looking totally uncomfortable, which she enjoyed watching immensely. "Vivienne, I said a lot of things I shouldn't have. But seeing you with him—I guess I was just—hurt."

With those words, all of her anger dissolved in an instant.

"And"—he paused, still avoiding her eyes—"that girl you saw…that was my sister."

And all the anger came flooding right back. *Sister? WTF?* "The blonde girl—she was your sister?"

He finally looked at her. "Yes, the blonde. That's my sister, Jen. She was home from college for fall break."

Vivienne let the words sink in. "So you were pretending she was your girlfriend?"

"Hey, I didn't say that." Brady turned defensive. "You just assumed that when she came out." He shrugged. "And I just kind of went with it. After seeing you with Chad, I guess I wanted to show you how it felt."

On one hand, she wanted to do somersaults—there was no girl! On the other hand, she wanted to smash her fist into something. She took a deep breath. "I can't believe this. Brady, the whole thing with Chad was fake—he made me do it."

Brady's normally composed expression began to falter. "What do you mean, he made you do it?" She could see a flash of anger in his eyes.

She knew it wouldn't be easy to tell him the truth, but she had to. She glanced back at the house. "Do you think we could go somewhere? My parents think I'm in bed and they would kill me if they saw me sitting out here this late."

"Okay."

Brady pulled out of the driveway and drove down the snowy street in darkness. "Any ideas on where to go?"

"There's an apartment complex right up there." She pointed. "See that brick building? If you go around back, there's a parking lot. We'd probably blend in there."

Brady pulled into the asphalt drive, where a lit sign read 'Clifton Cove Apartments.' He drove toward the back and parked in a space at the end of a long row of cars. It was darkest there. "Probably should kill the engine?" he asked.

"Yeah," she said. She reached into her coat pocket, pulled out a pair of gloves and slipped them on. She was already shivering and it was only going to get colder.

A million thoughts were running through her head. She had wanted this moment for so long, so she could explain what had really happened at the Halloween party. But she had also dreaded this moment for so long because she didn't know how Brady would react. He would react badly for sure, but how badly?

"So, you said the whole thing was fake?" he prompted.

Just spit it out, Vivienne. "Yes," she sighed. "Chad was waiting for me after volleyball practice that morning—the morning of the Halloween party. He was standing up against my car and he wouldn't move. He said his friends were giving him crap because of rumors that were going around school, about how I dumped him and stuff. So he said he wanted me to go to the Halloween party, and make a big—well, you saw it—so everyone would see that perfect Chad was the one who dumped me."

"Or what?" Brady asked impatiently.

She took a deep breath. "God, I feel so bad about this."

"It's okay, Vivienne, what is it?" He looked at her with reassuring eyes.

She looked out the passenger window into the darkness. "He told me he would go to the cops—and tell them about your dad's business."

She waited in the tension-filled silence, which only lasted a few seconds, but felt like an eternity. His voice was low and strained. "What *exactly* did he say?"

CHAPTER 44

Brady's stomach turned and he suddenly felt sick. *How did everything get so fucked up?*

Vivienne's voice was so quiet, he could barely hear her. "Chad said that it would only take one phone call and he could ruin your dad's business. He called it 'aggravated gambling', said it was against the law and your dad could get in a lot of trouble."

"Wait—how did he figure out my dad's a bookie?"

"That first night at Kirby's party, I think my friend Beth—actually my ex-friend Beth—heard Andrew calling you O'Connell. I'm sure she told Chad your last name." She paused. "He said your name sounded really familiar, so he looked it up in his dad's phone and saw *bookie* next to it. And then I'm sure he did a full-scale investigation on you and connected all the dots."

Brady's head was swimming. "Jesus, that guy's unbelievable."

The whole situation absolutely terrified him. If his dad's business was exposed, it would ruin everything. "Has he said anything to you about it since the Halloween party?"

She sighed. "No, not directly."

"What do you mean?"

"Well, Kendra called me earlier tonight. I guess she heard Chad's still talking about me and stuff. He still asks about you and me, if we're together, I mean."

Brady wanted to find Chad and beat his ass. He didn't care if the guy towered over him; he'd take his chances. "Do you think he'd still call the cops?"

"I don't know," she said quietly. "I wouldn't put anything past him at this point."

He didn't know how to respond. His head was throbbing, and his feelings were so conflicted.

He did feel really shitty about the way he had treated Vivienne. She was obviously only protecting him and he had immediately assumed the worst. "I'm really sorry about reacting the way I did. I was just going by what I saw at the party, you know?"

"I know. And I wanted to tell you Brady, but honestly I didn't know how. I know how much your dad means to you, and I literally couldn't get the words out. I just thought if I did what Chad asked, then it would all go away."

He wanted so badly to start over with Vivienne and put all the Chad stuff behind them. Just sitting next to her in the car was torture. Now that he knew the truth, he wanted to reach over and grab her and kiss her and...

Stop!

He couldn't do it. If Chad found out they were together—well, he didn't even want to think about it. He had no other choice but to proceed with caution. "You look really cold, and it's getting close to curfew. I'm going to head back."

She nodded.

"Vivienne, I need to think about all of this. The most important thing to me right now is making sure Chad keeps his mouth shut."

"I just want you to know how sorry I am—about everything."

He shook his head. "You can't keep blaming yourself. Chad is completely insane and you can't help that. I just don't know what to do yet, but I need get my head straight and figure it out."

They drove the rest of the way back to her house in silence. As much as he hated the thought, he needed to steer clear of Vivienne for a while. He couldn't risk Chad seeing them together—at least for now.

When he pulled up in front of her house, she was reaching for the door handle before the car even stopped. "Vivienne." He grabbed her arm. "I appreciate what you did for me—I mean the Halloween party and everything. And I am sorry about what I said to you. I didn't mean any of it."

She smiled at him, but he could see the hurt in her face. "I know." She got out of the car and walked quickly up to the front door.

Brady watched and waited until she made it inside. As he pulled away and began the drive home, his anger grew.

It burned like a fire inside of him, and although it was still cold inside the car, his body didn't feel it.

Maybe he should just confront Chad—tell him to back off, or else. But the asshole would probably laugh at him—and then kill him—and then call the cops anyway.

What the hell was he going to do? Brady's anger reached a boiling point, turning into full-on rage. He screamed out in frustration and punched the top of the dashboard.

And then he screamed out in pain. Holy shit that hurt.

CHAPTER 45

On the plane ride home from Boston, Vivienne felt trapped. Nestled in the window seat with nothing but gray skies on one side and her mom on the other, she found herself in an inescapable position. Mom knew something was wrong, and Vivienne didn't want to talk about it. She pretended to read her Kindle, but the truth was, she had been staring at the same page for the last twenty minutes, unable to get past one line in particular. *Even after they told her he was gone, she couldn't believe it, she wouldn't believe it.*

Her mom finally nudged her in the arm. "So what's going on?"

"What?" Vivienne acted distracted, as if she was deeply engrossed in her book.

"You were moping around the whole weekend. You seem upset about something."

It was true. Thanksgiving was the usual family affair at her grandparents' house: football games on the lawn, board games by the fire, a Martha Stewart-worthy Thanksgiving dinner. Everyone seemed to have a great time—everyone but her.

She had tried to smile and she had tried to laugh, but it was forced and fake. The entire weekend, her mind wandered to Brady. She thought about what he was doing almost every minute. Would he be spending Thanksgiving with his dad, or mom, or both? Did he like pumpkin pie or apple pie, or maybe he hated pie altogether? She pictured him in a button-down shirt and khakis, his unruly hair a little neater, his adorable smile a little wider—

Stop, stop, stop!

But Vivienne couldn't, no matter how hard she tried. The worst had been Thanksgiving Day. With Grandma and Grandpa's "no electronics" rule, she was forced to sneak off to the bathroom repeatedly to check her phone. She'd see a text message on her screen and a spark of excitement would rush through her. And just as quickly, it would disappear when she saw it wasn't from Brady. Vivienne had tormented herself with possible texts she could send him:

Just wanted to wish you Happy Thanksgiving—too formal.

Happy Turkey Day—too stupid.

I miss you so bad it hurts—too pathetic, but true.

Luckily, no one seemed to notice her internal misery. Grandma and Grandpa, her aunts and uncles and cousins, everyone thought she was fine. But Mom wasn't everyone, and Vivienne had been anticipating an interrogation the whole way home.

Vivienne shrugged. "No, I'm fine." she had to look away. She had prepped herself, but she was a terrible liar.

"Honey…" Her mom wasn't going to let it go.

"Mom, I don't want to talk about it," she said quietly. Even as she said the words, she could feel the emotions coming to the surface. She was on the verge of spilling it all.

"Okay, I won't push it," Mom said softly. She put her hand over Vivienne's arm and gave a gentle squeeze. "But if you ever want to talk about it."

That made Vivienne feel even worse and she couldn't help herself. "It's just…do you remember when I went out with that guy a few weeks ago?"

Her mom's eyes brightened. "Umm, Brian, right?"

"Brady, actually," Vivienne corrected. "Well, things didn't work out and I'm kind of bummed about it." *Understatement of the century.*

"Oh, I'm sorry, hon."

Suddenly, for some reason, Vivienne did want to talk about Brady. She wanted to tell her mom everything about him. She wanted to tell her how cute he was—how he could send her heart racing with just a look—how crazy smart he was—how he knew all kinds of things about stars and comets—how he could do a Rubik's Cube in twenty seconds—how he was the most amazing kisser ever (okay, maybe not that)—how he always said the right things and always made her feel safe.

But she blurted out the first thing that came to her mind. "Brady can do this crazy thing where you give him a problem, like with super huge numbers, and he can calculate it in his head in like two seconds."

"Wow." Her mom's eyebrows lifted. "That's interesting…"

"Well, he was in an accident when he was like eight and he said ever since then, his brain just does it automatically."

"Hmm…sounds like acquired savant syndrome. It's extremely rare."

"You know about it?"

"You'd be surprised at how much I know, Vivienne." Mom smiled. "Being a nurse can be a blessing and a curse. A blessing, because you know a little bit about everything. And a curse, because you know a little bit about everything."

"I think I'd rather not know." Vivienne put her hand on her mom's arm. "Sorry, Mom, but I don't think I'll be following in your footsteps."

"Why not?" Her mom frowned. "You do such a good job at the nursing home. The director told me all the residents love you there."

Vivienne shrugged. "It's just really hard. Emotionally, I mean."

"I know, hon." Mom sighed. "I only suggested working there because I really thought it would be good for you. Give you a different perspective on things."

"Yeah, I know. It's just seeing all the residents there alone, and hardly any family members coming to visit—it gets depressing."

"Vivienne, that wasn't my intention, and I would have no problem with you getting another job."

"No." Vivienne shook her head, remembering Gloria's words. "I don't want to leave." But she did want to do something—she just wasn't sure what.

"Okay, well don't worry yourself over it. It seems like you've already got a lot on your mind." Her mom handed her a pillow. "Here, lay back and relax. We'll be landing soon."

Vivienne took the pillow and propped it up between herself and her mom. She leaned into it and closed her eyes. The drone of the plane engine was the only sound, and in the blackness, her thoughts faded, her mind emptied.

She found herself unexpectedly nodding off, but there was no sanctuary, even in her dreams. She was on a beautiful beach and the sun was setting over the horizon, the sky ablaze in oranges and reds over an endless turquoise ocean. An image appeared in the distance—someone walking toward her, his hair wet from the waves, his bare chest tanned from the hot sun, his smile bright and playful—Brady. He scooped her up in his arms, pulled her close to his wet body and kissed her passionately, his lips hot and urgent. They fell into the warm sand together, locked in each other's embrace, and as he touched her, she trembled...and then everything started trembling...and then shaking...

Vivienne was jolted out of paradise to the sound of a brash voice over the loud speaker. "Ladies and gentlemen, we have landed in Cleveland, where the weather is light snow, and a chilly eighteen degrees."

Back to reality.

CHAPTER 46

"So are we officially done with the weight room—at least until January?" Jay asked.

They sat in Brady's room while Jay played Xbox and Brady watched. The swelling on his hand had gone down, but an ugly bruise remained on his knuckles. It still hurt too much to lift weights or even play video games. "Whatever."

"Look, bro, you have no other choice, you do realize that."

"Yes, I realize it," Brady said.

He knew he had to stay away from Vivienne. But he wouldn't stop looking for a way to fix it. "I just wish there was some way to get Chad out of the picture, you know."

Jay weaved and bobbed with his controller in hand, killing everything in his path. "Like blow his head off with a scattershot?"

Brady shook his head. "No, not kill him, Jay, just make him shut his mouth."

"Yeah, well, sorry, Rain Man, I don't think a threat coming from you is going to have a real big impact." Then he added, "No offense."

Brady leaned back on his bed. "I really want to text her."

"Dude, you can't do it," Jay said with warning in his voice. "You need to forget about Vivienne, like one hundred percent. And then hopefully Chad will forget about you—and your dad."

"Shhh!" Brady threw a balled-up sock at his head. "He's gonna hear you!"

"Sorry, but you need to get your head out of your ass and get over her—like yesterday." He grabbed a bag of Funyuns and began crunching loudly.

"I know." Brady stared up at his ceiling. "I can't help it. Trust me, I wish I could."

"Enlighten me, Brady. I want to know what makes this girl so special."

He knew he sounded pathetic but he didn't care. "It's like everything in my brain is so structured and predictable. Like every situation or problem that comes up, I can rationalize and make sense of. But with her, I can't. It's total chaos."

"And that's a good thing?"

"Yes, it's a very good thing." Brady smiled. "It's a beautiful thing."

"Well, I'm sorry, bro." *AintNoMockingJay* died and Jay threw down his controller. "But I don't see any solution to this problem."

Just then there was a loud knock at the door. Dad peeked his head in. "Hey I'm frying up some Italian sausage. You guys want some?"

Neither of them would ever refuse food. "Sure, Mr. O," said Jay.

Dad nodded. "Okay, I'll call you when it's ready." He closed the door, and Jay looked at Brady. "Dude, since when does your dad cook?"

His dad had changed since he'd started going to McGuire's. He cooked more, he cleaned more, and he definitely left the house more. He would go see the guys every Thursday night for business, and he would also go in for lunch at least a couple of times a week. Dad had started making short trips to the grocery store, and when Brady came home from school, he would actually find him cooking dinner sometimes. When they sat down to eat, Dad would tell Brady about the latest happenings at McGuire's.

Like how Pete Sands became the proud grandpa of a baby boy and passed out cigars to everyone in the bar while his wife Mary passed out cupcakes with blue frosting. And how they were going to have a surprise party for Liam, who had finally gotten tired of delivering mail and was retiring from the US Postal Service after thirty-nine years. McGuire's was really like a big family in itself, and now Dad was a part of it again. It had changed him.

"He's been cooking a lot lately," Brady said. "Ever since he started going to McGuire's he's been different, in a good way."

Jay took a sip of his Coke. "Even more reason to stay away from her."

"I know, Jay," Brady snapped. "Don't you think I get how messed up this whole thing is? I'm not going to risk my dad's business over a girl."

Even a girl like Vivienne Burke.

CHAPTER 47

After the long weekend of fake smiles and forced small talk, Vivienne was glad to be home. She was unpacking her duffel bag when Kendra called. "You need to come over to Beth's house, like, as soon as you can!"

"Okay, slow down! We literally just got home. What's up?"

Kendra's voice was almost frantic. "It's a long story, but we might have a solution to the Chad problem."

"What?!" Vivienne's heart leapt. "What is it? Tell me!"

"Seriously, Vivienne, get in the car and start driving. Like, now. Call me back when you're on your way."

"Okay, okay." Vivienne clicked off with Kendra and dropped her dirty clothes on the floor. Running downstairs and grabbing her coat, she yelled out to her mom, "I'm going to borrow the car for a little bit!" She didn't wait for a response.

As soon as she pulled out of her driveway, she called Kendra back and put her on speaker. "I'm driving."

"Okay, remember how I told you Beth had an idea about getting back at Chad?"

"Yes?"

"Well, it turns out, she might actually come through."

"Tell me!"

"Okay, so Beth was in the same gym class as Kristen Lane last year, and she remembered this one day in the locker room, she heard someone crying, and so of course she had to eavesdrop." Kendra paused to catch her breath. "Anyway, it was Kristen, and she was talking to Mia Mathers, saying she wanted to break up with Chad, he was such a jerk, yadda, yadda, yadda"—another quick breath—"and then she shows Mia something on her phone, and it must've been bad, because Mia looks like really shocked."

"What was it?!" Vivienne shouted.

"Well, Beth never knew. She thought Kristen was probably just being a drama queen and it wasn't a big deal. I mean Beth would never believe Chad was anything other than Mr. Perfect."

"But now that she knows the real Chad..."

"Exactly," Kendra said. "She starts thinking maybe there was something to it, so she decides to call Kristen."

Vivienne waited, her heart pounding in her chest.

"And apparently there was something—a video."

"Oh, please tell me it's bad, and please tell me Kristen still has it."

"Yes and yes."

A surge of hope rushed through her. "Did you see it yet?"

"No," Kendra said regretfully. "Kristen doesn't feel comfortable sending it to anyone, but she's sitting in Beth's kitchen right now—"

"What? She's there?"

"Yes, she's in town for Thanksgiving, but she's got to catch a plane back to Phoenix—like in an hour."

"Okay, okay. I'm like two minutes away!"

***

When Vivienne got to Beth's condo, she found Kendra hanging out the front door, holding it open. "C'mon!" she yelled, waving her in.

Vivienne trudged up the driveway, through the fresh snow. "I'm coming as fast as I can!"

Kendra's face was full of excitement. "They're in the kitchen."

Beth was sitting at the island and Kristin Lane sat next to her. Vivienne had forgotten how pretty she was. Her blond hair, almost white now, was pulled back in a braid, and her skin was tan from the Arizona sun. She looked great, but she also looked uncomfortable.

"Hey, Vivienne," Beth said cautiously. "You want some hot chocolate?"

"No, thanks, I'm good." She tried to hide the edge in her voice. She just hoped her ex-friend would be able to redeem herself—big time.

Kendra took charge immediately. "Okay, we don't have a lot of time because Kristin has to leave here in"—she glanced at her phone—"twenty minutes?"

Kristin nodded. She didn't look just uncomfortable; she looked scared.

"You want to tell Vivienne what you told me?" Beth asked it like she was speaking to a five-year-old.

Kristin's voice was quiet. "Beth told me what was going on with you and Chad." She paused as if saying his name was painful. "How he wouldn't leave you alone."

Vivienne nodded encouragingly.

"Anyway, when we first started going out, he treated me great and was really sweet. But after a few weeks, he started acting like a jerk. He started making comments about what I would wear, about who I was talking to...and it just got worse. I'm sure you know what I mean."

"I definitely do."

Kristen sighed and took a sip of her hot chocolate. "So I broke up with him, and then he begged me to take him back, and I did. He was Chad Sutton, after all, and my friends were pressuring me, and I guess I just thought maybe I was being too picky. Maybe he wasn't really that bad.

"And then one day, I guess we had been going out for like six months, I went to an outlet mall with my mom—like forty-five minutes away. We were in the parking lot, and—." She paused. "I spotted him a couple of rows over.

He was just standing there, staring at me. I couldn't believe it. I pretended not to see him and got in the car as if nothing was wrong, but that's when everything changed for me. It was like I snapped out of a trance or something."

Vivienne could see the familiar look of panic on Kristen's face. "Go on."

"So I broke up with him—again." Her words got faster. "I did it at school. I figured that way he couldn't flip out on me, in front of all of those people. And it worked. But, by the time I got home, he was there waiting for me at my house."

Vivienne waited, hanging on every word.

"He had this video on his phone." Kristin put her head down. "Of him and me…you know. He took it without me knowing."

"What?" Vivienne and Kendra said in unison.

"Yeah, and the way it was taken, you couldn't see Chad's face. So it was like me with any random guy." Kristen's voice cracked.

"Oh my God, he's such an asshole!" Kendra yelled.

Then Kristen was wiping away tears. "I'm sorry…it's just, I've kept this in for so long."

Beth quickly grabbed a box of Kleenex and handed it to Kristin. "It's okay. Tell her the rest."

"Well, I stayed with him…I did everything he told me to do. I pretended like everything was fine because I was so terrified of him showing the video to people. My grades were slipping, my parents thought I was depressed. They were right."

Kristen paused, taking a deep breath and letting it out loudly. "I only had one friend I could talk to about it— Mia, and she told me the only way I was going to get rid of Chad was to beat him at his own game."

Kristen leaned over the island and handed her phone to Vivienne. "Here, push play."

CHAPTER 48

Vivienne pushed the little white arrow:

Wood floor, sandals running, a girl screaming, "Chad, please stop!" Kristen's voice.

"You bitch!" he screams back.

The phone pans up again and there's a flash of the room, a room Vivienne immediately recognizes—Chad's family room. And then there's a face—it's quick, but it's clear—Chad. His face is red, his eyes black. "You bitch, you think you can break up with me?"

Kristen's shrill voice. "I'm sorry! Oh God, I'm sorry, Chad. Please!"

The phone pans down again to the wood floor and then the screen goes dark. In the blackness the screams are still there. "Please, Chad, stop, you're hurting me! Stop please!"

Muffled noises for a few long seconds, and the video ends.

Vivienne looked up to see Kristin standing over by the patio door windows. "The first time I watched that video, I threw up."

"Unbelievable," Vivienne said quietly.

"What you don't see in the video is him grabbing me by my hair and throwing me down on the couch. Once he did that, I guess he came to his senses, because he started babbling about how sorry he was."

"So, what did he do when you showed this to him?"

Kristin shook her head. "I didn't. I didn't show it to anyone except Mia."

"Why?" Vivienne didn't mean for it to come out as loudly as it did.

"Well, I went home, I watched the video and I had every intention of showing it to Chad. And then literally, that night, my parents called me downstairs and told me we were moving to Phoenix, as soon as the school year was over. I acted disappointed, but inside I cannot tell you the relief I felt. I mean, I just wanted to get away from him. A fresh start, you know?"

Vivienne and Kendra nodded together. "Sure."

Kristin sighed. "I know I should've been brave and all that, but I didn't want to make him mad if I didn't have to. I just kept telling myself, 'six weeks,' 'five weeks,' and then 'four weeks' until the last day."

Vivienne thought about how different things would've been if Kristin had shown someone the video. Vivienne never would've gotten messed up with Chad, but that also meant she never would've met Brady. It was so bizarre how one person's decision could have such a huge impact on another person's future, even when the two people were essentially strangers.

Kristin walked back over to the island and sat down. "I guess I'd always known Chad would move on to someone else and do the same thing, but I couldn't worry about it. I needed to get myself healthy, and I just wanted to forget he ever existed."

Beth chimed in, "And then I called her and told her what was going on with you."

"I'm sorry, Kristen, I just—" Vivienne started.

"No." Kristen put her hands up. "It's okay. I want to help, I do. He can't keep getting away with this."

"But," Kendra said, "what if Chad retaliates and sends out his video of—you know?"

Kristin shrugged. "Honestly, I don't care anymore. I have a new life in Arizona, new friends, people he doesn't know anything about. He can do whatever he wants, but he can't hurt me anymore."

Vivienne still held the phone in her hands. She pushed the white arrow again and watched until Chad's face appeared. She paused on it. His red, angry face was indisputable. She held it in front of Kendra. "I think this might actually work. There's no way he wants this getting out there."

"I think you're right." Kendra smiled. "He'll have to leave you alone after he sees that. In fact, I think he'll pretty much do anything you say."

Vivienne was suddenly feeling optimistic. "I hope you're right." She turned to Kristin. "I can't thank you enough. I really think this could get him off my back."

"I'll send it to you now." Kristin stood up. "I hope it works." She pushed some buttons on her phone. "I really have to go. My parents will kill me if we miss our flight."

After Kristin left, Beth began rambling off an apology. "Vivienne, I feel really bad about everything. I didn't realize how much of a jerk Chad was, and I wouldn't have told him anything if—"

Vivienne cut her off. "Beth, it's okay. He had a lot of people fooled. I'm just glad you thought of Kristin."

"Are you gonna send it to him?" Kendra asked.

"No, I think I have to show him in person," Vivienne said. "You know, face-to-face, see his reaction, tell him what I want."

"We could go with you, for like moral support," Beth offered.

"Actually, I think I need to talk to Brady," Vivienne said. "He's got too much to lose and I want to make sure he's okay with it."

"Yes!" Kendra agreed. "You two should show the video to Chad together. It would have way more of an impact, and it's probably smart to have a guy there anyway."

"Oh, I definitely agree it will make an impact," Vivienne said. "It'll make Chad more pissed off."

"Yeah, but you need to show him you are in control, Vivienne," Kendra said. "Tell him that video is going viral—to the entire student body—unless he promises to leave you and Brady alone for good."

Beth added, "And make sure you freeze it up on his face and zoom in. Make sure he sees that part."

"Okay." Vivienne took a deep breath. "But I don't even know if Brady is going to want to do this."

She looked down at the phone in her hands. There was only one way to find out.

CHAPTER 49

When Brady saw the number come up on his phone, he felt an instant wave of excitement—that quickly turned to panic. All weekend long he had thought about calling Vivienne, but Jay's words always came ringing back like alarm bells. *Do you realize what you are risking with her?*

Brady did realize it. His dad was sitting right next to him on the couch, munching on popcorn as they watched a *Breaking Bad* marathon on Netflix.

And he knew the smartest thing was to ignore the call, but he couldn't help himself. He got up and walked to his room. "Hey."

"Hey." Her voice was quiet. It seemed impossible that one simple word could cause such an intense reaction in him, but it did. He lay back on his bed and closed his eyes.

"I don't want to bother you, but something came up and I thought it was important to tell you about it."

"I'm listening." But he was cringing inside too, hoping it wasn't more bad news.

"Okay, so it's a long story, but basically I have this video I want to show you. It's of Chad and his old girlfriend—the one who moved away."

"Okay…"

"The thing is, the video is something I know he doesn't want anyone to see, and I was thinking of confronting him with it. I won't do anything, though, unless you tell me it's okay. The last thing I want to do is screw things up any more for you."

"I wish you wouldn't say stuff like that, Vivienne." He paused. He wanted to say so much more, but he had to see the video first. "Go ahead and send it. I'll call you back."

"Okay, bye." She clicked off.

A minute later a text came through with the video. He tapped the little white arrow and watched. He almost couldn't believe what he was seeing. Chad wasn't just yelling at his girlfriend, he was terrorizing her. The girl's screams made his stomach turn. It was crazy on a whole other level.

Brady called Vivienne back right away. "God, I don't know what to say. I guess I didn't realize how insane he really was. Did he ever—?"

"No," she said quickly, "he never got that bad with me. But now it's pretty easy to see what he's capable of."

Brady could feel his anger intensifying. "Is that girl okay—the one in the video?"

"Yeah, I just saw her, and she's really good, actually. She's about to get on a plane back to Arizona and she said she doesn't care what we do with the video, she just wants to stay out of it."

"I don't blame her."

"Brady." He could hear the excitement in Vivienne's voice. "I really think if Chad sees this, it will shut him up for good."

The implications of what she was saying suddenly hit him. If Chad was completely out of the picture, they wouldn't have to worry about anything. They could start over—nothing holding them back.

"What do you need me to do?"

***

An hour later, Brady was in front of Vivienne's house waiting for her. She came out the front door, a white hat pulled down low over her dark red hair. It had been one of the coldest Novembers on record, and that night was particularly brutal—temperatures in the single digits with gusty winds. He cranked the heat up a little higher and took a deep breath.

She opened the door and got in. "Hey." She smiled.

"Hey."

Was she as nervous as he was? He couldn't tell. "So, SweetBrews, right?" He tried to sound casual as he pulled away from the curb.

"Yeah. Same place we went to. I told him seven thirty." Her usual upbeat voice was gone. She sounded scared. "I'll go in and get a drink with him, tell him I don't want to fight anymore or some other lie, just so he's not expecting anything. Then you come in and catch him by surprise."

"Vivienne, are you sure you want to do this? I mean, I'll talk to the asshole by myself if you want."

"No," she said. "I want to see his face."

They were quiet the rest of the way to SweetBrews. Brady figured Vivienne was probably thinking some of the same things he was thinking. Like, *What if Chad doesn't care about the video? What if he just gets pissed off? What if he retaliates with a vengeance? What if this ruins everything?*

Brady pulled into the parking lot and drove to a spot far enough away not to be noticed, but close enough to still see the entrance. He wanted to ease her nerves a little bit. "Hey, did you ever notice that we spend a lot of time in cars? Like, I would bet at least fifty percent of our time together has been inside a car."

"Yeah, you're probably right." Vivienne laughed and then her smile faded. "There he is."

Brady watched Chad get out of his car and walk under the lights, toward the entrance. He was wearing a long black coat which he had accessorized with a hat—not a cap—like a hat Brady's grandpa would wear. Seriously?

Just then Vivienne got a text. She held up her phone. *I'm at the coffee shop. Where are you?*

She texted back, *Pulling in parking lot.*

"Well, here goes nothing." She gave a weak smile.

"It'll be okay," he reassured her. "I'll be there in a few minutes."

He watched Vivienne run to the entrance and then looked down at his phone to start counting the minutes. When four minutes passed, he got out of the car. Showtime.

Brady's adrenaline pumped as he opened the coffee shop door and scanned the inside. He spotted Vivienne in a booth in the far corner. Chad's back was turned away from him, and he wouldn't be able to see Brady coming—perfect.

Brady walked calmly to their booth and Vivienne didn't glance up at him once. In one swift motion he swung around to Vivienne's seat and slid in next to her. He put his arm around her and kissed her on the cheek. "Hey, Chad, nice hat."

The look on his face was priceless. "What the hell's going on?" His eyes flickered back and forth between Brady and Vivienne.

"Well, I'll tell you what's going on." Brady looked across the table at the douchebag, his eyes unwavering. "You're not going to bother Vivienne anymore, you're not going to sit outside her house like a pathetic loser, you're not going to talk about her to your friends, and you're not going to hang on to any delusion that she will ever be with you again."

Chad's psycho smile returned. "Wow, Brady, how valiant of you!" He laughed sarcastically. "Vivs, you have your very own knight in shining armor!"

Brady ignored the asshole. "And you're not going to tell anyone—and I mean anyone—about my dad's bookie business."

"Oh, really?" Chad looked amused more than anything.

Brady pulled out his phone. "Here." He pushed it across the table. "For your viewing pleasure."

Chad didn't touch the phone, but the curiosity on his face was obvious. "What the hell's this?"

"Just push play." Now Brady was grinning smugly.

Chad let out an exaggerated sigh and picked up the phone. He pushed the play button and squinted at the screen. Within seconds, the color slowly began draining from his face. The video volume was on low but it was still loud enough to hear the screams: *Chad, stop, please!*

When the video ended, he looked up and shrugged. "Is this supposed to mean something to me?" His tone was casual but Brady could see the fear in his face.

Brady took the phone and clicked on his camera roll. He had saved the frame in the video that clearly showed Chad's face, zoomed in on it, and raised the resolution. The image was clear and unmistakable.

He held the phone up in front of Chad. "That's you, isn't it?"

Another casual shrug. "Anybody could put my face into some video. I mean, there's no proof it's me."

Brady put the phone in front of Vivienne. "What do you think, Vivienne? Do you think that looks like Chad Sutton?"

Vivienne smiled and nodded. "Yep, that's definitely Chad Sutton. And the constant screams of 'Chad, please stop!' kind of reinforce the picture." She looked up at him. "Not your best look, Chad."

Chad looked over to the window, and Brady could see the panic in his eyes.

"It doesn't prove anything. I mean, it's just a guy and girl having an argument." But his whole demeanor had changed from one of arrogant confidence to one of timid uncertainty.

"You know what, Chad, you're right." Brady put the phone in his pocket. "So you probably wouldn't care if I told you my friend Jay is hard at work right now, making a list."

A part of Chad's left cheek began pulsating. "What list?"

Brady cleared his throat. "See, my friend Jay is a wiz with computers, like insanely talented. And he told me he could have this video sent out to the entire Richmond student body in a matter of seconds. Shit, he could have it sent to every resident in Richmond in a matter of minutes. And by the night's end, this video could be a viral sensation."

Vivienne nodded. "Could you imagine what people would think when they found out Mr. Perfect Chad Sutton is actually a raging psychopath?"

Chad pounded his fist on the table so hard that Brady and Vivienne both flinched in unison. "What do you want, Brady?" he growled.

Brady glanced around to see some customers glaring at them in disapproval. "Simple, Chad—leave Vivienne alone. Avoid her like the plague. No calls, texts, surprise visits, nothing. And forget about saying anything, to anyone, about my dad's business."

Brady leaned back in his seat. "If you screw up, my friend Jay pushes the send button, simple as that."

Chad stared back at them, his eyes daggers. "Brady, I wouldn't be expecting too much from her"—he nodded at Vivienne—"you couldn't get her legs open with a crowbar."

Brady smiled. "No crowbar necessary."

Vivienne let out a laugh, and Chad looked so pissed, Brady thought he might actually jump over the table and start beating his ass right there. But instead he just stood up. "Whatever."

"Oh, and Chad," Brady said, "you might want to ask your dad what really happened when your parents got divorced."

At that, Chad sat back down. "What the fuck do you know about it, Brady?"

"Well, your dad told my dad…some pretty messed-up stuff. Like when your parents got divorced, he told you a bunch of lies about your mom. Said she was into drugs, and stuff."

Chad's eyes were full of rage. "She was."

"No, Chad, she wasn't. Your dad admitted that he made it all up—he was bragging about it. Apparently, your mom fought like hell for custody of you, but your dad had influence with the judge and she didn't have a chance."

Brady could see Chad's eyes watering up and he felt a tiny pang of sympathy for him, just barely.

"You don't know what the fuck you're talking about."

Brady shrugged. "Just thought you should know."

Chad got up and practically ran out of the restaurant without ever looking back.

Brady and Vivienne sat for a moment in silence, the realization that Chad was out of the picture for good slowly sinking in.

"Well, I think that went well," Vivienne said, smiling.

Brady smiled back, and then he reached across the table and picked up the hat that Chad had left behind. "Do you think we should go tell him he forgot his hat?"

CHAPTER 50

In the short time they were inside SweetBrews, the snow had fallen fast and left a layer of white powder on the windshield. When Brady put on the wipers to clear it away, they scraped over a layer of smooth ice underneath.

"Gotta let this defrost for a minute," he said.

Let it defrost for an hour, let it defrost for a day, let it defrost forever! There was nowhere Vivienne would rather be than sitting in a car with Brady.

She tried to sound casual, something that never seemed easy around him. "I can't believe it's only November. This is like January weather."

He turned to her and smiled, that adorable, confident, calming smile, and she felt her stomach do a flip-flop. "Well, I don't think we have to worry about Chad anymore."

"I think you're right." She could feel herself melting inside a little more with every second next to Brady. She needed to tell him how grateful she was. "Brady, thanks so much for coming here. I don't know if I could've confronted him on my own."

"I bet you could have."

She wasn't so sure. "Well, I just wanted you to know."

"Hey," he said, reaching out and grabbing her hand. He gave it a quick squeeze. "I'm glad I did."

She glanced at his hand. Inside SweetBrews, she had noticed his knuckles were bruised up pretty badly. "Can I ask what happened to your hand?"

He smiled. "The truth?"

"Yes, please."

"I punched something."

She cringed. "It wasn't a person, I hope?"

"No." He tapped the dashboard. "Just this."

"Ouch." She cringed again. "Bet that hurt."

He looked away like he was embarrassed, which somehow, although she hadn't thought it was possible, made him even more appealing.

"Holy shit, it's cold!" He rubbed his hands together and gave her a sideways glance. "You're starting to look like Rudolph."

"Hey!" She immediately covered her nose with her hand. "Yours isn't much better, Mr. Buttchin!"

"Mr. What?!" He laughed.

"You know, you have that dimple." She pointed her finger at his face and quickly touched the small indent in the center of his chin. "Haven't you ever heard it called a buttchin before?"

"Uh, no."

Crap. "Oh, well, it's a good thing. It's like a sign of beauty or something."

"Beauty?"

Crap, crap, crap. "I mean—you know—handsomeness— if that's even a word." She couldn't stop rambling. "I mean, if I could trade in my freckles for a buttchin, I'd do it in a heartbeat."

"You're acting funny," he laughed.

Oh God, what was wrong with her? She was being a complete spaz! "Sorry."

He paused and gave her a look—that look. "For what it's worth, I like your freckles."

At that she felt the flames of embarrassment rise into her cheeks. "Oh God, I hope you don't think I was fishing for a compliment. Because I really hate them, and I say it all the time."

He shook his head. "And I'm saying that I like them. They—"

"Don't!" She closed her eyes. "Sorry, but if you say 'they give you character' I'll cry. I'll seriously cry."

"No, I wasn't going to say that," he said calmly. He paused a second. "Geez...now I'm afraid you won't believe me."

"Okay, I'm sorry." Why was she so nervous?

"Please stop it with the *sorrys.*"

She bit her lip, almost saying it again, and kept her eyes forward. For some reason, she couldn't look at him. But she could feel his eyes watching her.

"I was going to say, 'they are probably my favorite thing about you.'"

When Vivienne was eight, she'd asked for a new American Girl doll named Kit, and on Christmas morning when she came down the stairs, Kit was under the tree, sitting on Kit's bed with Kit's pinwheel quilt, wearing Kit's puppy-print pajamas. It was one of the happiest moments of her life, but it wasn't even close to this.

When Vivienne was in ninth grade and playing in the conference volleyball championship, and the score was tied, and on the last point she'd spiked the ball...

"Vivienne?"

"Huh?" To her immense humiliation, he was waiting for her to respond.

"Should we head back to your house, then?" he asked, for the second time apparently.

But Vivienne didn't want to leave. She wanted to stay with him, right there, forever. "Would you maybe want to come over for a little bit? I mean, my parents will be there, so it might be lame..."

"Sure." He smiled.

She tried to contain herself. "Cool."

The streets were quiet as they drove back, with only an occasional snowplow going by. They were icy, too, and Brady seemed preoccupied with trying not to slide off into a snowbank. As always, she fidgeted with the radio stations, she couldn't help it. If it bothered him, he didn't say anything.

Brady pulled down her street, and while they were still ten houses away, she could see the inflatables glowing in the distance.

Crap. She had forgotten about her dad. Her house was always the first one on the block decorated for Christmas. As soon as they came home from Boston, it was an annual tradition for her dad to start turning the front yard into a Las Vegas circus show.

Brady parked the car on the curb in front. "Those are interesting."

Three huge blow-up decorations stood proudly in the middle of the lawn—Mickey Mouse dressed as Santa, Frosty the Snowman, and a Christmas tree inside a snow globe.

Then she saw her dad, kneeling down in the snowy ground, untangling a massive cluster of electrical cords.

"He's just getting started," she said. "My dad's kind of like the Clark Griswold of the block."

Brady laughed. "Great movie."

She was starting to rethink her idea of having Brady over. The embarrassment had already started and they hadn't even made it through the front door. Once they went inside, they were trapped in the chaos of the Burke household, and who knew what would happen. "Okay, if my sisters say anything, please ignore them. And my parents, well...they're my parents."

Again she found Brady looking at her with that smile—the calm, everything-will-be-okay smile. "It's fine, Vivienne. I get the embarrassing family thing."

"Okay." She took a deep breath and opened the car door.

The first encounter would be her dad. As soon as they walked up the driveway, he dropped an extension cord and stood waiting for them, a big smile on his face. *It will all be over soon*, she told herself.

"Hey, Dad, I wanted you to meet my friend, Brady."

Her dad reached out to Brady and gave an aggressive handshake. "Hi, Brady, it's good to meet you."

"You too, sir. The decorations look great."

Sir, the decorations looks great! Her dad was going to eat that up. "Well, thank you, Brady." His eyes gave Brady a once-over. "Kind of an annual tradition. I've only just started—you should see it when it's all done."

Brady nodded. "I'm sure it'll be great."

Awkward silence lasted for only a second before Vivienne took the cue to leave. "Okay, Dad, we'll see you later!" She grabbed Brady's hand, leading him away.

She closed the door behind them, welcoming the warmth, but dreading what was to follow. Sure enough, Tess didn't disappoint. Before they even got their coats off, her little sister was walking from the family room and into the foyer.

Tess barely glanced at Vivienne, but then did a double take when she saw Brady. "Well, hello!" she said in her squeaky voice. "I remember you! Vivienne, are you going to introduce me to your boyfriend?"

Vivienne gave her sister the most threatening look she could manage. "Brady, this is my sister Tess. Tess, this is Brady."

Tess walked up confidently. "Nice to meet you, Brady." She shook his hand with her most grown-up effort, and then stood there and started giggling.

"I think it's past your bedtime, Tess."

She reluctantly walked away, still giggling.

"Sorry," Vivienne mumbled.

"This is all very entertaining, you know." Brady was clearly amused.

"I'm glad you're enjoying yourself."

"Vivienne, is that you?" her mom called from the kitchen.

"Uh, yeah, Mom, I'm home!" she called back.

She led Brady into the kitchen, where her mom was packing lunches. "Mom, I wanted to introduce you to Brady."

Her mom put down the peanut butter knife and wiped her hands on a napkin. Vivienne could see the surprise in her eyes. "Oh, hello, Brady, it's so nice to meet you." She shook his hand politely.

"It's nice to meet you too, Mrs. Burke."

She gave Vivienne an approving look. "Would you two like something to eat? I could make you up some peanut butter and jelly sandwiches."

"No, Mom, we're good. But thanks."

They walked into the family room, where Morgan was sitting on the couch watching an episode of *Teen Wolf*. She was also talking on her phone, while simultaneously painting her toenails. She clearly had no intention of giving up her space.

Vivienne and Brady looked at each other. "Do you want to hang out in my room for a little bit?"

He smiled. "Uh, that's a no-brainer."

"C'mon." She led him up the stairs, and just as she reached her bedroom door, she heard Tess yell from somewhere down below. "Vivienne and Brady, sitting in a tree, K-I-S-S-I-N-G!"

She quickly pulled Brady into her room and slammed the door. Holy humiliation.

CHAPTER 51

The minute they got inside Vivienne's room, Brady felt a rush of relief that the parent introductions were over. But the relief was immediately replaced by nervous excitement. "So, your parents don't care if you have boys in your room?"

She smiled. "Well, this is the first time I've had a boy in my room, so I guess not."

A small feeling of satisfaction came over him just hearing that. He looked around the dimly lit room, the only light coming from a small lamp on the bedside table.

"Sorry, I know it's kind of a mess," she said as she began picking up clothes off the floor.

It didn't look messy to him at all, not compared to his own room. "It looks pretty clean to me." He glanced at the bed, which in contrast to the rest of the room was made up neatly with a down comforter and white furry pillows. He looked away quickly.

"Oh, go ahead and sit down," she said.

He sat on the bed, and then slowly leaned back, sinking into the pillows. The sweet smell of Vivienne surrounded him, and he immediately thought of her lying in that very spot, wearing only a t-shirt and...*Stop, Brady, just stop.*

He looked for a distraction and noticed a keyboard in the corner of the room. "Do you play that?"

She glanced over. "Yeah, piano lessons for ten years."

"That's awesome. Will you play something for me?"

She looked at him with a shy smile. "Do I have to?"

"No." He gave her a sad face. "Not if you don't want to."

"Fine." She walked over to the keyboard. "I'll do a short version of what I played at the last recital. Just remember, this sounds way better on the piano."

She pulled up a small chair from her desk and began playing. He recognized the song right away—"Clocks" by Coldplay.

He closed his eyes, listening to the ebb and flow of the music. She was an amazing player.

When she finished, he began clapping. "Why didn't you tell me you could play? I told you that story about the savant who could play piano, and you didn't even mention it."

She shrugged. "I'm not sure. I really don't tell people, but if I see a piano, like at somebody's house or something, I always get on and play. I see those black and white keys and—I don't know, it's like a magnet drawing me in. I just have to tinker with them."

"Probably how I feel when I see a Rubik's Cube."

"Exactly." She smiled. She leaned over in the chair, resting her elbows on her knees. "Now, tell me something about you that I don't know."

He said the first thing that popped into his mind. "I play baseball."

"Really?" She seemed genuinely surprised.

"Why, you don't think a guy who knows stuff about meteor showers can play sports too?"

"No." She paused. "I mean no, I don't think that." She got up and walked over to the bed. "I wanted to show you something."

"Okay..." His mind flooded with the possibilities of that statement.

She went to the bedside table and took something out of the drawer. It was a small leather notebook, old and worn. She pulled a tattered photograph out of the yellowed pages and handed it to him. It was a young soldier, who eerily looked a lot like him.

"This is Gloria's son?" he asked.

"Yeah, kind of weird, huh? He was only two years older than us."

Brady shook his head. "It's crazy that he probably died in some jungle somewhere, halfway around the world."

"And how many other nineteen-year-olds died too."

"I read somewhere that over sixty percent of all the casualties in Vietnam were eighteen- to twenty-one-year-olds." He stared at the face of Gloria's son, smiling proudly. "God, it makes me feel so guilty worrying about all the stupid stuff we worry about, you know?"

"I know. I'm just so glad I got the picture back." She tucked it back into the notebook.

Then she sat down on the bed next to him. "You know what's weird? You remember when you were talking about the energy, and how we all share it?"

"Yeah…" He really didn't want to get into another philosophical discussion at that particular moment.

"Well, I think the energy is so negative at Shady Oaks that every time I go there, I absorb some of it. I don't know why it bothers me so much, but it does."

He paused. "Please don't take this the wrong way, Vivienne, but have you ever thought about just quitting?"

"Many times. My mom just asked me the same thing. But I always go back to that day with Gloria when she told me how much the residents appreciated me being there."

"Well you can't feel guilty about it. I'm sure that's not what Gloria intended."

"No, I know. But I seriously don't want to quit. I just…want to make it better somehow."

"Well, last week we had this assembly at school with some reps from OSU and Bowling Green. They said one of the best things you can have on your college application is volunteer work. Do you guys have a bulletin board at school where you can post stuff?"

"Yeah…"

"So talk to the people at Shady Oaks and see if you can organize something so students can volunteer there. Even if one person signed up, it seems like it would make a huge difference."

"That's actually a really good idea. They could do games or crafts or whatever, or even just read to them."

He smiled. "I'll be the first volunteer."

Their eyes locked and he knew he had to kiss her. But before he could make a move, she abruptly said, "Close your eyes."

"What?"

"Just do it."

"Okay." He closed his eyes. His heart was pounding so hard, he thought she must be able to hear it through the silence.

"Hold on," she said.

Suddenly the pillows were ripped out from behind him and he fell flat on his back. "Seriously?" It came out in a nervous laugh.

Brady heard a click, and even with his eyes closed, he could tell that she had turned off the light. "Okay, now you're scaring me," he joked.

"Ha-ha."

Next, he felt her lie down alongside him, the length of her body pressed against his. Her hand reached for his, and their fingers interlaced. Then he felt her breath on his ear. "Okay, open them," she whispered.

He opened his eyes. Above them were hundreds, maybe even thousands, of tiny blue lights strewn across the ceiling. They were dark blue pinpoints of light, scattered randomly, giving it the feeling of a true nighttime sky. He suddenly felt like they were back at the tower, under the stars.

"Wow, that's impressive, Vivienne." And it was.

"I got blue ones so I could leave them on at night. The white ones were way too bright."

"This would be pretty cool to look at every night." *Especially if you were next to me*, he thought.

"I know it's not quite an octillion, but it still makes me feel good when I look at it."

It makes me feel good when I look at you.

Brady couldn't wait another second. He propped himself up on his elbow and admired her profile. She turned to him and smiled, her eyes glittering with the reflection of blue light.

He put his hand on the side of her face, feeling her soft skin, and then leaned into her, finding her lips in the darkness. When their mouths met, all the feelings from their first kiss came flooding back: warmth, comfort, excitement, wanting.

He could never get enough of her. Her kiss, her scent, her touch—just her. Something was happening to him and it was more than just an intense physical reaction. When he was with Vivienne, things just felt right. Life felt right.

And from that moment on, *he* wanted to do everything right.

He didn't want to rush anything or take things too far, especially when the entire Burke family was downstairs. He used every ounce of self-control to keep himself in check and slowly pulled away from her. He rested his forehead against hers. "I don't want to get too carried away. I can't seem to control myself around you."

"The feeling's mutual," she whispered.

"Maybe we should continue this another time?"

"Yeah."

He tried to move off of her, but her arms were still wrapped tightly around him and she wouldn't let go. "I don't want you to go."

He sighed. "I don't want to go either." He leaned down and gave her a quick kiss, not trusting himself to do anything more. "But if I don't go now, your parents might never let me come over again."

She frowned and slowly released her arms.

He sat on the edge of the bed, ran his hands through his hair, and took a deep breath.

Vivienne crawled over and sat next to him. She picked up his bruised hand and gently kissed his knuckles. They sat in silence for a second and then she began giggling.

"What's so funny?" he asked.

"I don't know." She lifted her hands in the air. "I guess I'm just happy."

He looked at her smiling face. "I'm happy too."

No truer words were ever spoken.

CHAPTER 52

It was the Sunday before Christmas, and Brady would be picking her up soon. They were going to McGuire's Pub to watch the Browns game.

Apparently, if the Cleveland Browns won the game, they would win their division, and clinch a playoff spot. Brady said it was a huge deal because the Browns hadn't done that since 1989, which was like ten years before they were even born.

She looked at herself in the full-length mirror. She was wearing her new Browns hoodie Brady had given her as an early Christmas present. He had taken her to Dick's and even let her pick it out. She had scoured the racks for the most fashionable thing she could find, which was not an easy task. The colors were hideous and their logo was just a helmet. And although they had adopted a cute-looking bulldog, it unfortunately wasn't on anything in her size.

She settled on a white hoodie with "Browns" written across the front in orange script. Her favorite part was the cute little elf on the sleeve, which Brady was all too happy to tell her was an old mascot from the 1940s, when the Browns were actually good. *The 1940s, seriously?*

Once she had asked him why he tortured himself. "Why not pick another team—almost any team would be an improvement, right?" Not a good idea.

He shook his head. "Vivienne, it doesn't work that way. You don't just 'pick' another team. When you're a Browns fan, it's ingrained in you. I mean, it's like literally part of your DNA. My dad, my grandpa, my great-grandpa, all Browns fans. And we've been so bad for so long that it just makes us more fanatical."

He looked at her with such seriousness, she had to suppress a laugh. "See, it's kind of like the 'want what you can't have' principle magnified times a thousand. The longer you go without something, the more you want it." He paused and gave her a teasing smile. "Do you really think Patriots fans have the same kind of passion Browns fans do? They can't. They're numb with success. It goes against the laws of the human psyche."

"Now you're an expert on the human psyche?"

"Trust me, Vivienne, the Browns will grow on you. And then you're doomed like the rest of us."

Well, that was encouraging. But Brady loved them, so she would try.

She did one last check of her makeup and then grabbed her phone. She glanced at the newly framed pictures sitting side by side on her dresser. One was a selfie of her and

Brady at the ice skating rink. She hadn't skated for years, and Brady had never skated. It was like the blind leading the blind, and they'd both spent most of the time sitting on the ice with wet butts. But snuggling up by the fire afterwards made it all worth it.

The other picture was the photograph of Gloria's son, Michael, which Vivienne had put into a small silver frame. For some reason, she thought Gloria would've wanted her to display his picture. It just didn't feel right keeping it hidden away in the old notebook.

And there was something else she thought Gloria would be happy about. Four students from Richmond High had volunteered at Shady Oaks so far. Well, three, really, because she had sort of guilted Kendra into doing it, but it was still awesome.

Her phone beeped with a text from Brady: *Here* ☺.

She ran down the stairs, yelled goodbye to her parents, and practically skipped down the driveway to Brady's car. She was about to jump in the backseat when she noticed the front passenger seat was empty. She opened the door and got in. "Hey, where's your dad?"

Brady didn't answer. He leaned over and kissed her before she could say anything else. Honestly, she would be perfectly happy just sitting in the car, in her driveway, kissing Brady. Nothing was better than kissing him.

"The sweatshirt looks good on you," he said with a smile on his face—that smile, the smile that still made her stomach do a flip-flop. He was wearing a Browns jersey and a Santa hat made out of orange fur, with a giant white pom-pom on top. He looked ridiculous—ridiculously hot.

"Nice hat." She smiled. It seemed like a permanent smile was pretty much plastered to her face every second she was with him.

"My dad wanted to keep the phone line open a little longer since it's such a big game—make sure everyone got their bets in. I told him I'd go pick you up and then we'd come back to get him."

"Oh, okay."

She had asked Brady if all of his dad's customers bet on the Browns, wouldn't he want the other team to win? That's when Brady had explained the concept of "laying off," where Mr. O'Connell would go online and put a big bet on the Browns too. That way, no matter the outcome, it was a wash. Words like 'wash' and 'laying off' were all part of Brady's vocabulary, and now they were part of hers too.

"So Jay's gonna be there, right?" she asked.

"Yes. Don't worry, he'll be there."

Since Vivienne and Brady had been spending so much time together, Kendra was feeling a bit left out. "Well, you might as well set me up with Jay," she'd said one day.

"Really?" Vivienne was all for the idea, but surprised Kendra would even consider it.

Kendra shrugged. "I mean, he's Brady's best friend, he can't be that bad, right?"

"Right," Vivienne had said confidently, but she really had no clue.

When Brady told her about the big game and how Jay would be there, Vivienne thought it was the perfect opportunity.

"It's just, Kendra is definitely going to be there," she told Brady. "She's volunteering at Shady Oaks this morning, but then she's coming to McGuire's at halftime. She said that it would look more casual—not so set up—if she came a little later."

Brady laughed. "Okay, then."

"What?" Vivienne asked.

"Do all girls do that?"

"Do what?"

"I don't know, like, plan things so they look 'casual'? I mean, does it really involve that much thought?"

She eyed him silently. "Brady, for our first date you took me to a lookout tower in the middle of God knows where to watch a meteor shower! You're going to tell me no thought went into that?"

He smiled. "Okay, I guess I should rephrase that. Guys might plan things out sometimes, but we don't sit around talking about it with each other. When I told Jay that Kendra was going to be there, he was like, 'Oh. Cool,' like he didn't think anything of it." He added, "They might hate each other, you know."

She gave him a playful punch in the arm. "Nice, Brady! Can you please show a little optimism?"

"Sorry." He shrugged. "But remember, I know Jay a lot better than you do."

"I guess everyone can't be as perfect as you." She rolled her eyes.

"You got that right."

And he was perfect to her—completely, undeniably, without question perfect. She had never felt as happy as she felt at that moment.

As she looked at him driving, in his stupid hat, with his adorable grin, her stomach tickled, her chest ached, and her cheeks burned.

Then, as they turned the corner, Brady's house came into view.

And her stomach dropped, her chest thudded, and her cheeks went cold.

"No," Brady whispered.

A police car was sitting in his driveway.

CHAPTER 53

Brady blinked his eyes hard, as if somehow that would make the car disappear. Maybe he was seeing things.

Black and white, shiny red and blue lights on top, Fulton Police written in large black letters across the side. His stomach lurched. It was definitely a cop car.

"Fuck!" he yelled, almost smashing his fist into the dashboard for a second time.

He saw Vivienne flinch from the corner of his eye.

"I'm sorry." He put his head back on the seat and looked up. "I just can't believe this."

"Brady, I am so sorry." She sounded on the verge of tears.

He turned to her and put his hands on her shoulders. "Vivienne, it's okay." Her face was ashen. She wouldn't look at him.

"Don't worry, okay? We'll figure this out. I'll just…" He stopped. He'd just what? He didn't know what the hell he was going to do.

Panic filled her eyes. "Do you think Chad called them? I can't believe he did that…I mean, he hasn't even looked at me funny. He completely ignores me at school…" Her voice was getting louder and more frantic.

"Come here." Brady pulled her into his arms and held her tightly. No matter what happened, he wasn't going to put the blame on Vivienne. But he would put the blame on Chad, and do whatever it took to ruin him, starting with the video.

Vivienne's voice was shaky, muffled against him. "What are you going to do?"

"I'll go in and see what's going on, okay? You just stay here, and I'll come back as soon as I can."

"Do you want me to leave? I could call Kendra to pick me—oh crap, she's at Shady Oaks. I can call—"

"Slow down," he cut her off. "Just stay here. Let me find out what the hell's going on first. If I can't take you home, I can call Jay."

She nodded. "Okay."

"I'll be right back."

Brady opened the car door and stepped out into the cold December air. He took in a long, deep breath and began the walk up the driveway. His legs felt heavy and his head woozy. He glanced into the police car on his way, noticing the metal cage barrier between the front and backseat. A sickeningly real vision of his dad sitting in the back materialized, and Brady had to steady himself. He concentrated on his steps, one foot in front of the other. *Just walk, Brady…just walk.*

***

"You need to call me back, right now!" It was the second voice mail Vivienne had left her best friend. Kendra was probably in the middle of story time or playing a game of gin rummy. *Please check your phone, Kendra!*

Vivienne felt like she was going to puke. How could this be happening? Why would Chad call the police? He knew they had the video of him! Did he really just not care?!

She stared at the small brick bungalow, her heart in her throat. She could just imagine what was going on inside. Cops putting cuffs on Mr. O'Connell. "Sir, we are charging you with aggravated gambling. You have the right to remain silent…"

This was all her fault. What would Brady do? Would he blame her and break it off? Of course he would. *Crap, crap, crap.*

Just then her phone lit up—Kendra. Before Kendra said a word, Vivienne was babbling. "Oh my God, Kendra, the police are here, at Brady's house! We were coming to pick up Mr. O'Connell for the game—and there was this cop car in the driveway—and Brady went in—and I'm just waiting—and I don't know what to do!"

"Okay, Vivienne, calm down! Say that again, because it was a little hard to understand you."

So Vivienne repeated the story. "What am I going to do, Kendra?"

"Okay, just stay calm until Brady comes out," she said. "Whatever happens, I don't think this is a deal breaker for you guys. It's like you guys are seriously in love with each other—it's pretty sickening, actually. But the point is, you'll figure this out."

"Kendra, that is all fine and good, but this is major. Brady's dad means everything to him." Vivienne could feel the tears welling up. "I just don't get why Chad would do this. I mean, since when does he not care about his precious reputation?"

There was silence on the other end. A long silence.

"Kendra? You there?"

"Crap, I just thought of something," she said quietly.

"What?! What?!" Vivienne screamed into the phone.

"Well, I was going to tell you at McGuire's. Beth just texted me today. She heard something about Chad."

"Kendra! What?! Tell me!"

"She said she heard Chad was moving to St Clair."

"What?" Vivienne's anxiety went through the roof and she was finding it hard to process what she was hearing. "What do you mean? Why?"

"His mom lives there," Kendra sighed. "I don't know all the details, but Beth said he's moving in with his mom over Christmas break."

"Oh my God." Vivienne couldn't believe the irony of it all. Brady had told Chad about his dad's lies, and Chad had probably worked things out with his mom because of it.

And maybe Chad didn't care who saw the video since he'd be starting over in a new school.

Chad was having the last laugh.

"Unbelievable," Vivienne said quietly. "You do realize Brady was the one who told Chad the truth about his mom."

"I know. This sucks," Kendra said. "Hey, I'm sorry, but I've got to get back to Bingo."

"I guess I'll just sit here and wait for the cops to bring Mr. O'Connell out in cuffs."

"Don't think that way. Just text me as soon as you can. It'll be okay."

No, it wouldn't be okay. It was so frickin' far from okay.

Vivienne slumped down in her seat. Snowflakes began falling—the big fat ones that plopped when they hit the windshield. Beautiful, delicate, perfectly unique—shattered, destroyed, obliterated, as they hit the glass.

CHAPTER 54

After Brady went through the back door, he felt a throbbing pain start between his shoulder blades. His muscles were in knots and his heart felt like it was going to beat right through his chest. He forced himself to stop and take a deep breath. *Breathe in, breathe out...*

When he entered the family room, he found his dad sitting on the couch, wearing his Browns jersey. His hands were clasped in front of him, twiddling his thumbs. A cop was sitting in a chair across from him, with his back to Brady. They were drinking coffee.

"Hey!" Dad shouted, a big smile on his face. "There you are! Brady, come here!"

What in the hell?

As Brady cautiously walked closer, the cop turned around. "Hey, Brady, you ready for the big game?"

WTF? It was Eagle Ears Bob.

"Oh, hi, Bob. I didn't know that was you," Brady said, trying to hide the nervousness in his voice. "I didn't know you were...a police officer."

Bob smiled his familiar, quiet smile. "Oh, your dad never told you?"

Brady looked at his dad. "No, he didn't."

"Well, I don't really like to advertise it at McGuire's. Don't want the guys to get skittish around me, you know? When I'm off duty, I just enjoying having some company like everybody else there."

Brady nodded. He was dumbfounded, at a loss for words.

"Well, I better get going." Bob stood up and put on his police cap. "I'm so pissed off I got called into work, but Officer Scott's wife went into labor and I can't really argue with that one. I'll be watching the game, though, you can bet on that." He winked at Brady and gave him a pat on the shoulder. "Go Browns!"

"Yeah, go Browns!" His voice came out in a squeak.

Brady turned and watched Bob, or maybe he should say Officer Bob, go out the door.

As soon as he was gone, Brady was yelling, "Dad! What the hell? Seriously?" He began pacing. "When were you going to tell me Bob was a cop?"

His dad shrugged his shoulders as if that little tidbit of information was of no real importance. "I don't know, I thought I did tell you that. What are you so jumpy about?"

"What am I so jumpy about? Oh my God, Dad, I thought you were in trouble! I pulled up to the house and there's a cop car in the driveway!"

His dad laughed. "So that's what this is about? Brady, I already told you the cops don't care about this small-time stuff. Shit, half of the Fulton station bets with me."

"What?!" Brady shouted.

"See?" Dad picked up a piece of paper. "Bob was bringing these over."

Brady looked at the rows of names and numbers, neatly printed in blue ink. "Those are bets from cops?" He couldn't believe what he was hearing. "Eagle Ears Bob was bringing over bets—on the game?"

"Jesus Brady, don't be so naïve. Cops like to have a little fun too." His dad picked up the coffee cups and carried them into the kitchen. "Besides, I give 'em a break and don't charge them any juice—just to show my respect and appreciation, of course." He winked.

"I can't believe this." Brady fell back on the couch, his head spinning.

His dad emerged from the kitchen and glanced at his watch. "It's getting close to game time. I'm going to go put these bets in the computer." Just business as usual.

"Dad, I thought you were getting busted! I told Vivienne to wait in the car—Shit!"

Vivienne was still sitting in the car! Brady felt a massive rush of relief and a surge of newfound energy. He jumped off the couch. "I've got to go get Vivienne!"

"Well, go get her, then!" His dad laughed. "I'll be there in a minute."

Brady didn't have to worry anymore, and neither did Vivienne. All there was left to worry about was opening that car door, taking her into his arms, and kissing her like he'd never kissed her before.

And that's exactly what he did.

CHAPTER 55

The inside of McGuire's was an explosion of brown and orange. It was jam-packed, people standing shoulder to shoulder. As soon as they walked through the door, Maggie came rushing to greet them. "Where have you been?" she shouted over the noisy crowd. "I reserved a place for you at the bar, but I can't hold it forever!"

She led Mr. O'Connell through the crowd first. "Don't say that bum leg never got ya anything, because you're getting the best seats in the house!"

The energy was palpable, the room so full of excitement, it felt like the air itself was vibrating. All the big-screen TVs were tuned in to the pregame show, and the announcer's voices blared through the loud speakers. Chants of "Here we go, Brownies!" reverberated throughout the bar.

Brady held her hand through the crowd, making quick stops along the way to say hi to friends. Vivienne spotted a familiar face, Jimmy Rainey, wearing a hat that looked like a dog with big floppy ears hanging down the sides. She smiled at him and waved.

"Beautiful Vivienne!" he yelled out in a booming voice. "So good to see you!"

When they finally reached the middle of the bar, they found Mr. O'Connell sitting next to two empty barstools. As soon as they were in their seats, Brady turned to her, grinning from ear to ear. "Wow, this is pretty crazy, huh?"

She glanced around the room at the different faces in the crowd. Some old, some young, but all with one common thread—they were all Cleveland Browns fans, and they had all suffered.

Brady had told her about the 'Factory of Sadness' as he liked to call it—Red Right 88, the Drive, the Fumble, all of it. And how up until this year, they had pretty much been a perpetual joke.

But now they weren't, and she couldn't even begin to imagine the excitement and happiness they all must be feeling. She obviously hadn't been a fan long enough to understand, but Brady had, and she could see it all over his face.

She watched his profile as he yelled over to someone down the bar, "Yeah, I think it's going to be a good game for him—he's due!"

He glanced over and caught her staring at him. "What?" he asked, his eyes sparkling.

She smiled. "Nothing."

He put his arm around her and pulled her close to him. "I'm just excited—and nervous! Shit, I'm nervous as hell!"

Vivienne grabbed his hand in hers. "I've got a really good feeling about this."

"A good feeling about the game, or about us?" Brady asked, smiling—that smile.

She looked him in the eye and said as sincerely as she could, "Both."

In that one moment, it was as if they were the only two people in McGuire's. The thunderous noises around them all seemed to fade away. Whatever it was between them, it felt real, and safe, and good.

Vivienne liked how it felt—to fall in love.

***

"Do you think the Browns will win?" Vivienne asked.

A thought flickered in Brady's brain, but then he quickly dismissed it as fast as it came. Did he just think that? He couldn't have.

Could he actually think that if the Browns lost the game, he would be okay with it? That if the Browns lost the game, he might not get depressed and boycott his Browns gear, or feel like punching someone when they said "there's always next year"? That if the Browns lost the game, he might not be sad at all?

Because when he looked at Vivienne, and she looked at him, he couldn't imagine being sad about anything—even the Cleveland Browns losing a chance at their first division championship since 1989. He looked into her green eyes and he couldn't be sad.

"I'm not sure," he answered honestly.

"What's your best guess?"

"You and your best guess! Okay, I think they will win. There."

She seemed satisfied with that, and he leaned down and gave her a kiss, a kiss that was meant to be quick, but turned out to be a second too long.

A familiar, loud voice put an end to it. "PDA much?" It could only be one person. Brady reached around Vivienne and gave Jay a fist-bump. "You ready for this?"

"As ready as I'll ever be!" Jay looked at Vivienne and gave her a thumbs-up. "Love the sweatshirt, good choice."

She smiled back. "Thank you, Jay."

He immediately began scanning the bar.

"She's coming at halftime," Brady said.

"Dude, I'm just admiring the scenery. It's a beautiful thing."

Brady looked at Vivienne and smiled. He couldn't give Jay any more material. They had gotten ridiculed too many times to count, and Brady had promised to keep any displays of affection to a minimum.

At halftime the Browns were leading by three. The game was a nail-biter. It seemed like there was no other kind with the Browns.

Jay's eyes had been glued to the door since the end of the second quarter. When Brady saw Jay suddenly stand a little taller and start touching his hair, he knew that could only mean one thing.

"Kendra! Over here!" Vivienne waved over the crowd.

When she finally made it over to the bar, Brady stood up and offered her his stool. "Hey, Kendra."

"Hey, thanks." She wiggled out of her coat. "Wow this place is insane!"

"I know, right? I love that sweater, by the way, is it new?" Vivienne asked. Girl talk.

Kendra glanced down at it. "Uh, no, I got it a long time ago. I just never wear it—I mean, it's brown." She glanced up at Brady and Jay. "No offense, but I hate brown."

Jay made his first attempt at humor. "As long as you don't hate the *Browns.*"

Kendra smiled. "Well, of course not," she said, and then Brady heard her mutter to Vivienne, "This is so bizarre, I know nothing about football."

"It's okay, just cheer when everyone else does. That's what I do. It's actually pretty fun."

The four of them watched the rest of the game together, yelling, cheering and high-fiving.

Brady still hadn't gotten the thought out of his head: *If the Browns lose, I won't be sad.* Could it be possible?

In typical Cleveland Browns fashion, the game came down to the final play. Four seconds on the clock, Browns down by two points. They had a chance to win it with a forty-seven-yard field goal. A tough kick—but not impossible.

Brady and Vivienne stood quietly, along with all the other petrified fans, holding their breath. If the kick was good, they won. If the kick was no good, they lost. This was it.

All eyes were fixated on the screen as the announcer's voice boomed over the loud speakers with the play-by-play. "Stacked blocker's out front, the ball's snapped back, the kick is up, the kick is…good! The kick is good! The Cleveland Browns have won the division! The first time since 1989! The Cleveland Browns are division champs!"

Absolute pandemonium.

They were jumping so high and screaming so loud, it was almost like a dream. Hats flew through the air, car horns beeped outside, and beer cans were tossed around. Brady high-fived everyone, hugged everyone.

He grabbed Vivienne, lifted her off her feet, and twirled her around. And then he did something he hadn't planned, but something he knew he had to do. Maybe it was too soon—maybe he was just caught up in the moment. Maybe it was a lot of things. He didn't really care. He knew what he felt, and it was real.

Right then, right there, in the middle of the chaos, the oh-so-beautiful chaos, he pulled her close and said into her ear, "I love you."

About the Author

Alex Tully lives outside Cleveland with her teenage son and daughter, her husband, and a golden retriever named Trooper.

Her debut novel *Hope for Garbage* is a contemporary coming-of-age story and is available on Amazon.

Visit: www.alextullywriter.com for more!

Regarding my beloved Cleveland Browns…I'm tired of waiting 'til next year!

I'll make my own happy ending ☺

32848985R00192

Made in the USA
Middletown, DE
20 June 2016